W9-AYB-703

Champagne
Life

Dear Reader:

How far would you go if your marriage was in financial decline? Well, find out how one couple deals with their growing debt in *Champagne Life*.

Naomi and DeShaun are living the high life, like the title suggests. Their satisfying marriage and job security allow them happiness…until their employment takes a downward spiral and they face money woes.

The couple takes a plunge by sacrificing their morals in hopes of rescuing their situation. DeShaun, a waiter for a high-end restaurant, constantly attracts attention. When a wealthy couple, particularly the wife, adores his service, he falls for extravagant gifts. With Naomi's blessing, he provides companionship and all's well until he actually falls for the wife, Jenn.

Sometimes no matter how clever one sets up a plot to use or abuse a situation, it often backfires. Such is the case with this desperate couple.

You can check out how Nicole Bradshaw sets up the novel with its ebook prequel, *Caviar Dreams*.

As always, thanks for supporting the authors of Strebor Books. We try our best to bring you the future in great literature today. We appreciate the love. You can find me on Facebook @AuthorZane and on Twitter @planetzane.

Blessings,

Zane

Publisher
Strebor Books
www.simonandschuster.com

ALSO BY NICOLE BRADSHAW

Unsinkable

A Bond Broken (original ebook)

Caviar Dreams (original ebook)

ZANE PRESENTS

Champagne Life

Nicole Bradshaw

STREBOR BOOKS

NEW YORK LONDON TORONTO SYDNEY

Strebor Books
P.O. Box 6505
Largo, MD 20792
http://www.streborbooks.com

ISBN 978-1-59309-485-0
ISBN 978-1-4767-0393-0 (ebook)
LCCN 2013933672

First Strebor Books trade paperback edition January 2014

Cover design: www.mariondesigns.com
Cover photograph: © Keith Saunders/Marion Designs

10 9 8 7 6 5 4 3 2 1

Manufactured in the United States of America

For information regarding special discounts for bulk purchases,
please contact Simon & Schuster Special Sales at 1-866-506-1949
or business@simonandschuster.com

The Simon & Schuster Speakers Bureau can bring authors to your live event. For more information or to book an event, contact the Simon & Schuster Speakers Bureau at 1-866-248-3049 or visit our website at www.simonspeakers.com.

This is dedicated to the Whitaker family.
I think about us every single day.

Acknowledgments

As always, I'd like to thank the Lord for giving me a gift that I try to work on each day.

Thank you to Zane for allowing me to continue to do what I love to do (and get paid for it.) Many of you don't know, being a writer puts you out there for the world to see, so be kind to a writer this month. Thanks to Charmaine and Strebor for combing through my books to correct all my errors. (I try to keep them at a minimum, sorry. LOL!)

Thanks to my family and friends who "like" and comment on all my posts, even when they don't feel like it, especially Steve, my little/big brother. Thanks to Pops for hooking me up by sending out all those manuscripts when I wasn't able to—and not one complaint either. Don't think I don't appreciate it. Thanks to Dawn for talking my ear off about all those reality shows. Okay, I actually enjoy our talk/gossip for hours at time. They give me great story ideas. Thanks to Sharon for passing around all my information to potential readers. You probably don't know this but I do look to you for spiritual inspiration. Thanks to all those people in my life, good or bad, who have influenced me one way or another. The funny thing is, you probably don't even know it.

Most importantly, thank you to my family. Neal, Savannah, Brandon and Dylan, I love, love, love you guys so much—yes, even when I'm frustrated. Thank you so much for putting up with me. I know I can be a teenie bit difficult sometimes.

Finally, thanks to my mother who helped raise some great kids. I know you're looking down on us, proud of who we have all become.

Seven Months Earlier

He scrunched up his face and narrowed his eyes. The tiny, protruding purple vein in his forehead began pounding. Slowly, he balled up his fists. "Nah, man," he said between clenched teeth. "I don't believe I heard you properly."

"Stop it," I begged, but it was too late. He didn't even glance in my direction. His eyes were fixated on his mortal enemy, the man who had just told him that I was having his baby. "Did I hear you correctly? Did you say my wife was having your baby?"

I grabbed his arm, but he snatched it away, never once looking in my direction. "Please, let me explain!" I yelled.

The pulsating vein on his forehead was joined by another in his right temple. His breathing was heavy, like a wild beast on the hunt. I had never seen him like this before.

He took another step toward his enemy. The two men were standing toe-to-toe. Neither was ready to back down.

A gust of wind swooshed the front door open and the unseasonably warm winter rain landed in tiny droplets onto the foyer marble floor. The booming thunder was no match for the bedlam taking place inside our refurbished contemporary Philadelphia home. I would have given anything to be standing outside in the rain right now, to be anyplace but here.

I lowered my voice, attempting to calm him down. "Just go." All he had to do was turn and head for the door; that was it, but it was too late. With his left hand, my husband, who stood over six feet two inches tall, snatched up the much smaller guy, by the collar of his white shirt. He balled up his hand and, with his massive fist, struck the guy in the jaw. There was a cracking noise as blood gushed from the corner of the guy's mouth. He crumpled to the ground and landed with a hard thud. The fight was practically over before it began.

"Oh, God, please!" I screamed. "Stop it! You're going to kill him."

My husband raised his fist again and down it went, crashing against the side of the guy's face, his eye already starting to swell.

I reached for my husband's arm, but he yanked it away before I could grab hold. "You have to go! Now!"

The scene may have been chaotic, but for a brief second, he looked up at me and our eyes connected. His eyes glassed over, almost as if an evil force had taken over. We had been together for several years, first as friends and then as lovers, but today, at this moment, it was as if I had never seen this person standing before me.

I thought the fight was over when my husband stumbled backward, but he still had the guy's collar in his grasp, causing the guy to fall back with him. They tousled on the floor for several minutes. The tables had turned; my husband was now the one on the bottom, his face being pummeled with fists of fury.

I grabbed the guy by his shoulders and tried pulling him off. "Stop it!" It was no use. A sharp, burning sensation traveled up my right side. I had been accidentally elbowed in the midst of the chaos. Seconds later, a stinging sensation moved down my left cheek and I realized I had been struck in the face. The blow didn't quite knock me out, but disoriented, I fell back. I reached up and held on to the wall to steady myself. Through blurred vision, I glanced over in the direction of the two men, who were still wrestling about on the floor. This time my husband was back on top and pounding the guy with his fists. Blood was everywhere.

I scrambled over to my purse and rifled through it, looking for my cell. When I looked up again, I could only make out the silhouette of two bodies rolling about on the tiled floor of the hallway.

I located my cell and immediately tried to dial, but my vision was so blurred, I couldn't make out the numbers.

Clumsily, I punched in 9-1-1.

"This is nine-one-one emergency," the operator said. "What is your emergency?"

"I need help." My hoarse voice came out in a whisper. *"Please. They're going to kill each other."*

"Please, ma'am, slow down. I can't understand what you're saying."

"I need help."

The guy stood over my husband while holding a round, light-colored object in his hand. There was a huge crash and pieces of my opaque wedding vase scattered everywhere.

Disoriented and with blood oozing from every orifice on his face, the guy on the floor grabbed a long, sharp sliver of the broken vase. He extended his arm and held out the jagged edge like a sword in a bullfight.

Like a bull, my husband stood up and charged, right toward the sharpened edge. There was a scuffle and the guy fell to the floor, a deep crimson liquid swelling from under his body

My legs buckled from underneath me and I fell to the ground. The faint sound of approaching sirens was the last thing I heard before everything went black.

Part I

Naomi and DeShaun

One Year Earlier

Sunday afternoons were my time of solace. At the age of twenty-eight, before getting married, I lived in a sexy, single apartment in downtown Philadelphia. I said sexy because the place always reeked of sex; not in the overpowering, recently finished getting down and dirty way; more like in an artsy way. More specifically, I took pleasure in displaying the sensual nude paintings on my walls of black men and women alone and as a couple. Back then, I liked to walk around naked when I was at home, especially in the sweltering summer months. It was my apartment and I did as I pleased. My single Sunday afternoons consisted of sticking in a Paulinho Moska CD and doing a little baking. It was something I enjoyed. Now, at thirty-two, things were definitely different. I was married and didn't hang out much with girlfriends because my husband had become my best friend. I had an older sister, but to say we weren't close was an understatement.

Back then, I never invited guys over much. I preferred to keep my space just that; my space. DeShaun and I dated a year before I even brought him over to my spot. I didn't want him becoming like the guy before him, who took all of two weeks to move out of his momma's place and into mine—without paying rent, a power bill or even a measly cable bill. That definitely wasn't going to happen again. DeShaun had his own spot and I had mine. My momma didn't raise no two-time fool. You got one mess up; twice was not an option.

"Move a little closer to the cage," DeShaun said. "That way I can get the full shot of your sexy body."

I inched myself closer to the edge of the birdcage. It was in the middle of the summer and we were in the midst of a heat wave, the second one of the season. My peach-colored sleeveless summer dress stuck to my thighs as tiny droplets of sweat rolled down my back and settled inside the tip of my crack.

"I feel disgusting," I complained.

DeShaun narrowed his big, doe-like gray eyes and scanned my body up and down as if he wanted to take more than the picture. He rubbed the tiny, coarse stubbles of hair on his chin and licked his thick, juicy lips. "I like sweat. That's why I married you."

I stared him up and down, almost in disbelief that he was my husband. I never ever thought I would get married, especially to a man that was six years younger than me. Add the fact that he was born and raised in the Bahamas and this four-year marriage was damn near mission impossible.

He reached inside his back jeans pocket and pulled out a washcloth. He wiped away the sweat from his deep mocha brown face and neck. "Here. Let me wipe you down now."

"Ewww," I squealed. "Get that nasty thing away from me."

My married Sunday afternoons consisted of DeShaun and me visiting the bird sanctuary, a hobby I hadn't acquired until three years into our marriage. The admission was free from eleven until closing and we usually carried our own snacks. In the late afternoon, we'd sneak off to our cherry tree in the sanctuary quad and enjoy whatever goodies I had baked early Sunday morning. Today it was apple turnovers that Mom had taught me how to bake from scratch, and a bottle of wine that Mr. Stiles, DeShaun's boss, had given him. His boss was always giving him bottles of wine. I figured it was because he recognized that DeShaun was such a hard worker and Mr. Stiles needed him much more than DeShaun needed that crap waiter's job.

His smile was wide and mischievous. "A little closer."

I squeezed in next to the cockatiel as much as I could, with the scorching steel bars pressed against my left shoulder. The bird squawked and I jumped, but I pressed up against the bars once again. "Hurry and take the pic." My dress, matted down with beads of perspiration, pressed up against my leg. Damn, it was hot. The lingering scent of the birds was far from pleasant.

"Now smile." DeShaun lifted his head and took in whiff of the air. "Damn, girl, is that you or these nasty birds?"

"Very funny. Shut up and take the picture. It's hot as hell out here."

He raised the camera and focused. I pulled my sun hat over my spiky, cropped cut and gave my silliest, toothiest grin. "How does this look?"

Click.

I lunged at him. "Oh, no you didn't! Delete it now!"

He held the camera above his head. "That's what you get for trying to be cute."

"Oh, so I have to try now?"

"Yeah, well, you know how it is when you're an old lady," DeShaun said. "You have to work at it."

"Is that so? And I'm only thirty-two, thank you."

"And a beautiful, sexy thirty-two you are." DeShaun's smile faded and he got those tiny wrinkles between his brows, the way he did whenever he was deep in a thought. "Do you know how much I love you? If I paid you five hundred bucks, would you let me take you right here?"

"First of all, you ain't got five hundred bucks," I said. "And second, if I did take the money for that, wouldn't that make me a prostitute?"

"Well, then let me hit it for free."

"If I *was* a prostitute that would make me stupid."

He laughed. "Bring your sexy body over here."

I inched up alongside him and delicately ran my fingertips up and down the panther tattoo on his sweaty bicep. Today we both were in a playful mood. "I dare you." I leaned over and gently licked away the drips of sweat from around his tat. "I have on a sundress and guess what?"

"What?"

"I don't have any panties on."

DeShaun's smile widened. "Seriously?" He moved in closer. "You freak. Why don't you have on any drawers?"

The real reason was that I hadn't done the laundry before we had left, and the only undergarments clean were my monthly big drawers. Plus, I wanted to wear my cute sundress since I had recently lost five pounds and big ol' drawers were not cute under a sexy sundress.

Instead of speaking the truth about the laundry situation, I winked and told him, in my best Marilyn Monroe knock-off voice, "I wanted to be sexy for you."

"Keep playin', girl. You know if you start it, I'll finish."

I knew that, which was exactly why I was tempting him. I reached up, pulled down the right side strap to my sundress, and let it rest against my shoulder. "Well?"

My excitement traveled south. He could do that even before laying one finger on my body. It took a truly gifted man to be able to do that to a woman. DeShaun was a man who was endowed with many gifts.

He grabbed for my wrist. I moved back. He glanced over his shoulder. When the coast was clear, he reached for my waist again, this time securing his arms around me so I couldn't get away. He steered me toward a shaded corner of the sanctuary. I felt my back against the jagged edge of a limestone rock. "Do you think—"

"Shhhhhh." He placed his opened mouth over mine and kissed me…hard.

An older couple had wandered into our sanctuary section, so he pressed his body up against mine to back me further into the corner. A tiny drop of sweat trickled down his forehead and dripped onto my shoulder. We stayed mushed up against each other, listening, until the voices faded around the bend.

DeShaun took a step back. He was watching me. He liked to see how incredibly crazy he made me. He wanted to witness me on my knees—literally—begging for it. He unbuckled his belt and his khakis dropped around his ankles. I dropped to my knees. He grabbed the back of my head and pulled me toward him. After all these years, you'd think I'd be used to his size, but DeShaun required effort every single time.

When I finished, I stood up and he kissed me, his lips starting at my forehead, working down my cheek and finally finding a home on my lips. His sweaty cheek rubbed against mine as he reached down for the hem of my dress. He pulled it up around my waist and felt around, trying to find out if I told the truth about not wearing any undergarments. When he realized I hadn't lied, he quickly stepped out of his pants and kicked them to the side, where they landed in a bush. This was ridiculous. We were like oversexed teenagers doing it in the bushes while the parents were inside watching television.

But, I couldn't stop.

While he was pulling his shirt over his head, I fumbled around with the buttons on my dress. Unable to wait, he ripped open my dress, popping two or three buttons in the process. Seconds later, he was inside me. He placed his mouth over mine to keep me quiet. The more he pushed, the more I wanted to scream. We did this for ten minutes, until he finished. Quickly, he retrieved his pants while I hurriedly fastened the remaining buttons on my dress.

"Are we crazy, DeShaun? Why are we acting like dogs in heat? We're grown adults, not seventeen-year-old kids, getting it in before Momma comes home."

"You like it that way." He fastened his belt buckle. "You're a freak."

"If I am, I learned it from you."

"Let's go home and finish this conversation—in bed." He tugged at my elbow, but I pulled back.

I shook my head. "Oh, no, you don't. Sunday is my bird sanctuary day. Besides, they recently opened up a new Avocet exhibit."

He shrugged and threw his hands up in the air. "Don't know what the hell that is, but if that's what you want to do, we'll do it."

We lasted a total of seven minutes in the Avocet exhibit. I spent the entire time holding my dress closed where he had popped the buttons. We visited three other exhibits and between each, I found myself swatting away DeShaun's hand from my backside as I tried to read about each bird. DeShaun hated birds almost as much as I hated sitting around the house, watching football. He hated the way the birds smelled, especially on a day like today. He hated the squawking sounds they made. He didn't much care for the birds at all; however, he trudged along with me on Sundays because I loved them.

That was one reason I adored him.

"Did you know the macaw typically mates for life and can have a long lifespan together with his partner in the wild for more than half a century?" I asked, swatting away his roaming hands.

He kissed my neck. "Like us." This time, his kiss was tender and sweet. His tongue licked away a bead of sweat dripping down my face.

Right then and there, I decided it was time to go home. We drove seventy miles an hour to get home, and when we did, we spent the rest of the afternoon in bed.

I searched the entire upper shelf for the bottle but could not find it. In the cabinet, I pushed aside the canned spaghetti sauce, the box of instant mushroom noodles and even the canister of dehydrated gravy, which I had only used once for a Thanksgiving dinner two years ago. I still couldn't locate the four-ounce bottle of real vanilla. I didn't splurge on much. My purses could come from Walmart and my sandals from Payless, but my baking supplies and my lip glosses—they had to be top-notch.

I opened up the next cabinet and began frantically searching. I reached behind the package of brown rice and found the box of mac and cheese I had searched for last week and a single dusty pack of beef-flavored ramen noodles. Those noodles had to have been stashed back there from last year or so.

Since buying this house, DeShaun and I hadn't changed a thing in our three-bedroom, two-story contemporary home outside of Philly. We made a few updates here and there, like stainless steel appliances since I loved to bake, and minor updates to the three bathrooms, but other than that, I considered our cozy place perfect. DeShaun wanted to add another bedroom for all the kids he wanted, but thank goodness I was able to hold him off that—the kids and the bedroom.

I pulled open the cabinet above the sink.

Aha! There it was, hiding behind the box of instant mashed potatoes. I poured a teaspoonful of vanilla into the wet mixture and stirred.

You could not pay me a million dollars to enjoy cooking, but baking, that was a different story.

When I was a kid, Mom introduced me to baking by way of homemade apple pie made with granny smith apples. She taught me how to treat and slice the apples so that they were thin enough to properly cook, but thick enough to hold on to the gooey sweetness of the sugar and cinnamon mixture. One holiday—I wasn't sure if it was Thanksgiving or Christmas—we woke up early, before the sun rose, and spent the morning peeling and slicing apples. It was a moment when I remembered being truly happy. By the time the sun was high in the sky, the entire house smelled like the sweet sensation of Momma's homemade apple pie. My mouth watered from merely thinking about it.

"What smells good in here, Mimi?" DeShaun entered the kitchen, wearing only a beige terrycloth towel wrapped around his midsection.

We had spent the entire Sunday afternoon, making love. While he slept, I was full of energy, so I hopped out of bed and started baking chocolate chunk cookies, one of DeShaun's favorites.

"It's a surprise." I sifted through the bottom kitchen cabinets in search of the electric mixer.

He dug his index finger into the open bag of flour and flung it at me. I ducked and the flyaway flour missed. He then dipped his finger into my batter. "I put it on you that good that you had to jump out of bed and bake me cookies? Now that's what I'm talking 'bout." He raised his finger to his mouth and sucked off the chocolaty goodness. "Mmmm, this is almost as good as *your* sexy chocolate." He smacked my backside. He took four fingers and dunked them into the mixture once again, this time producing a big chunk of batter and shoveling it into his mouth.

"Hey, I need that, you know."

"It tastes different."

"Really?"

"Yeah." Greedily, he licked off the remaining batter on his fingers. "Am I tasting a hint of peanut butter?"

"Yup. I'm trying something a little different. What do you think?"

"You should sell these things. They are damn delicious."

"Aw, thanks." With mitted hands, I went to the oven and pulled out my first batch. I reached over to the counter and stuck in the awaiting second, and last, batch.

He sidled up next to me. "How long is that going to take?" He grabbed my waist and then planted a small peck on my forehead, then my cheek.

"Why?"

He looked down, grinned and then tugged at the hem of my lace boy short panties. "I'm ready for round two."

"Hmmmm, really? Didn't we have round two about an hour ago? I think we're up to three."

"Whatever, I just know I'm ready." He whipped off the towel wrapped around his waist and let it fall to the tiled floor. Standing in his nakedness in the middle of the kitchen, I saw his member slowly rise to attention and salute me. "Hurry up and finish those cookies," he said, turning and heading back into the bedroom. "I'll be waiting for you."

I turned off the oven, pulled out the last batch of underdone cookies and placed them onto the countertop. I scooped up several fully baked cookies from the last batch. I licked away the warm, melted chocolate chips from my fingertips as I headed back into the bedroom

Tonight we were having dessert in bed.

Naomi

Mrs. Leanora Pritcherd was a stodgy old lady who reminded me of those demons in horror movies. She looked sweet and innocent on the outside, but once you got to know her, you realized she was Satan's second coming, disguised in a pink and blue floral dress that she wore at a minimum twice a week, and yes, she was in the bank that often, which, for the life of me I couldn't understand why. Perhaps loneliness or boredom was the bane of her existence. Mine was spotting her on the curb Monday mornings, waiting for Percy, the bank guard, to unlock the double glass doors. As soon as he did this morning, Mrs. Pritcherd made a beeline straight for my counter. She clunked her brown leather purse onto the marble countertop and pulled out a tattered, stained handkerchief stuffed with coins. She told me she wanted to open a new account.

She may not have dressed the part, but Mrs. Pritcherd had plenty of money. She had a savings account of over sixty-seven thousand dollars. I also knew she had at least two other accounts with different banks. On several occasions, I thought about what I would do with all that money, the first being to get rid of those damn credit card bills. After that, DeShaun and I would go on vacation; it didn't matter where, just somewhere.

I wondered if she would even notice if a few bills were gone.

Customers—usually older folks who didn't have direct deposit—

filed in as soon as the doors opened. In most cases, they deposited their social security checks or the meager paychecks from part-time jobs since they couldn't afford to retire. The thought of someday not being able to relieve my weary mind and body from the hustle of the grind gave me nightmares.

Each week, as the older folks handed me their deposit slips, I reminded them that direct deposit was an option and even gave them the necessary paperwork. Every Monday, they returned bright and early, with their check in hand.

"I need the best possible rate." On this particular morning, Mrs. Pritcherd was more incensed than usual. "You banks are always trying to cheat me out of my money."

I glanced at the line of impatient customers behind Mrs. Pritcherd. Half of them looked to me, pleading with their eyes to tell her to hit the road—or at the very least, go to the next teller.

"Yes, ma'am," I told her. "I'll be sure to give you the best rate possible."

Several customers groaned and grudgingly changed lines.

"Is there a problem?" Jeremy Butler, another teller, walked up behind me. He stood so close, I could smell the cinnamon on his breath from the breakfast bun he ate this morning. "You've been on your feet all morning, Naomi," he told me. "Why don't you take a break? I'll handle Mrs. Pritcherd."

"I'm supposed to be on my feet. It's what we do. Besides, I only got here thirty minutes ago."

He placed the palm of his hand on the small of my back. "I got this. You go take a break."

I shifted away from his inappropriate touch. "I'm fine. Go ahead and do whatever it was you were doing."

"I'm only offering because Rebecca wants you to finish up filing that stuff."

"What stuff?"

He shrugged. "I don't know. She told me to tell you to file some junk." He turned to Mrs. Pritcherd, who was fidgeting impatiently on the other side of the counter. "I'd be more than happy to take care of Mrs. Pritcherd."

Mrs. Pritcherd wasn't going to make this easy. She nodded in my direction. "I normally deal with her."

In a perverted sense of justice, I smiled, hoping she would insist I deal with her. Normally, I would relish in someone taking away a headache, but Jeremy was a jerk; a real jackass whose aunt was the branch manager. Being the stereotypical pretty boy type with light skin and curly hair bothered me about him, too. Jeremy Butler was *that* guy who always got what he wanted, today, yesterday and forever. I had overheard him talking about his days as homecoming king and being president of the Kappa Alpha Psi fraternity during his single year at Howard University. He never finished college, though, and I never cared enough to find out why.

"She has been my teller since I started coming to this bank," Mrs. Pritcherd complained.

"It's warm in here, isn't it?" Jeremy unfastened the top button of his white polo shirt. I rolled my eyes. It pissed me off that a few of the younger, thirsty girls stared at him like he was the flyest cat in the world. To me, he was kind of short and looked scraggly with his five o'clock shadow.

Did Mrs. Pritcherd just check him out, too?

"I understand you normally deal with Ms. Knowles, which is precisely why I am going to treat you as my special customer. When we finish here, I will personally walk you over to our new accounts department." When Jeremy flashed a grin and gave a wink, it was all over for old lady Pritcherd. It was also all over for my breakfast.

She took a second to respond, but eventually that old woman cracked a crooked smile, exposing stained, chipped dentures. "I suppose that's fine," she said, finding it difficult to keep her sour demeanor. "Start off with cashing in this loose change." She reached into her bag and pulled out a glass jar. "I have at least one hundred dollars' worth of change and I want to use that to start my new account."

"I'll be going on break now." I grinned as I headed off to the back, toward the lounge. Served him right.

When I got to the back, I made sure the room was empty before flipping off my black peep toes. I headed straight for my purse stashed away in the closet reserved for bank employees and pulled out my phone. I quickly dialed.

"Hey, baby," DeShaun said when he answered the phone. "You never call me during the day. What's up?"

I was relieved to hear his deep voice. "Are you busy?" I reached down and massaged my aching dogs, starting with my big toe and working my way down to the littlest piggie.

"Nah. Mr. Stiles is taking a long lunch, but let him tell it and he'll say he's scoping out new locations for another restaurant."

"Is he really considering opening another one?" I whispered into the phone, making sure Rebecca, my manager, or anyone else couldn't hear me. "I thought you said he was in over his head with the current restaurant."

"He is, but when you've got money, you're looking for ways to blow it."

"Do you believe he'll make you manager of this new restaurant?" I asked.

DeShaun hesitated on the other end, taking a second to clear his throat. "I don't know. He claims I'm the front-runner, but that's what dude from the last restaurant said."

I sighed, desperately wanting to tell him to quit these waste-of-time positions. Every restaurant he worked in promised him a promotion, and every one of them fell through for one reason or another. I was getting sick of it. Unlike me, DeShaun was a patient guy with these jobs. He had to be. I'm not professing to be better, but I did graduate college. DeShaun barely graduated high school and came right out of school to work full-time as a busboy at some greasy Bahamian/Chinese restaurant on the island of Freeport to help support his mom.

I shook my head. "That's not right. You should be the front-runner. You have been at that crappy restaurant the longest and practically running the entire joint singlehandedly. And when he does make you manager, he needs to come up off the dime and pay you what you're worth. Don't let him shortchange you."

"Relax, baby, I got this."

The door to the back room swung open. "I have to go. I'll see you tonight."

"Are you my heart?" he asked.

"Always my heart." I shoved the phone back into my purse. When I looked up, Jeremy was standing there, looking at me with a cherry Kool-Aid grin on his mug.

I slipped my feet back into my shoes. "What are you staring at?"

"Was that your husband?"

"Were you listening? And where is that paperwork I'm supposed to file anyway?"

He shrugged. "I guess Rebecca took care of it after all."

"Whatever."

The corners of his mouth turned upward into a sly grin. "Oh, and don't worry about me saying anything to the boss lady. Besides, I know her older sister. We're tight like that." He flipped up his collar and winked—a move that irritated me even more.

Without warning, he pulled his shirt over his head.

I quickly turned away. "What do you think you're doing?"

He looked down at his bare chest. "Oh, sorry. Changing my shirt." He reached into the locker and pulled out a light pink long-sleeve button down. When he buttoned up the last button, he reached into a gym bag and pulled out a brush. He furiously attempted to brush the strands on his head straight, but each lock boinged back into a fluffy curl.

Everyone in the office couldn't stand Jeremy. In the beginning, I tried to stay impartial, but he irritated me the way a gnat buzzing in your ear would. He had started working as a teller only four months ago, but being that the manager was his auntie, he strutted around like every cent in the bank was his. I had heard at one point, he even cussed out a senior teller at another branch, something about she didn't adhere to new procedures regarding bank loans. He was a cocky son-of-a-bitch, but even so, I gave him the opportunity to prove me wrong.

Unsurprisingly, he didn't.

The younger girls at the job swooned over his muscles, curly hair and light eyes. To me, he looked like any other light-skinned dude that worked out. I only knew his daily exercise regiment because in case you didn't hear him brag about how much he benched that week, he wore these ridiculous dress shirts that fit like the Baby Gap—exactly like the pink one he had changed into. On numerous occasions, I found myself staring at that poor middle button on his shirts, wondering when it was going to give.

"So what did hubby have to say?" he asked, placing the brush back into his bag.

"Are you really asking me that?"

I never put my business out there. The only thing Jeremy knew about me was that I was married. That was only because for some reason, he confided to me that he considered getting the same style of my wedding ring for his then-girlfriend. According to him, he didn't because my ring was way too small and she liked extravagant things. I wanted to tell him that was probably the exact same reason she dumped him—too small—but opted not to since I needed a paycheck and he was the nephew of the manager. To this day, I still believe he didn't see the ignorance in his statement.

"Your husband works at a restaurant, right?"

"How in the world do you know that? Do you have connections to the FBI? Are you having me followed or something?"

He laughed. His laugh even sounded pretentious.

"Not at all. I heard you mention something about him being made manager of a new restaurant or something to that effect. Want some water?" He handed me a paper cup filled with lukewarm water.

I shook my head and he quickly retracted the cup. "Being the manager would be a good thing, right?"

I hesitated, deciding whether to give in to my desire to garner a second opinion on such a touchy subject between my husband and me. I treaded cautiously. "I guess so."

"If that's the case. Why do you sound like it's the end of the world?"

I shrugged, realizing this wasn't a conversation I wanted to get into.

"He's got a job and you're sitting there acting like it's the worst thing in the world. I will never understand what women want from a black man. You want us to get a job, we get one. Then you don't want us to have that job you begged us to get. Maybe it's me, but I don't understand it."

"First off, you must be eavesdropping hard on my conversations to know that much about my husband. Second, you're right. You don't understand it." There was a slight tinge of defensiveness in my tone. "Nobody is begging any of ya'll to get a job, but you damn well should have one. What adult doesn't work? I've had a job since I was fifteen. I can at least expect you to have one by the age of twenty-one, can't I?"

"Don't get mad. I'm simply saying, it seems like ya'll don't know what you want anymore and us fellas are paying the price for it."

I stood up and headed for the door. "I'm not having this conversation with you. I have enough problems without getting into some philosophical discussion as to whether or not the chains holding down the black man are real or not."

"That's cool, but that's precisely my point. You women won't tell us what we need to do to please you, and I'm guessing that's because you don't even know yourself. But, on the other side of the coin, I do feel you, though. You look good and you're somewhat successful, and you said you've been working since you were fifteen. I get that you're trying hard not to be like *that* stereotypical black woman who has it going on, but—" He trailed off.

"But what?" I was like a tiny fish, trailing after the dangling bait, and he was the fisherman, reeling me in.

"It's really none of my business, and I don't mean to be rude, but, you *are* that black woman and you could have any man you wanted. I find it odd that you chose a waiter, of all things—not that it's a bad thing," he quickly added. "I don't blame you for not wanting to be in the working class all your life. Hell, I want the exact same thing. Let me ask you something. Doesn't he want to better himself? Didn't you say he had his bachelor's degree in something?"

"I never said that." I wished I hadn't taken this jagged road that could only lead down a dangerous path.

"And don't you want to get your mom off your back?"

"How do you even know these things?" I never told anyone that Mom constantly nagged me about marrying some "island coconut" from the Bahamas, not even DeShaun—*especially* not DeShaun.

"Don't be angry. I accidentally heard a few things when you were talking to your mom on the phone before. Let's be real, there's more privacy at Thirtieth Street Station than there is in this back room. In my defense, as soon as I realized you were on your phone, I'd turn around and leave. I'm sorry. I didn't mean to pry. I feel like—"

"Feel like what?" Again, I was that same fish swimming toward the wriggling worm on the hook.

"I feel like you're expecting too much from him. Maybe that's all he's capable of. You chose him, and maybe now, you have some regrets, but again, that's my opinion."

"You're absolutely right. That is *your* opinion. And what my husband and I talk about really is our business."

"I realized you'd be angry," he said. "But, you wouldn't be if there wasn't at least a grain of truth to what I'm saying." He hesitated, waiting for me to make the next move. I stood up and headed for the door.

"Wait! I apologize for offending you. Let me make it up to you."

As I turned the doorknob, I felt myself relenting a bit. Lately, I was sounding more and more like my uptight psychologist mother when she was given an opinion that didn't agree with her own.

I took a deep breath and swiped a page from my father's life playbook, which helped him become one of the nation's top black surgeons. Who cared what Jeremy thought? He was only expressing his opinion, no matter how wrong and wacked out of an opinion it was. "Nah, I'm cool."

"Seriously, Let's talk. I could use your thoughts about some things, too."

"Like what?"

"Go to lunch with me and I'll tell you."

"No thanks." I stood there for a few seconds, trying to come up with an excuse, but after thinking about it, I realized I didn't need one. I did not want to go to lunch with him or anyone else from the bank. I did my job and went home; that was it. I wasn't interested in making friends.

"Why not? It's just lunch, not some hot, steamy sex session in a seedy motel after-hours." He laughed.

"Comments like that are precisely why."

"I was kidding. If we go today I can get us a long lunch." He winked. "I'm in good with the supervisor."

I shook my head, getting impatient. "No, thank you."

He cocked his head to the side as he rubbed the stubble on his chin with his thumb and index finger—something DeShaun did. "Why not? It's only a burger. It won't kill you."

"I'm having lunch with my husband today, sorry."

"Tomorrow?"

"No thank you." I turned and walked out the door, shutting it behind me. From behind the closed door, he yelled, "Hey, you owe me. I took on old lady Pritcherd for you. Do you know how many pennies that bag had? And I'm not referring to the container."

I shook my head and went back to my counter.

"You come with me to lunch and I'll make it worth your while."

I started to say no, but something about the way he said it made me consider it for a brief second. "No." I said the word, but it was a softer "no." By his sly grin, he knew it, too.

I walked out the door, thinking I was an idiot for even being tempted by this man.

DeShaun

"My good man," Mr. Herjavec began, "I want to surprise my wife with a birthday party she'll never forget, and I'm coming to you to iron out all the details. Can you handle that?" DeShaun nodded. "I'll do whatever necessary to make sure Mrs. Herjavec enjoys her day."

The restaurant was crowded, more than usual for an afternoon service. Today, the Toastmasters were having a luncheon for their annual Women's Day and one of DeShaun's usual customers, Mr. Herjavec and his wife, were two of the 157 attendees. The spacious room was crammed with overzealous patrons who had nothing more to do with their money and time than to spend it dining on overpriced chicken breast, garlic bread and a choice of two sides.

Mr. Herjavec placed his, tanned, well-toned arm around DeShaun's shoulders. His pungent cologne stung the inside of DeShaun's nostrils. "It's Jenn," Mr. Herjavec corrected. "You've known us for several months now. It's okay to refer to the both of us by our first names."

DeShaun, eager to get away from Mr. Herjavec's grasp, nodded. "Jenn and Berti, it is then."

Berti Herjavec was a decent guy, but a little too touchy feely for DeShaun's taste. Berti was that guy who gave you a hearty welcoming hug and kissed you on both cheeks every time he saw you. He frequented the restaurant on several occasions, picking up the sometimes over a thousand-dollar tab to enjoy one evening with family and friends. He loved to tell the story, especially when drunk, of his parents' trek over to the U.S. from Croatia with only thirty dollars in their pockets. At the age of forty-seven, Berti's father, Dmitar Herjavec, set up shop in New York with a distant relative of the family who had moved there years before.

Mr. Herjavec gave a quick nod and took his arm from around DeShaun. He reached inside the pocket of his crisp, white shirt and produced an expensive-looking timepiece. The platinum-colored watch was attached to a tiny silver chain and contained a huge diamond stuck smack dab in the center of one of the links.

Berti lifted the watch toward the sun, squinted and checked out the time. "It's getting late. I'm meeting the head of the Department of Defense this afternoon to hopefully garner another govern-mental contract. I hate working with those old boys, but I do love that money, you know what I mean?" He ran his fingers through his salt and pepper hair, smoothing down the spiked pieces.

Berti may have been older, but in no way did he look it. One evening when he wrote out a check for a $700 dinner with friends, DeShaun saw his license. According to the date on the license, Berti was sixty-three years old.

"What are you doing over there?" His wife, Jenn, sauntered across the room from the other side of the restaurant. "We need to go now. Have you forgotten we are meeting Leonard and Tina for drinks in an hour? I need to go home and change."

Jenn Herjavec clunked across the room, her heels clicking the marble floor with each step. For such a short woman, her limbs were long. Her pinned-up, raven-colored hair accentuated her long, slim delicate neck.

Her neck was the only thing that was slender about her. She preferred to show off her curvaceous body in maxi, spaghetti-strapped dresses that clung to every curve. Her dangling gold earrings weighed down her lobes like tiny anchors, but matched her shimmering-tanned skin tone perfectly. The only time a wrinkle became visible on her face was when she frowned while waiting on her husband.

Overhearing a few of Berti's conversations, DeShaun realized Mrs. Herjavec's teeth were as fake as her breasts. Her face was round and her cheeks, constantly flushed. Even though Mr. Herjavec was trim, and looked good, DeShaun pegged the misses at least fifteen years younger than her husband.

"I'm coming," Berti said. "Just thanking our waiter for his impeccable service." Berti leaned over and whispered, "Impatient, but I guess that comes with the territory of Armenian women, huh?"

Jenn sighed. "I've already thanked him."

Thank him, she did. After DeShaun had brought over the $250 lunch check, Jenn had graciously handed him a crisp one hundred-dollar bill as a tip. When she handed it to him, her fingertips lingered in the palm of his hand. Mr. Herjavec was standing not fifteen feet from them when she whispered, "You're such a delicious waiter." She was a little tipsy when she said it. In fact, Mrs. Herjavec was always drinking—during brunch, lunch, whatever. During late night suppers, Mrs. Herjavec always had a glass in her hand, usually filled with a red port wine. Every once in awhile, she ventured into the harder stuff, but those were usually reserved for special occasions.

"It isn't necessary for Stiles to be involved in our plans," Mr. Herjavec told DeShaun. "I'd prefer this dinner be between you and me. Your manager has a way of overpricing his menu." He slapped DeShaun on the back as he gave a hearty laugh that echoed throughout the dining room. Berti's rings sharply smacked against his shoulder blades.

"No problem, but I'll have to clear getting the time off with my boss. Plus, if you need a few other servers for your party, I'll have to clear them too."

"Fine. Do what you must, however, do not include Stiles in on the original plans. The prices he charged me for our last soiree were ridiculous. Forty dollars a plate for lobster?"

The truth was, DeShaun thought Mr. Stiles didn't charge enough, especially considering the plate came with risotto and truffles. Where his manager went wrong was providing sub-par service for guests who didn't mind shelling out the cash, especially for private progressive parties, where guests went from house to house dining on delicious delicacies for each course. DeShaun bet he could get away with charging double and not one complaint would leave Mr. Herjavec's lips after the event.

Mr. Herjavec wrapped his arm around DeShaun's shoulders and gave a rigid hug. "I'm trusting you to gather your best men for the event. If all goes well, there will be a big tip in it for you. Plus, if you do a good job, I can refer you to all of my old chaps." Mr. Herjavec stuck out his hand, but DeShaun wasn't fast enough to respond. Mr. Herjavec reached down and grabbed DeShaun's hand and shook it ferociously. He shook his hand so hard, his rings dug into DeShaun's palms.

"Yes, sir," DeShaun said. "I will handle everything."

"Wonderful!" Berti reached up, grabbed DeShaun's face and double kissed his cheeks.

Jenn grabbed her husband's arm. "Are we ready yet?"

When Berti hushed her, she turned and walked away, her heavy steps angry and tired. "I don't have all day." Her flowery perfume scent lingered in the air.

"One second," Berti turned to DeShaun. "She is impossible to please."

"I heard that." She shot a quick look at DeShaun and smiled with a twinkle in her deep green eyes. "And for the record, I can definitely be pleased."

DeShaun watched Mr. and Mrs. Herjavec walk out the restaurant doors.

"Yo." One of the service waiters walked up to DeShaun. "Stiles wants to see you right away."

DeShaun nodded, still watching the Herjavecs. Berti attempted to hold open one side of the restaurant's double glass doors for her to exit, but for some reason, she opted to walk through the other door, leaving him to trail behind her. They seemed like polar opposites. Berti was more on the friendlier side while his wife was colder toward people. Berti was also a frugal man. He may have spent money, but it was for things he deemed well worth it, like the expensive family dinners or parties for business associates. His wife dropped money on anything she wanted to, regardless of its worth to her. Mrs. Herjavec would probably explode if she didn't spend at least a thousand dollars a day on something frivolous.

"You wanted to see me, Mr. Stiles?" DeShaun asked, when he stepped into his manager's back office.

"Did you know Damien was leaving the restaurant to go to school?"

Damien was Stiles' son-in-law and had absolutely no experience in the restaurant business. It wasn't a total shock when Stiles hired Damien to run the entire operation. Nepotism was alive and festering in today's businesses, but DeShaun figured Mr. Stiles was too cheap to let his business be run into the ground by some inexperienced kid, family or not. Then he found out Mr. Stiles was barely paying the twenty-one-year-old kid and understood why he was hired in the first place.

"I do remember you saying something about that," DeShaun said.

"Well, I'm thinking you are the best candidate to take over his position. How do you feel about that?"

How was he supposed to feel? If someone had asked him how he felt about the situation two months ago, he would've answered in one word—cool. Mimi wanted him to get the position, and for awhile, he did too. Now, there was more to it than that, plus the fact that he knew what Damien was paid. That would be a downgrade, considering he wouldn't receive tips as a manager. It was the tips that were keeping him financially afloat. He was good at his work, but he wasn't sure if being in the food service industry was what he wanted to do long term. Even managers in upscale restaurants didn't make six figures and, although that kind of money was a long way off, taking this position would almost guarantee he'd be struggling for much longer than he needed to.

He didn't want to decline either. Mr. Stiles took a chance and hired him when his work permits weren't straight. He owed him a lot.

"That sounds like a great opportunity." DeShaun left it at that. His manager could take that any way he wanted to.

Mr. Stiles shuffled around a few papers on his desk. "Great. I'll send the paperwork to Corporate later this week. And I do understand that the tips would be greatly reduced, so, therefore, I am recommending a one-hundred percent raise with your new promotion along with two extra weeks' vacation time."

DeShaun couldn't believe it. It was like his boss had read his mind. Old man Stiles was finally coming up off the dime. He must've realized how much DeShaun was worth to the company. With the extra vacation time and money, he and Naomi would be able to make trips back to the Bahamas for vacation and visit his family, whom he hadn't seen in over four years since moving to the States.

"That would be greatly appreciated." DeShaun turned to leave but then remembered something. "I need to speak with you."

"Let me just make a few calls to corporate and we can get the paperwork going with your new position. Now, you do under-stand that this position wouldn't take effect for the next few weeks. Damien isn't leaving until the end of the summer, so I'd suggest training with him to get a feel for your new position. When he's gone, you will be fully ready to handle the responsibility."

"Yes, sir." DeShaun turned to leave.

"You wanted to speak with me about something?" Mr. Stiles picked up the phone on his desk and began dialing.

"Oh, yeah. I almost forgot. I spoke with Mr. Herjavec."

His boss paused mid-dial and raised his brow. "Oh? What did he want?"

"Nothing big." DeShaun attempted to muster up as much casual-ness as he could. "He wants me to get together a service team for a party for his wife. I'll schedule M.J. and Luke to work the party and keep Reggie and Malcolm on the schedule here at the restaurant."

Mr. Stiles gently placed the phone back onto the cradle. "I heard nothing of this. Why did Mr. Herjavec not see me on this arrangement?"

"That's the thing," DeShaun shrugged. "I suppose he didn't want to bother you."

Mr. Stiles reached up and scratched his temple with his stubby, nail bitten index finger. "That's really strange, DeShaun."

"How so? I've worked parties on my own before."

"Yes, but he's always come to me first. I don't understand why Mr. Herjavec is coming to you rather than to me. We have spent much time and money on his social affairs and all of a sudden, he wants to cut me out?"

"I don't think he's cutting you out." DeShaun hoped to minimize the situation. He didn't realize it would be this big of a deal. "Maybe he understands how busy you are and wants to save you the headache of trying to prepare a small gathering for his wife."

The truth was, Berti had invited over 200 guests for his wife's birthday party, but now was not the appropriate time to spill that bit of information.

"Since when has Berti Herjavec thrown a small party?" Mr. Stiles asked. His boss may have been the guy to hook DeShaun up with a job, but when it came to money, that didn't matter. Business was business.

"I'm only telling you what Berti, I mean, Mr. Herjavec, told me."

Mr. Stiles picked up the phone. "I'll give him a call. Continue service while I get this straightened out, please."

DeShaun walked out of the office, closing the door behind him.

Dammit! He hoped he hadn't messed up a gig that could bring in plenty of cash.

Naomi

The waitress came around with my bacon fried shrimp appetizer. When she set the hot plate down, a droplet of grease splattered on my arm.

"Sorry about that," the waitress said. I looked at her nametag. Her name was *Shanteska*.

"That's fine," I told her, inspecting my arm. *Was Shanteska happy with her job as a server? Was this her only goal in life or did she have other dreams that never came to fruition?* My parents wanted me to have what they called, a serious profession. To them, that meant a doctor or a lawyer. They would even accept me being something artsy like a writer if I was serious about it and made millions of dollars from publishing deals and movie rights. To my parents, money equaled success. I harbored some guilt by the fact that my parents spent tons of money for me to obtain my undergraduate marketing degree, and yet I was still looking to do something I enjoyed while making money. To date, I hadn't found either. I figured going back to school to obtain my Masters was the best option at this point. If the opportunity presented itself, I would surely take it.

I took a big, sloppy bite out of my burger. Immediately, I soared into heaven. That was one of the perks about eating alone. You could be as greedy as you wanted with no apologies.

A big splotch of ketchup dripped from the burger and onto my shirt. I grabbed the napkin on the table, dabbed the tip in water and began blotting at the stain.

"You sure look like you're enjoying that burger." Jeremy stood there, looking down at me with a satisfied smirk on his face. "You're tearing through it like it was your job."

"What are you doing here?"

"Stopping in to pick up lunch." He watched me blot away. "You know, you really should use seltzer water. It'll keep the stain from setting." He grabbed the first waiter that walked by. The kid carrying two plates full of food in his hands and one plate nestled in the crook of his arm looked irritated. "Hey, can you get us a bottle of seltzer water…quick?"

The peeved waiter nodded and headed toward a corner table to drop off the food. He then went back into the kitchen and a minute later returned with two blue bottles in his hands. "Anything else?"

I took the bottles. "No, thank you." I opened up one of the bottles, wet another napkin and began blotting at my blouse. After a few minutes the stain faded.

"Told you."

"Thanks."

"You're welcome." He hovered over my table like a vulture would a carcass. "So, where's your husband? You know, the one you're having lunch with today."

"Couldn't make it."

"That so?"

Shanteska, the waitress, walked up and placed a small stack of napkins onto the table. She looked at Jeremy. "Will you be joining her today?"

He looked down at me. "Do you mind?"

I wondered how rude would it have been to tell him that I was really looking forward to having a nice, quiet lunch by myself, but he looked so pitiful, looking down at me.

I took another bite of my burger. "Sure."

Shanteska, obviously excited to get more of a tip, bounced back toward the kitchen to get an extra set of silverware. Before she disappeared behind the swinging kitchen door, Jeremy called out, "I've already ordered. You can put my food on a plate and bring it out to me. It should be a veal parmigiana for a Jeremy Butler. Thanks."

A few minutes later, Shanteska returned with a steaming hot plate of food and sat it in front of Jeremy. She disappeared back into the kitchen.

"Let me order you a drink." He turned around, looking for a waitress. "What are you having, a martini?"

"A martini at lunch?" I asked. "It's only noon, plus, I'm not a big drinker."

"Then let me get you something lighter." He looked at Shanteska, who had come back over to our table. "Give us two wine coolers, please." He turned back to me. "Is that light enough for you?"

"Make it one for him," I told Shanteska.

"Oh, c'mon. Stop being such a little girl. Did you forget I am in tight with the manager?"

"Would you stop saying that?"

"Saying what?"

"How you know the manager, how tight you are with the manager, *anything* at all pertaining to the manager. We get it. Everyone gets it. She's your aunt. You don't need to remind us every single day. And I told you, I really don't feel like drinking this early."

"Okay then, bring over two beers," he told the waitress, ignoring me. "Beer is like drinking soda with a little extra kick."

This guy was unbelievable. "Didn't you hear me?"

"One beer. That's it."

I threw my hands in the air, flopped back into my seat and surrendered. "Fine. Bring the beers. Make mine light, please." I had no intentions of drinking it. I simply wanted him off my back.

When the waitress returned, she plopped down two beers onto the table and left.

Jeremy lifted up the tip of his plate and peered under it. "No extra napkins? Who does that? The waitress sees we're eating greasy food and she doesn't leave extra napkins."

I shrugged and took another bite. Burger crumbs fell down the front of my blouse. "It's not that serious."

"That burger must be good," he commented.

I nodded, taking another full bite. "Sure is."

He took a sip from one of the bottles of water on the table and then one from the beer bottle in front of him. "I'm not trying to be a dick here, but I can't stand incompetent people. Sometimes servers have to be the most ignorant people in this world. How hard is it to slap some extra napkins onto a table?"

"Oh, let it go, please." I stuffed a fry into my mouth. "And most times it's not even the server's fault." I felt the personal need to defend servers, especially since my husband was one. "The restaurant tells the servers to only give out extra napkins if the customer asks for them."

"That's not the only issue. She's slow, she's sloppy and she has a bad attitude. "

"She's fine to me."

"I forgot. I'm sorry."

"For what?"

"I forget your husband does this for a living. I really should know when to shut the hell up sometimes." He took a bite of his veal. "At least the sandwich is good." He took another drink from the beer bottle. "Maybe your husband should get out of the lower end of the restaurant business and look into becoming a chef or some other higher-up position."

The flush rushed up to my cheeks. At that moment, I was embarrassed for my husband. Not really for him and what he proudly did for a living, but by the fact that Jeremy, a bank teller, thought that DeShaun was on the lower end of the food chain at his job. I expected this from my parents, whom I only speak to on a monthly basis, but coming from a co-worker, it left me speechless. It was best to let that comment go, however, I made a mental note never to have lunch with this ass again.

"You really should come to the gym with me some time."

The last time I went to the gym, I was still single. "I'm not much of a workout person."

"Really? You're in great shape. It gets harder for women to keep that *BOOM POW!* as they get older, you know."

"I'm not old." I took a bite of my burger and downed it with a swig of beer. One tiny sip couldn't hurt. The ice-cold beverage felt refreshing going down.

"Go one time with me and I'll show you how to lift weights properly. If you like it, you'll continue. If not, then you can go off and be fat, old and happy. Just look at Deb over there."

"Who?"

"Deb, over in the corner. She works at the Lower Merion branch. You've probably never seen her. She rarely comes to the office. She was there the other day for only a quick minute. She's only thirty but looks like she's over forty with that extra weight. Nice girl, but if you don't watch it and hit the gym every once in a while, you'll end up looking way older than you are."

"Oh, gee, thanks." I took another tiny swig from the bottle. "When you put it like that, how can I refuse?"

"So you'll go with me tonight after work?"

"Nope."

"I thought you couldn't refuse me?" Jeremy said. "What about tomorrow night?"

"It's called sarcasm and nope."

"You seem busy this week, so how about a week from Thursday? We can sweat a little. When we're wet, we can begin the real exercise."

I glanced up from my burger. "I don't think so."

"One time," he begged. "It will be fun."

"I said, no." I was beginning to understand why he got on people's nerves so quickly.

"Am I getting on your nerves?"

I stuffed the last of my burger in my mouth and started in on the fries. "It's cool, but I don't think it would be right if I hung out with you, that's all."

"It's not a big deal. It would be two co-workers getting together after hours and you know, if something happens after that, we can take it from there."

I dropped my fry onto the plate. "Dude, really? Don't you get that you make women feel totally uncomfortable when you make comments like that?"

"I was kidding."

"If that was your idea of a joke, your sense of humor sucks."

"Wow. That stung."

"I don't mean to hurt your feelings, Jeremy, but you sometimes have that reputation of being, well, creepy."

"Seriously? I thought I was being funny."

"Really?" I asked incredulously. "I'm not trying to be mean. I simply want to tell you the truth."

"No, no, I get it," he said. "I thought I was being friendly. I didn't know you thought I was some serial rapist or something."

I looked at the hurt expression on his face. "I'm sorry. I shouldn't have said anything."

"No, don't be. I'm glad you did." There was an uncomfortable silence as he took a sip of his beer. "I'm uncomfortable around pretty women so I over compensate by trying to be this confident guy with all these jokes that apparently aren't funny."

"You really didn't know that?"

"Seriously, no. I feel like an idiot. I always do this."

Oh, God, please don't let him tell me his life story. All I wanted was a quiet lunch to myself, not some psychology session. I got enough of that from my mom, with wanting to talk about my feelings all the time.

"I've always done that," he said. "When I was younger, I had absolutely no confidence and now I work out and take care of myself and feel good. I want to make sure everyone understands how good I finally feel inside."

I put down my fry and set aside my plate. I was about to channel Mom, the psychologist, for a quick second. "I get that. I really do, but all you're doing is pushing people away. You can have confidence without telling the world how great you are. You feel good on the inside, people will see that by how you act, authentically."

"I never told anyone this," he said. "But, in college, I was seventy pounds overweight and let me tell you, college is not the place to be when you're fat. Trust me on this." He laughed nervously, finally showing an authentic emotion. "I don't even know why I'm telling you this."

Jeremy didn't seem that bad of a guy, but he was always so hot and cold. That time at the bank with old lady Pritcherd and her jar full of change, he wanted to genuinely help me out. Minutes after that, the smug Jeremy resurfaced and he was back to making inappropriate comments.

"Seventy pounds isn't all that heavy."

"It was bad," he said. "And add that with being a virgin. The fellas were relentless."

"You were a virgin in college?"

"See? Even you want to laugh."

"It's not that, it's just that I never pictured…that…from you."

"I was, and right up to my senior year."

"Contrary to popular belief, that's a good thing," I told him.

"I don't know why, but it feels good to finally tell somebody. You know what I mean?"

I nodded. "I do."

"Do you have any deep secrets that you haven't told anybody?" he asked.

That I did, but unlike him, I most definitely wasn't going to divulge any here today sitting in front of a plate full of grease and a light beer. "Maybe."

"Most people do," he said. "I was tired of hiding my past. It wasn't like I killed somebody. I know I shouldn't be ashamed of being fat and a virgin throughout college, but I was a guy, and it was embarrassing."

The waitress came back and asked us if we would be having dessert. Jeremy looked at me and I shook my head.

"Not a big dessert fan?" he asked.

"I prefer to bake my own."

The waitress smiled, told us to have a good day and placed the bill down onto the table and left.

Without hesitation, he grabbed the bill, reached into his wallet and placed a twenty on the table. "You bake?"

"A little."

"What's your favorite thing to bake?"

"I'm a big fan of chocolate chip cookies."

"Me too." He took a sip of his beer. "I mean I was, but I had to knock that out in college with my big ass."

I waited until he laughed before I chuckled a bit.

"Well?" he asked.

"Well, what?"

"You were giving me your deep dark secret."

I normally didn't tell people my private business, but watching Jeremy tell me something about his past, I felt his relief. It prompted me to want to do the same. "Okay, mine's a college secret too."

"Really? I pictured you as the homecoming queen or the captain of the cheer squad."

"I was those, too."

He laughed. "Should've known."

"But that's not all I was." I had never told anyone about my college days, not even DeShaun, but it seemed okay at that point. "During my freshman year, I needed money for books so I danced as a stripper."

"You're lying. That sounds like a movie."

"Seriously, it's true."

"How the hell did you get into college then?"

"I had a partial scholarship, plus my parents made a lot of money and paid for the rest."

"So what was the problem? Why didn't you hit up your parents?"

I couldn't believe I was telling him this. Even DeShaun had no idea of my dancing past. "When I was in college, I was a bit of a fashion freak and totally into myself." I hesitated for a second, deciding if I should give him the entire story or the condensed version. I settled on the shorter story.

"My parents gave me money for books, but I spent it all on clothes and shoes. I had to make money somehow and my roommate knew this girl who knew this girl, and to make a long story short, I danced at a local spot for a month."

"Topless or full nudity?"

"Only topless, but that was bad enough." I thought a second. If I was going to come clean, I was going to come clean completely. "Okay, I lied. It was full nudity."

"Get outta here!" he exclaimed, but quickly added, "but hey, I don't judge. You had to do what you had to do. At least you had the sense to figure out how to get money."

"The whole ordeal was so disgusting. Men looked at you with their tongues practically hanging to the floor. When I danced, on the stage, I could look down and see the bulges in their pants getting bigger and bigger. I was seventeen years old and the first time I stepped onto that stage to dance, I felt like a little girl. Eight minutes later, at the end of the routine, I had felt like a hoodrat who had been around the block a few times."

The longer version of the story went something like this; dancing for a month, dabbling in drugs in order to force myself onto that stage every night and even a few times being approached by "movie producers" who wanted to feature me in their films.

"It's still embarrassing when I think about it." I was glad to finally admit that to someone. No one, except for my freshman roommate, Tanisha, knew about my dancing days as "Victoria." Last I heard, Tanisha was doing adult movies under the name, "Wicked Wanita."

"Your secret is safe with me. I told you about my fat, back-brace-wearing days, and you told me about your dancing days. I'd say we're even."

"Back brace, too?" I didn't know whether to laugh or feel sorry for him. "You had it bad."

He laughed. "Well, now we know something about each other that no one else knows."

I grabbed my purse and stood up, ready to leave. For some reason, his last statement made me feel slightly uncomfortable as well as a tad bit guilty. Another man knew something even my husband didn't. I wasn't sure how to feel about that.

DeShaun and Naomi

DeShaun prepared dinner almost every night. He didn't have to be at work until after six most evenings, so often times I walked through the front door and was met with the sound of food sizzling in a frying pan and to the smell of various spices. Tonight, as I unlocked and entered through the front door, I heard no sizzling and there was no scent of spices wafting in the air.

DeShaun was at the kitchen counter with his back to me. "Hey, you're home." There was something sexy about seeing him prepare food at the kitchen counter he'd refurbished for me. He spent the last of our savings to install the granite countertop because he knew I wanted it. Plus, the fact that he was completely nude was a plus, too.

I glanced down at his tight body and felt myself getting slightly turned on. "Are you kidding me? You cannot be serious."

He raised his arms and in a slow motion, turned around wearing a grin as wide as the Grand Canyon. Aside from two white chef's hats on both heads, a pair of white tube socks was the only other thing he wore. He handed me a glass of wine. "For you, my love."

"You are crazy. You know that, right?"

He eased his way up to me. "I thought we'd try something a little different tonight." Little D poked my thigh as DeShaun took the glass from my hands and raised it to my lips. "Taste this. It's good, right? The restaurant changed wine sellers. I knew you'd like this one."

With DeShaun still holding on to the glass, I took a quick sip. "This is really good." I took the glass from his hand and took another sip. "It's delicious." With my free hand, I reached down and cupped Little D. "And so is this."

DeShaun took a step back. "Hey, hey, hey. Before you go and get yourself all worked up, I've got good news to tell you. In fact, I have two pieces of good news."

I looked at his naked butt and laughed. "Is that what prompted this little outfit, or should I say, lack of one?"

He looked down. "This old thing?"

"You are stupid." I couldn't help but laugh. "So what's this good news?" I glanced down at Little D, who was standing at full attention in his tiny white chef's hat. "You ordered some Viagra or something?"

"Nope. That's all you. But the good news is that Berti and Jenn Herjavec came in for lunch today."

"Did she corner you in the pantry and rip off your clothes again?"

DeShaun was always telling me stories about Mrs. Herjavec and how she flirted with him right under her husband's nose. I never got jealous. Maybe it was because he told me every time she flirted with him, or maybe it was because I was secure in my marriage and didn't feel she posed any threat. In some weird perverted way, it excited me to hear about another woman wanting my husband. That meant I had something special.

DeShaun grabbed the glass from my hands and took a sip. "No cornering this time, but she did drop me a one-hundred dollar tip."

"Oooo, good. Now I can go shopping."

DeShaun refilled my glass and handed it to me. "Are you trying to get me drunk?" I took another sip.

"And if I am?" He gently took the keys from my hand and set

them down on the table. He backed me up against the counter top and began unbuttoning my blouse while gently kissing my neck.

"Hold on a sec. All I had to eat today was a burger for lunch. You have to feed me before you get all this." I suggestively smoothed the palms of my hands down my pencil skirt. "You want this, you gotta pay for it. Wait, that doesn't sound right."

He kissed me again, this time on the lips. "A burger, huh?" Little DeShaun was now stabbing at my thigh. "Since when is Miss Savings Queen spending money going out to lunch?"

"First off," I said, reaching for the half-empty glass of wine on the counter behind him and taking another sip. "It was only a burger. And second, I didn't pay for it."

He stopped kissing. "You walked out on a check? Oh, that's tacky, even for you Mimi."

"Who said I walked out? If you must know I went to lunch with a co-worker. He paid for it."

"He?"

"Yup. Some tall, handsome bank teller who whisked me off my feet and carried me to lunch in his awaiting chariot." I enjoyed teasing him about other guys as much as he teased me about other women. I think it even turned him on a bit, the same way it turned me on when he told me about the women at the parties he serviced. "He said his name was Prince something or other—Charming, I think."

"Oh really? I thought the only dudes at the bank were that short stubby guy and the dude with the bad psoriasis who spits when he talks."

I playfully smacked him on his shoulder. "Stop that. You know Scott has a lisp."

"Did he spit all over your food when he said, 'Passth the thsalt, pleath'?"

I laughed. "You are so ignorant. Did you know your momma raised an ig'nant son? And for the record, I didn't go with Scott."

"Who then?"

"Jeremy. You remember him, don't you?"

"You mean the guy you hate?"

"I don't hate him—not really. He actually turned out to be cool."

"Oh, he did, did he?"

"But he doesn't compare to you in the least, my Snookums."

"Does he still have that big, pointy peanut head?"

"You mean like yours? Yup, he does."

"HA! Funny. You seem to like *this* pointy head poking you." He grabbed my waist and pulled me to him.

"That reminds me," I said, in between his kisses. "I got your message at work. Sorry. I couldn't pick up, but you would not believe who came into the bank today?"

"Who?"

"The President—"

"Obama?"

"No, you goof," I said. "And would you let me finish? The president of the Maxum Corporation."

"Who?"

"The makeup company."

DeShaun shrugged.

"I only wear their lip gloss all the time."

DeShaun shrugged again. "Hey, if they make you look like that, I'm down."

I took another sip of wine. "They opened an account with us. Dude walked right in and basically, slapped down like a million bucks onto the counter and asked to open up an account. It was nothing to him. It was like he was ordering a cup of coffee."

"Did you snatch up a couple hundred-dollar bills 'cuz I sure could use some new kicks."

"I wish. He was with like ten bodyguards. Must be nice to have cash like that." I polished off the rest of the wine in my glass and poured another one. "What was your other news?" I asked, drinking up the wine in two gulps. "You said you had two pieces of good news to tell me."

"Well, it's not million dollar news," DeShaun said. "But Stiles is ready to offer me the managerial position."

"Wow! That is good news. Congratulations!" I tried to muster up a little more enthusiasm but my thoughts were elsewhere. I was thinking about old lady Pritcherd and all those other people who waltzed into my bank with all that money. As I poured another glass of wine, I felt him watching me.

"Am I interrupting your happy hour?"

"What? I took another sip. "I said, 'Congratulations.'"

"Really? That's all I get? You sounded more enthusiastic talking about dude who came into the bank with all that cash."

"What are you talking about? I am happy for you."

"I want you to be happy for us."

"I am, baby. I really am. I'm happy for you, I'm happy for me, and I am especially happy for your big peanut head." I reached up and rubbed his bald head.

He smushed his naked body against me. "Isn't my big peanut head the reason you married me?"

"Nope." I kissed his nose. "I married you for your smoking hot body. I also married you for your sexy smile." I planted another kiss on his lips. "I definitely didn't marry you for your money."

He took a step back. "What's that supposed to mean?"

I unbuttoned my blouse and slinked up to him, wrapping my

arms around his bare waist. "Oh c'mon, you didn't marry me for my money either. We're both broke."

"That's different. I'm broke so I don't have any money and I'm just a waiter. You're only broke because you refuse to ask for money from your rich-ass parents. You could have it if you wanted it."

"So? Either way it's broke," I said. "How would it look for their grown married daughter, asking for money?"

"So what you're saying is, I'm not doing a good job taking care of you?"

"One thing has nothing to do with the other. Stop putting words into my mouth. I'm simply saying that I refuse to go back to my parents with my tail tucked between my legs and ask them—the people who didn't want me to marry you in the first place—for money."

"Oh, that's right. How could I forget? Your parents wanted you to marry Mr. Money Dude with a shit load of money. Maybe Mr. President-Money-Bags-the-one-who-apparently-shut-the-whole-bank-down-so-you-couldn't-talk-to-your-broke-ass-husband-for-two-seconds is single."

"Knock it off."

"You could always go back and see if you can get another lunch out of Mr. Peanut Head Teller Dude while you're at it. See if he can spring for something a little more high-class than a burnt burger."

"Yeah, maybe I will." I stormed out of the kitchen.

That should've been the end of it. I should've stomped out of the house, ran upstairs, did anything other than say what escaped my lips. If I had, we could've been having make-up sex within the hour. But, in the heat of the moment, I wasn't thinking. I turned and stood in the kitchen doorway. Before I controlled it, I spewed out, "I'll bring you back a doggie bag of our scraps."

DeShaun had never placed hands on me and I never thought he ever would, but right then and there, I understood that those were some serious "check yourself" words. And while I never condoned violence against a woman for any reason, I had to admit I wouldn't have been surprised if he would've come at me. He didn't, and I was thankful for that.

DeShaun

"What has gotten into you tonight, D?" M.J., one of the bartenders, and DeShaun's best friend asked. "You've been stomping around here like a bitch who caught her man cheating. And old man Stiles is on your ass too? You'd better act right; you know that old, Italian dude is looking for a reason to fire one of our black asses. I ain't tryin' to be the one tonight."

Tonight, it was a full house at the restaurant and there was much money to be made, but DeShaun was in no mood. Two nights ago, after the argument with Naomi, he couldn't think about anything else except her throwing his lack of finances in his face. That pissed him off.

DeShaun shoved past M.J. "Man, I don't have time for this. I don't care if he does fire me. He'd be doing me a favor by getting rid of me."

M.J. raised his brow. "Oh really? How much of a favor will it be when you get your lights shut off and your raggedy car repossessed?"

DeShaun shot him a warning look. "Watch it, man. I'm not in the mood."

"I'm only trying to tell you that firing you won't affect those rich, white folk." M.J. nodded toward the outside patio, where guests chatted with one another while sipping champagne. "Look at 'em, so happy with all their money. You're merely a skid mark in their designer drawers. And look at the missus. Your black ass ain't even good enough to spit shine her Red Bottoms. You can probably use your bald shiny head to buff her kitchen floors. Hey, if you're lucky, you might be able to call yourself Bojangles and dance the jig at one her parties. Call her up and see if you can—"

"Do you ever run out of jokes?" DeShaun cut his eyes. If his boy didn't tone it down tonight, they would probably come to blows by the end of the night. But he didn't want to lose the business over some stupid fight. Stiles, his manager at the restaurant, was still pissed that the Herjavecs didn't contact him for their party. He didn't want to blow this gig, or his job for that matter, if the other party didn't work out for whatever reason.

M.J. raised his hands in the air. "C'mon, man, you know how I do. I like to bust your chops."

DeShaun looked into the crowd and singled out Jenn amongst all the partygoers. She was grinding on some dude who was a friend of the Herjavecs. DeShaun only knew the guy as Liam and that he owned several fabric factories overseas. Liam's hands rubbed up and down Jenn's thighs. She was getting into it too. She lifted her leg and wrapped it around his waist as she threw her head back.

DeShaun spotted Mr. Herjavec at the other end of the grounds, talking to a few of his business colleagues. It was hard to believe that he didn't catch his wife on the dance floor, moving like the featured dancer at the strip club.

"You will never be in their rich world," M.J. said. "You could maybe be their personal server or butler, but that's it. Maybe you should change your name to Jeffrey. What about Benson?"

"Seriously," DeShaun warned. "Knock that shit off."

DeShaun was tired of talking about how much money everyone else had and how much money he *didn't* have. When he and Naomi had that huge blow out, he was ready to grab a bag and walk out the front door for good. He didn't remember ever being that angry at his wife. He would never hit her, but after that scraps comment she threw at him, he was closer than ever before. Naomi had apologized as soon as the words left her lips. They had even made love that night, but something was different. He saw it in her eyes as she laid underneath him during their lovemaking. When he ran his fingertips down her thigh, her body tensed up. He wasn't certain, but he believed she even faked it that night. When he had rolled off her after reaching his climax, Naomi hopped out of the bed, asked if he wanted a glass of water and disappeared down the steps before he even gave an answer.

Granted, sex with his wife wasn't always fireworks and explosions. Not one married couple he knew could say sex with their spouse was, but he and Naomi, at the very least, always left each other satisfied. That evening he was fulfilled—physically at least, but was she?

DeShaun looked out at the sea of porcelain white faces in the restaurant. He had never noticed before, but those old school folks with money seemed to have paler skin, as if a sun-kissed complexion indicated less prestige and power. On the contrary, the younger affluent crowd—meaning age fifty and younger—seemed to not mind a little tint to their complexions. Mrs. Herjavec was part of the tanned crowd but mostly because of her Armenian heritage, although DeShaun heard her talking about hitting the tanning salon a few times.

This evening, Mr. Herjavec was in rare form during his wife's party. He made rounds with several different men and women throughout the crowd. Although DeShaun couldn't hear what they were saying, Mr. Herjavec's actions suggested business. First, he'd start off by walking up to a couple. He would shake hands with the men and kiss the women on the cheek. Then the small talk started. DeShaun imagined them talking about vacationing at the Hamptons or visiting a local winery, the shit white folks did. Then Mr. Herjavec would start in on business. DeShaun could tell because every time Mr. Herjavec talked business, he used his hands a lot. By the end of the conversation, business cards were exchanged, they'd shake hands once again and off he'd go to another couple. It was like that every single time. That was probably why Mr. Herjavec never noticed his wife drunkenly blowing kisses at DeShaun.

As Mr. Herjavec exchanged business cards with the gentleman, Mrs. Herjavec sauntered up behind her husband and put her arms around his waist. She planted a kiss on his cheek. Without missing a syllable, Mr. Herjavec bent down and placed a gratuitous sloppy, wet kiss on her cheek, no doubt for show. He then took hold of her arm and gently pushed her to the side. Mrs. Herjavec smiled politely to the couple and headed off, probably in search of another drink.

"Can a lady get a glass of champagne around here?" Countess Vargas, one of the richest women on the East Coast, was standing dangerously close to DeShaun. She leaned in and whispered, "It gets sooooo hot in here. What does a girl need to do to help cool her off?"

DeShaun handed her a glass of champagne from his tray. "Is this good?"

Countess Vargas reached up and patted down her silver-colored bouffant wig. "This is splendid."

Countess Vargas had diamonds the size of chandeliers hanging from her earlobes and wore a diamond detailed necklace that was equally as stunning. Her husband, Count Vargas, had died years ago, leaving her more money than she knew what to do with. The latest conquest to her boy toy collection was a young kid named

Esteban Molina, who, if you didn't know, spoke like he only came to the U.S. a week ago. He had actually been in the U.S. for over twelve years. He and DeShaun used to work private parties together a few years back, but that was way before the Countess decided to deal with Esteban on a one-on-one basis. DeShaun had seen Esteban at four or five parties with the Countess, which was a record for her. Most guys didn't last two or three. Rumor had it Esteban was handpicked by the Countess because of his lack of English-speaking skills, which meant for the Countess, she wouldn't have to put up with any backtalk. The poor kid had no idea what he was getting into when he hooked up with her. If Esteban thought he was getting an old lady who preferred a quiet game of chess, he was sadly mistaken. The Countess had a libido that would put any twenty-five-year-old to shame.

The Countess took a sip of wine. "Perfect." She reached around and grabbed DeShaun's backside. DeShaun jumped, almost knocking over the remaining glasses on his tray. "In fact, *you're* perfect."

"You have to stop doing that," DeShaun whispered. "Your boyfriend is right over there." DeShaun felt weird referring to any man as the Countess's boyfriend, especially one so young.

The Countess looked over. She extended a veiney, ghostly white manicured hand in the air and waved to Esteban, who stood alone at the other end of the room, looking completely uncomfortable amongst the crowd around him. Esteban may have no longer been a waiter, but he definitely wasn't accepted into this crowd. People with any hint of color rarely were.

"It doesn't matter," she whispered. "He enjoys watching me with other men."

Like he had a choice.

DeShaun studied the Countess. She had to have been closing in on eighty and was not very attractive either. On some occasions, she could even be classified as downright revolting with her stale cigar and brandy breath. The Countess was skeletal thin and insisted on wearing the boldest reds in lip and nail color to contrast her pale complexion. Her completely gray hair was always pulled back into a puffed-up bun that made her receding hairline even more prevalent. Even though her husband left the Countess close to one billion dollars, the talk was that she had already blown through a good portion of it before she turned seventy, buying men, jewels and toys like it was going out of fashion.

"If you ever change your mind, you know where to find me." The Countess reached down and grabbed DeShaun's package. The remaining champagne glasses toppled over on the tray, making a loud, clinking noise. Everyone in the party turned.

When Jenn looked over, she saw DeShaun. Immediately, her expression brightened. She waved her arm high in the air to get his attention.

"Looks like her highness is beckoning you," M.J. said. "She probably wants you to blow on her soup to cool it off. Must be nice to be white."

"Nah. They're exactly like us."

"Are you crazy, man?" M.J. said. "They'd be exactly like us if they had bad credit, had on the lesser side of ten bucks in the bank and were standing here in this penguin getup, running around like Kunta Kinte, with a tray in their hands. When that day happens, then you can say some shit like that."

DeShaun sighed, tired of listening to his boy's rantings. He grabbed a glass of champagne from the tray M.J. was holding and headed off in Jenn's direction. When he reached her, she instantly grabbed him and gave him a small peck on his lips.

"What was that for?" DeShaun asked, surprised. Mr. Herjavec was less than thirty feet away, talking to another couple.

"We're celebrating the graduation of my son, Berti's stepson. With his stepdaddy's money and influence, Kyle has finally managed to eke his way out of college after seven years. What a proud Momma I am," she said with a slight slur. "That's much better than his broke deadbeat father could have done."

"Uh, congratulations," DeShaun said.

"The party is more for us than for him. Do you know how much yearly tuition is at Harvard?"

DeShaun shook his head.

"Too much. And he even had the nerve to graduate with an art history major. What in the world does he plan to do with that?"

DeShaun shrugged. "I don't know."

"I'll tell you one thing," Mrs. Herjavec said, leaning closer. "If he plans to sponge off Mommy and Daddy, he'd better think again. The upkeep on this face and body is expensive. If Kyle wants to mooch, he'd better find himself a sugar momma. Am I right or am I right?"

Not knowing how to respond, DeShaun simply nodded.

"I'm only kidding," she said, taking a sip from her glass. "I would do anything for my only child."

DeShaun grew increasingly uncomfortable. "That's good."

"Let me ask you something, DeShaun," Jenn said. "Do you consider me attractive? I've had work done but nothing major. You should see what some of these women do around here and I don't think they look half as good as me. I'll tell you what, DeShaun." She leaned in closer and whispered in his ear. "What you see is mostly hard work with only minimal help from a plastic surgeon. What do you think? Do I look good to you?"

DeShaun pulled back. "You look good."

"How about great?" she asked. Her eyes drifted downward toward DeShaun's mid-section. "I bet you could handle this, couldn't you?"

Mrs. Herjavec swigged down the last of the contents in her glass. It was official. She was drunk. "Women would kill to look like me. Don't you agree? These women are jealous of my Armenian heritage. You know why? Because their old white asses are falling apart, and there's nothing they can do about it. Look at my wavy, dark hair. It's beautiful, isn't it?. And I don't have to wear those god-awful wigs or extensions, either."

"Mrs. Herjavec?"

"Please call me Jenn."

"Jenn." DeShaun took another step backward, but she took another step toward him, this time closer than before. "You look good. I'm sure Mr. Herjavec appreciates it."

"HA! I wish he did. Now you, I bet a man like you would appreciate all I do to stay looking good. If you think this is good," she said, running her thick fingers down the side of her dress, "you should see what I look like naked. Don't let the extra pounds fool you. I'm thick in all the right places. Isn't that what black men like—a thick woman?"

"I really need to get back to work." He grabbed an empty tray from the table and practically sprinted back to the kitchen. As he plopped the tray onto the countertop, she grabbed his backside and held on tight.

"You didn't believe you were going to get away from me that easily, did you?" She pressed her body against his. Her full, firm breasts heaved up and down against his chest. He felt her erect nipples through his shirt.

"We shouldn't be doing this," he whispered, looking around to make sure no one was nearby.

She didn't care. She leaned up and grabbed the back of his head. She drew him to her and planted a sensual kiss on his lips. "That feels good, doesn't it? If you like that, I have something that will make you feel even better."

She hiked up her skirt mere inches from exposing downtown. Quickly, she grabbed his hand and guided it down the inside of her bare thigh.

He snatched back his hand. "You're very attractive, Mrs. Herja—Jen, but I can't do this. I'm married and so are you."

"I'll be frank. A woman like me can give you so much. I would even pay you, if that's what you want."

"What?" DeShaun couldn't believe what he was hearing.

"I enjoy bestowing gifts on people who are my friends. I want you to be my friend, DeShaun. I want you to be my *very special* friend."

The kitchen door swung open. They both quickly parted.

"Thank you for showing me where the glasses are." She rushed back out to the party.

M.J. walked up to DeShaun and raised his brow. "What the hell is going on here?"

"Thanks, man." DeShaun grabbed a towel and headed out the door back to the party.

"For what?"

"Trust me. You don't wanna know."

DeShaun

"What were you doing with my wife in here?" Mr. Herjavec bellowed behind them. "I hope not anything inappropriate." Tiny creases were gathered between Mr. Herjavec's bushy brows. Slowly, the creases disappeared and the corners of his mouth turned upward. "Relax, my good man. I'm joking. Now stop being so serious and join us for a drink." He picked up a glass of champagne and offered it to DeShaun. "Did the lovely Missus happen to tell you why we are celebrating?"

DeShaun took the stem of the glass and followed him out to the crowd gathered on the marbled stone patio. He was tempted to take a long, slow swig from the flute but decided against it. It wasn't like he didn't down a glass or two at these parties, it was just that tonight, he didn't feel much like drinking.

Mr. Herjavec headed out to the center of the crowd. He grabbed a fork from the buffet table and clinked it against the champagne glass in his hand. The crowd quieted down. When he had everyone's full attention, he held up his glass. "I would like to say a special congratulations to my stepson, Kyle," he announced. "He recently graduated from Harvard University."

Cheers and whistles sounded from the crowd.

"I'd also like to give a special thanks to my beautiful wife, Jenn, who helped make this night possible."

The crowd oohed and aahed at the special toast.

"For if she didn't cut down on the Botox and her collection of overly priced designer shoes," he continued, "we never would have been able to make the tuition payment."

The crowd laughed.

The look of disappointment and shock washed over Mrs. Herjavec's face, but only for a second. She quickly recovered and stepped into the center of the crowd, joining her husband.

"Well, dear," Mrs. Herjavec said. "It's better than spending it on hair replacement sessions and Viagra, from which I never seem to benefit from." Mrs. Herjavec raised her glass. "I will drink to that." She took a sip. "Lord knows, I deserve it."

Sounding more like a comedy roast than a special toast, the entire crowd roared with laughter. Even Mr. Herjavec chuckled a bit.

As the crowd dispersed and resumed their conversations, DeShaun turned and headed back toward the kitchen.

"Excuse me." Mrs. Herjavec walked up to DeShaun. He could smell the scent of her floral perfume before she even reached him. "Could you please get more hors d'oeuvres from the kitchen?"

"Yes, ma'am."

She grabbed his arm, leaned in and softly whispered, "I'll tell you what else you can get me—a man that knows how to please a woman."

DeShaun pulled away, but that didn't stop him from becoming excited. "I'll get those hors d'oeuvres right away."

Mrs. Herjavec's thick, crimson lips turned up at the corners as she said, "What I need has nothing to do with food." She reached down and grabbed him—right in the balls. Her grip was aggressive, not painful. "Wow, nice, *real* nice." She grinned.

Politely, DeShaun grabbed Mrs. Herjavec's hand and removed it from his privates. "I'm married."

"As am I. That only means we need to be discreet."

"What about your husband?"

"What about him?" Mrs. Herjavec squeezed in closer, so close, he felt her warm, breath on his neck. It smelled like fresh mint, which was surprising considering all the liquor she downed this evening.

"I'll let you in on a little secret about Mr. Herjavec. If you're not a young black boy with a tight body, he has no interest." She looked DeShaun up and down. "You'd better watch out."

DeShaun quickly walked away. He turned around as he headed back to the kitchen. Mrs. Herjavec was watching him.

When he pushed open the kitchen door, he ran right into M.J., who was rinsing champagne glasses in the sink. "What's up with that look on your face? Lemme guess, Mrs. H. asked you to pet her dog, Fido," M.J. said, laughing.

DeShaun shook his head. "It was more like her kitty cat that needed petting."

Naomi

*T*oday was One. Tiring. Day. That was the only thing on my mind the entire bus ride home from work. This morning, my car would not start and, of course, DeShaun had picked this day to run early morning errands. When I hopped into the car and turned the ignition, my heart sank to my stomach when all I heard was a *click* instead of the sound of a smooth-running engine. I had to take the bus to work.

When I finally got to the bank, an hour and forty minutes late, the power went off. We still needed to continue with work as usual, while dealing with irate customers, as well as the rush of sweltering heat that made its way inside the doors every time someone entered. Then, later in the day, one of the branch managers pulled me aside to tell me my attitude needed adjusting. Apparently, I was not representative of the excellent customer service that the bank had to offer.

What wasn't representative of the excellent customer service was getting your lights turned out because your corporate office forgot to pay the light bill. That was some straight ghetto mess, right there. I could not figure out how in the world a bank, of all places, forgot to make an electrical bill payment.

I had no idea how long I would be able to put up with that place. The stress of the bank was beginning to get to me, so chances were, a forced smile on my face wasn't an option, which was rule number one in the Customer Service Guide Book. *Make customers feel appreciated with a friendly word and a smile on your face.*

Oh, please.

It wasn't that I couldn't excel in this position, it was more like I had no incentive to shine. For the past several months, I felt like I was wasting my time doing something I loathed—but wasn't everybody? The economy didn't allow for picking and choosing anymore. If you had a job, you kept that job. Unfortunately, bills were beginning to surpass our earnings. Every evening, I came home to at least one overdue notice jammed inside the mailbox.

At the end of the long day, I barely caught the bus and ending up sitting in one of the last seats available, which happened to be next to a woman with allergies.

Aaaaaachoooooooooo! The woman sitting next to me sneezed.

"Excuse me, please." I stood up and carefully eased by her to sit somewhere else. I plopped down into an empty seat near the door, as far away from Sneezy as possible. As soon as I sat down, my purse slipped from my shoulder and landed on the dirty bus floor. It hit the ground and the contents spewed out and all over the place. At that exact moment, the bus stopped and let off passengers

I scrambled beneath dirty shoes to gather my belongings. *Of course.*

On days like this, it felt like I was holding rocks on my shoulder. While I could lift the weight for awhile, it would eventually wear me down. There was never a break. There was never a moment to breathe. The worst part was, DeShaun and I had our first real fight in months. He never mentioned it but even now, I was still feeling guilty about the doggy bag comment. Sure, we fought about dirty laundry and undone dishes, but our last argument—that was one for the books.

As soon as I walked through the front door, I spotted a pile of mail on the hall table. Against my better judgment, I picked it up and sifted through it. Every single envelope contained a tiny clear window in the middle, which only meant one thing— a bill. The one exception was a pale green envelope from a solicitor, asking me to donate funds to a Fireman's charity ball.

Some of the bills were yellow, some were white. A least two of them were pink. My spirits lifted a bit when I picked up one lone envelope with no window, no color, nothing— just a plain, white envelope.

The outside of the envelope read *McIntyre, Roth and Associates.* My heart skipped because I immediately recognized the name. I had forgotten all about the law firm that I interviewed with some time ago. About three weeks back, in one of my positive life moments, I had decided that I should go back to school. I thought about practicing law, but due to financial reasons, realized that was out of the question. That same day, I was leafing through the newspaper when I saw the ad for an administrator for McIntyre, Roth and Associates. I spent my entire lunch break, getting together a detailed resume to fax. I didn't have much experience and what experience I did have, I embellished a bit. The one thing I had going for me was my degree in Marketing from Hampton University, but since I was applying for a job in the legal field, I didn't know how much that would help. Two hours later, I snuck away from my counter and to the back room to fax off my resume.

Thirty minutes after that, I received a message on my phone that McIntyre and Roth wanted an interview with me.

I had done some research on the firm and found out that they reimbursed up to seventy percent of tuition for employees that qualified. This had to be a sign. *Think positive.* The firm had to be contacting me to give me the job, right?. This would change our lives. This job would finally give me something fulfilling to do with my life other than dealing with old women and their pennies. This could be the beginning of a brand new lifestyle. Screw late bills, overdue notices and definitely screw having only $46 in the account.

My fingers fumbled with the envelope as I ripped open the letter. I couldn't read it fast enough.

Dear Ms. Knowles,

Thank you for your application. We have reviewed your qualifications and feel as though you may be a suitable fit for our administration position. We would like to schedule a second interview with you at your earliest convenience.

Thank you and have a great day.

Jim McIntyre, Esq.

/lw

McIntyre, Roth and Associates

Philadelphia, PA 19120

While it wasn't an offer letter, it was still good news. They wanted to schedule a second interview. I took a deep breath and one of those burden-ridden rocks fell off my shoulder and clunked to the ground.

One down, three hundred and seventy-six more to go.

I heard the lock at the front door. I raced to tell DeShaun my semi-good news but stopped in my tracks when I saw his expression.

"What happened?"

He clanked his car keys onto the hall table.

"What is it?" I asked again.

"You wouldn't believe it."

"Believe what?" I was getting impatient.

"I was fired today."

A part of me was relieved that the news wasn't a death. The other part of me wanted to double over and puke out a lung. It felt like I was kicked in the gut—and in a sense, I had been. Life circumstances were rearing its ugly head once again. A grain of happiness was apparently too much.

"What happened? I thought your manager was about to give you a raise. You were a guarantee for that managerial position. What the hell happened between last week and today? How could you have possibly screwed that up?"

"He's a jerk," DeShaun said. "And he can kiss my ass for all I care. If that bastard thinks I need that job, then he can kiss my black ass twice. I don't need him or anyone else."

"Are you serious? Of course, you need that job. We can barely make ends meet now. In case you haven't done the math yet, less money in our pockets means less money to pay the bills."

"I know that!" He was getting angry and I didn't care. I was getting angry that he even had the nerve to be angry for something he did. *Who the hell got fired from a service job? My husband, that's who!*

I threw my hands in the air. "Now what are we supposed to do? Do you think I can deal with this right now?"

"Stop being so dramatic. I'm the one that got fired."

His constant reminders of the obvious burned me up. "Yes, you did," I said through clenched teeth. "And what did you get fired for anyway?" I tried to keep my expression calm, but on the inside, I felt the flames searing right through me.

His angry expression softened. He shook his head and let his gaze drop to the floor.

What did that mean? What was he so ashamed of...aside from the obvious?

"Why did you get fired?" I asked again.

He shook his head. "It was stupid. It wasn't my fault. Stiles had it in for me ever since Mr. Herjavec wanted to cut him out of the planning of some big party."

"I didn't ask if it was your fault. I asked why you got fired. It's not a difficult question."

He shot me a warning look.

"Did you finally snap and hit that pig bastard? What?"

He shook his head again.

What the hell was that look?

I was beginning to reach my boiling point. "What then?"

"I was fired for stealing," he finally mumbled, but quickly added, "It wasn't my fault, though."

"Please tell me you are joking. For stealing? Really? I would have more respect for you if you had told me you clocked him."

He shot me another look.

"Are you serious?"

"Are you?"

DeShaun looked up, his gaze connecting with mine. "Why can't you support me? Is it that hard?"

"How can I support you for doing something so stupid?"

"Gee, I don't know," he said. "How about, maybe because you're my wife and I would support you, regardless?"

The fact that he would want to me fall in line with this absurd mess angered me even more. "Of course, you would support me. I would never do anything so idiotic. Stealing? You want me to support that? Let me ask you something; do you have any idea how difficult it is to support your spouse when he has minimal earning potential? When we first got married, I supported the both of us financially. Oh sure, you finally decided to get a job— as a waiter! What the hell? That's okay for high school but don't you think it's time to put your big boy boxers on and get a real job?

It's easy for you to have to deal with me because I have potential. I've secured a steady job at the bank and while it doesn't pay much, it's still twice as much money as your job pulls in."

I avoided his gaze, not because I had regretted what I said. I didn't want to see his hurt expression when I told him the truth—his truth, our truth. I wasn't going to take it back. He had to hear this. I couldn't go on like we had been. It was too tiring. "I make money, I keep myself up. I work hard. You married up. You should be damn proud to tell people that I am your wife. I'm a good catch."

"Up until now, I thought I was, too," he said. "I had no idea that you even felt this way. I realized you were unhappy about our financial situation, but damn—. " He walked past me and toward the front door, knocking into my shoulder. Without even turning around, he said, "I'll call you later and tell you where I'll be staying for awhile."

The front door slammed shut. He was gone.

Naomi

I walked into the immaculate downtown Philly office building of McIntyre, Roth and Associates. The spacious lobby was contemporary in design, containing two plush butter-colored leather sofas on opposite ends, one leopard-print lounge chair and an art deco style glass table situated in the center. The paintings on the walls featured different countries around the world. One I recognized as Paris, another, Venice, Italy. A third painting was of a Caribbean location, maybe Aruba or Jamaica.

I was nervous as I headed toward the receptionist's desk. My nude-colored heels clicked against the black and gray expensive-looking checkered tile floor.

I hated wanting something so badly, but the truth was, I needed this position. This job would mean more money, but most importantly, it meant future career growth, something I was lacking working at the bank. It was rare that a smaller company, such as McIntyre, Roth and Associates paid employees to go back to school, but if the company was willing, so was I.

"Good morning." I smiled at the receptionist at the front desk. She was a young, neatly dressed black woman, wearing a tight, stylish high ponytail. From her formal style of dress, I was glad I'd chosen my black knee-length pencil skirt, that hugged my hips, and my tan blouse I'd purchased on sale from Nordstrom. I'd opted to spike up a few strands of my cropped cut and purposely had chosen gold-studded earrings and a matching necklace to complement my skin as well as bring out the subtle bleach-blonde highlights in my hair.

The receptionist looked up from her computer. She had a friendly smile as she asked if she could help me. That's when I noticed her hair color. She somehow managed to match her make-up with the red streaks in her hair. Her nails were short but well-manicured. I glanced down at my own, wishing I had taken the time to, at the very least, polish them up with a clear gloss.

"I'm here for a noon interview with Mr. Roth," I told her. The silver accented name plate on her desk read, *Stephanie Merchand.*

Stephanie began furiously typing on her keyboard. When she stopped typing, she ran her finger down the screen, stopping half-way. That was when I checked out the band on her ring finger, a diamond white gold eternity wedding band. That ring cost a fortune, at least, two-thousand dollars. The band was accompanied by a one-and-a-half-carat diamond engagement ring with accented micro pavé diamonds in platinum. Her ring was the exact same engage-ment ring I had yearned for; only DeShaun and I couldn't afford it. Stephanie Merchand must have married very well.

I decided that if I got this job I would treat myself to a nice ring, exactly like the one Stephanie wore.

"Ms. Knowles?" Stephanie said. "They're ready for you now."

I stood up and smoothed down my skirt.

I felt completely confident. This position was as good as mine; I could feel it. It had to be, especially with DeShaun and me in the position we were in, financially as well as emotionally.

Naomi and DeShaun

"I'm glad you're back. I missed you."

"It was only a couple of days," DeShaun said. "We needed to cool things down a bit."

DeShaun took a seat in the antique Bergère armchair I had purchased on one of our many excursions into the city. I loved that chair. With its gilded shine and the flower pattern upholstered back and armrest, it reminded me of the chair my grandmother used to have in her house in Garner, North Carolina.

I took a seat across from him on the couch and propped my feet up onto the matching footrest. I took a long, drawn-out sip from my glass of wine and allowed the liquid to slide down my throat and warm up my body, putting me in a more relaxed mood.

"In any case, I'm glad you're back." I took another sip. "You sure you don't want another glass?" I asked, holding up my wine.

He shook his head. "I've already had three."

I swirled the remaining contents inside the glass and then downed the rest of the wine in one giant gulp. I reached over to the coffee table for the bottle and poured another glass. "You sure? Last chance."

"I'm good. Thanks."

I tipped the bottle and poured out the last few drops into my glass. "How about a cookie then?" I lifted the plastic container with the cookies inside. "They're your favorite, chocolate chip."

"Nah, I'm good."

He didn't seem the same this evening. "You sure you're okay?"

He nodded. Even though DeShaun was back home, things were definitely tense between us. I got that he was upset, but I felt as though that discussion—or argument—needed to happen eventually.

I sat back and took another sip. "So, how was that party the other night?"

"More of the same. When rich people get drunk, they get crazy."

"Uh-oh. What happened this time?"

I had come home from work late in the afternoon and found DeShaun, snoring like a wild boar on the couch. He was fully dressed, laying in bed with his shoes still on. Normally that drove me insane, however, at that point, I was just glad he was home.

Within the course of several hours, he had grown massive stubble on his upper lip and chin area. When I found him on the couch, he was sleeping in the same clothes he had on when he left the night before. His untucked, unbuttoned, white shirt hung loosely and his jeans were unbuttoned and unzipped, exposing his Fruit of the Loom blue and white striped boxers. I had watched him sleep, feeling a twinge of guilt for making him hurt, the man that I had vowed to love forever.

He stretched out his legs and rested his head against the arm of the couch. "I'll tell you what happened. It was more of the usual, rich drunk people dressed in casual designer duds, stumbling around the party barely able to stand. That's what happened."

"Really? Did the Countess hit on you again?"

"Of course."

"What about Mrs.—?" I thought for a moment. "The one that gets drunk at every party and throws herself at you, what's her name?"

"Liana Edison?"

I shook my head. "Doesn't sound familiar."

"Marcia Nicholson?"

"Sheesh, how many women hit on you?"

He shrugged. "Comes with the territory."

I took another sip of the wine, allowing it to slide down my throat and relax me. "I cannot remember that one chick, the one who was dirty dancing with that British dude at that party for that rich couple."

"That could be anybody." He furrowed his brow and thought a moment. "Ohhhh, you mean Jennifer Herjavec."

"Is that the one with the husband who's an arms dealer for the DOD?"

"That's her." DeShaun shot up from the chair and headed for the kitchen. I heard the refrigerator door open and seconds later, I heard the sound of him removing a cap from a beer bottle. "You want a beer?" he yelled from the kitchen?

I reached over, grabbed the bottle of wine and emptied the remaining droplets into my glass. I downed that in one point five seconds flat and then said, "Sure."

He returned with two beers in hand and a bag of sour cream and onion chips. He handed me one bottle and placed the other onto the table along with the bag of chips. "Be right back." He disappeared back into the kitchen. As I sipped on my beer, I listened to the drawers, cabinets and refrigerator open and shut. A few minutes later, he returned with a six-inch turkey sub on a paper plate. "I cut it in two in case you wanted half."

I wrapped my mouth around the sandwich and took a colossal bite. Breadcrumbs dropped from my mouth and onto my shirt. The combination of turkey, ham, cheese and lettuce with a touch of mayo tasted like heaven on a paper plate. The only thing that would make the sandwich better was crunched-up sour cream and onion chips stuffed in the center. One thing you couldn't say about me was that I was a dainty eater.

I eyed the bag on the table but before I could grab for them, DeShaun reached for the bag and handed it to me.

"Go ahead. Mess up your sandwich like you always do."

"You know me so well." I crunched up a handful of chips and strategically placed them onto my sandwich.

DeShaun grabbed a handful of chocolate chip cookies and shoved them into his mouth. "These are really good." He shoved in another mouthful of cookies. "What were we talking about?"

"The slut who keeps hitting on you at the parties." I could barely get the sentence out with my mouth full of lunchmeat potato chip bliss.

"Oh yeah." He took another swig from his bottle of beer. "Mrs. Herjavec was so drunk, at one point, I thought I was going to have to escort her out of the party. She was stumbling around and even tripped a couple of times. I can tell you, she will definitely have a major hangover tomorrow."

"Wow," I said. "So, the rich actually get drunk to that point, huh?"

"I've seen it all."

He gave me a few more horror stories about the lifestyles of the rich and famous, during which, we shared another quarter sub, which would technically only make that a half sandwich, so I didn't feel like a total pig. Between the both of us, we had almost two bottles of wine, which was mostly me, and four beers, which was mostly him.

After feeling more relaxed, DeShaun moved from the chair and sat next to me on the couch. He gently ran his fingers up and down my arm. The sensation tickled.

"I don't know what's happening to us, Mimi. Why are we always fighting so much lately?"

I shrugged. "I don't know. We're both under a lot of stress. You lost your job and I despise mine."

"Even before I lost my job, we were fighting over small things."

"We're under tremendous financial stress, I guess. When the other smaller issues pop up, it pushes us over the edge."

I was sounding like my mother, who was an expert at diagnosing situations. The truth was, I had no idea why we were picking at each other so much. One evening, after hearing Mom and Dad argue, I saw her in the bedroom, crying. I would never forget what she told me, a ten-year-old little girl, at the time.

I had innocently asked if she was going to be okay. Her initial response was to reassure me that all was well. As I was about to leave the room, feeling satisfied that Mommy was going to be all right, she called me back, sat me down on the bed and told me something I would never forget.

"Mimi, honey, you will find that perfect man who will love and trust you with his life. You'll feel the same way too. Always remember that marriage is something that is constantly evolving and the dynamics of that union will change several times throughout the course of that union. The person you marry is inevitably going to change. So are you. Sometimes those changes are minor and you won't even notice them. Other times those changes define the course of your marriage. Changes are due to external as well as internal factors. As the marriage evolves, so must we."

I listened to my mother, but at ten, had no idea what she meant. I did remember leaving the room and rushing to the dictionary to find out what *inevitably* meant.

I was feeling those changes.

DeShaun shook his head. "I can't keep doing this, Mimi."

"I know. I can't either, but what should we do? How do we fix this?"

"I don't know. I guess we keep on trudging along, hoping something will give. That's what we've always done."

"That's my point," I said. "Trudging along and doing nothing is exactly what has gotten us nowhere. It seems like we keep trying to get ahead but keep getting knocked back further and further, until we find ourselves scraping to get back to position we were originally in, which is the position we were trying to get out of in the first place. Does that make sense?"

DeShaun nodded. "I feel that way, too."

"So what do we do?"

DeShaun shook his head. He didn't have an answer either. I didn't tell him about my interview with the law firm. I didn't want to get his hopes up, but now may have been the best time to expose a little bit of that proverbial light at the end of the long, dark tunnel.

"I had an interview with a law firm. I didn't want to say anything. I didn't want to get our hopes up and then have them smashed to the ground again."

DeShaun nodded, knowing exactly what I was referring to. A week ago, he was in a position to become the manager of a restaurant and making more money. Days after that, we found ourselves scrambling around trying to decide which bills we could put off. At this rate, showering at the gas station around the corner was becoming more of an option.

"It went well." I attempted to downplay it and conceal my optimism. "It's a decent company and if I qualify, they'll pay for schooling. I could even take paralegal courses or get my Masters. It's a good option."

"That sounds great," DeShaun said. "In the meantime, I'm looking for work. I even got a tip about a catering company from M.J. He's worked for them as a side gig a few times. I'm going to put in an application next week. Plus, there's that party Mr. Herjavec is having for his wife. That should pay pretty well."

"So we're on the right track. Maybe you'll make more contacts at the Herjavecs' party and one of them will use you for another party."

"True, true," DeShaun said. "And if that doesn't work, I can always become Mrs. Herjavec's escort for awhile."

"Don't forget about the Countess." I playfully swatted his backside. "Those women would love that and I bet both would pay triple for a piece of your sexy self, probably triple what you and I could make an entire week combined. Not to mention, you'd be able to hit all the high society parties. Those people were always having parties, or is it called a soiree when you're rich?"

"Parties?" DeShaun said. "Mrs. Herjavec probably wouldn't let me out of the bed long enough to go to any of those parties."

"Yeah, and you'd come home sore and with bruises on your body from swinging from the chandeliers. But, hey, it would be worth it to have these damn bills paid."

"Speak for yourself. You wouldn't be the one needing a hip replacement at forty." He stood up and limped around the couch, feigning like he had a bum leg.

We both laughed so hard, our sides hurt.

"By fifty, I'll be in a wheelchair," he said, making another lap around the couch.

"And I'll push you around."

He came around and plopped down onto the couch next to me. "Oh, man," he said, out of breath. "I do love you, Mimi. I just don't want you to stop loving me."

"Are you serious? That could never happen. Sure, we have our issues, but we'll find a way to deal with this. We always do."

He stretched out his arm around me and then leaned in to kiss me. "You're right." At first, his kiss was a quick peck, but then he leaned in again. This time his kiss lingered as he rubbed his hands up and down my back. He pulled my shirt over my head and I pulled down his jeans. I slid off the couch and onto my knees.

With my teeth, I pulled down his Fruit of the Loom boxers and went to work. When I finished, he scooped me up and carried me to the bedroom. Gently, he laid me down onto our bed and stepped out of his jeans and boxers bunched around his ankles.

"Now, I'll do you."

Naomi

I woke up and performed the daily bare minimum. By that, I meant I showered, brushed my teeth, unwrapped my hair and threw on a pair of black pants and a pink silk blouse. I skipped the moisturizing, skipped breakfast and skipped the gas station on the way to work, which I would probably regret when I was sitting at the gas pump with every other nine-to-fiver. I even skipped calling in to the supervisor when I realized I was running late and wouldn't be there in the next ten minutes. Bare minimum.

The fact that I *had* to go to work now more than ever stabbed me right in the gut. I needed to before, but at least in previous circumstances, I was able to fall back on the standby that DeShaun was working and pulling in a salary too.

For the past few days, DeShaun had been searching for a job and had even followed up on that catering tip his ex co-worker, M.J. gave him. Two days ago, he called the company and they had yet to return his call. I urged him to call at least two more times after that, treading dangerously into stalking waters, but the bottom line was; we were desperate. A few days ago, we received an overdue notice via mail from the power company. That really pissed me off. Three months back, we had overpaid them and it took two billing periods to get a measly fifty-six dollars returned. Now that we were four days late, PECO was sending notices and calling, asking for their money like a pimp would his whore. Dang! I got that they wanted their money, but three calls in under an hour? If I didn't have the money the first time, chances were, I probably wasn't going to have it forty-five minutes later.

When I arrived at the bank, thirty-seven minutes late, Percy, the security guard, opened up the door for me. In his usual fashion, he gave a pleasant good morning, nodded and then tipped his security hat.

I wished I loved my job *half* as much as he did or, at the very least, could fake like I did.

I ignored the who-does-she-think-she-is, sideways glances from the other tellers and headed for the back room. I dropped my purse onto the floor of the employee closet and went straight for the bathroom.

I looked into the mirror and studied my reflection. Instead of looking like I was in my early thirties, my reflection screamed that I looked like I was at least forty—and not one of those gorgeous forty-year-old women who kept themselves up. I looked like that forty-year-old woman with three pain-in-the-ass kids, all under the age of six, that whined all damn day long and sucked the little bit of life I still had right out of me.

Hell, with the bloating that was popping up in my mid-section from all the late night stress snacking and the period that was due in a couple of days, I looked like a beat down, pregnant forty-year-old hag.

I splashed some cold water on my face and dabbed it dry with a wad of scratchy brown paper towels. I gave myself another quick once over and then headed to my counter to face my adorning fans, also known as picky, irritating customers.

"Something is wrong with my account," the next man in line said. "I don't know what happened, but my interest was miscalculated. Your bank is off by more than twenty-three dollars."

I tried so hard not to roll my eyes. Twenty-three dollars, huh? My life was falling apart and this dude was bitching about a derisory few dollars? I wished that was my only issue.

I hadn't heard from MacIntyre, Roth and Associates since the interview, and quite frankly, I was getting worried. The interview went well, or so I thought, and I e-mailed the follow-up thank you response, so why was I getting the silent treatment? For the past two days, I replayed the entire interview in my head, combing through every single detail.

Professional attire? Check.

Pleasant demeanor? Check.

Confident attitude? Check.

The other day, feeling slightly insecure, I gave DeShaun the details about the interview.

"What if another applicant was more qualified?"

He simply smiled and shook his head. "Not possible."

"But I had read up on the company to find out what they looked for in employees," I told him. "They wanted passionate, smart, articulate people. I possess those qualities, don't I?"

Again he nodded, more sure than I could ever be. "You're the most passionate person I know."

When I questioned whether or not I may have been overly confident, he kissed my cheek and that was reassurance enough. I only wished I was as confident as he was.

Jim McIntyre, the person who interviewed me, asked what I could bring to the table? I rattled down my qualifications like my life depended on it, which often times during the interview, I felt like it did.

"Do you think I got the job?" I had asked DeShaun like he was The Oracle. Every single detail raced through my mind. Maybe they had many more applicants than I had anticipated and decided on hiring a fresh-out-of-college kid who would demand much less money and minimal health benefits as opposed to someone who had dependents.

DeShaun had embraced me and said, "Take a deep breath, Mimi. Remain positive and the job will come through."

He was right. I had nothing else to go on. A little bit of hope would keep me moving.

"Did you hear me?" The man at the counter stared me down. "Something is wrong with my account. I don't know what happened, but my interest was miscalculated. Your bank is off by more than twenty-three dollars."

I punched his account numbers into the computer. The man had over seventy-five thousand dollars in his savings account and he was bitching about twenty bucks.

"I am so sick of you people trying to pull this." The man's voice got louder with each word, capturing the attention of nearby customers. "I put my money into your bank and expect to get the correct interest. How hard is that?"

I took another deep breath, trying to maintain my composure. "Sir, I'll take a look and take care of it."

"You're damn right you will!"

That was it. I had enough. "Excuse me?" I felt the hot blood pumping through my veins and for a second, I imagined myself reaching across the counter and wrapping my fingers around his scrawny neck. I had it with these people I was so sick of everybody complaining about nothing. At least they had money in the bank to complain about.

The man opened his mouth to say something else, but before he could, I felt a tap on my shoulder. When I turned around, Jeremy was standing there, with a composed smile on his face. "Why don't you allow me to handle this gentleman?"

I glared at the customer. "You don't have to do that."

The composed smile remained on his face when he said, "I insist." Before I could protest further, he grabbed hold of my shoulders and steered me toward the back room.

"These people are so annoying," I whispered, angrily. "Seriously, who gives two craps about his stupid twenty dollars?"

Jeremy stepped up his pace as he continued steering me to the break room.

"Shit! I'll give him the twenty dollars to get the hell off of my line!" I called back, hoping the old bastard heard me.

"Chill," he whispered. "Take a few minutes and get yourself together. When you're ready, you can come back up to the front and I'll let you deal with the jackasses. Deal?"

"Thanks." I opened the door to the back room and headed straight for my purse. I pulled out my phone and dialed. I called DeShaun's cell but a recording came on. The phone was "out of service," which translated into the bill had not been paid. I didn't need the recorded voice to tell me that. I thought he had at least another week before his service stopped. That only meant one thing; my phone was next. I gave it another two or three days, tops.

Several minutes later, Jeremy came to the back room. "Is everything all right?"

I flopped into the refurbished lounge chair and flicked off my left shoe with the toes of my right foot. I did the same with my left shoe. I reached down and squeezed my toes hard, like I was ringing out a wet dishtowel.

"It's the usual," I sighed. "I was seriously about to strangle that old dude if he didn't get off my case about his stupid twenty-three dollars."

Jeremy watched me rub my aching feet. "Yeah, I could tell that. And the funny thing was, it wasn't our mistake. He miscalculated."

I hopped up. "What? You mean he brought that mess to me and got me all riled up for nothing?"

"Woosah, woosah. Take it down for a minute," Jeremy said. "I can read the morning headlines now, *Black woman teller strangles elderly white man with big ears.*"

"You noticed those ears, too?"

"How could you not?" he said. "Ever notice that when you massage yourself it never feels as good as when you're being massaged by someone else?"

"Huh?"

"Your feet."

I looked down. I forgot I was still rubbing them. "Oh."

"What did you think I was talking about?" He thought a second. "Oh, I didn't mean it like that. I only meant that it feels better when someone else rubs your feet as opposed to doing it yourself."

"Yeah. I got that now," I said, still rubbing.

"Well?"

"Well, what?"

"Do you want me to do that for you?"

"Nah." I squeezed my big toe. "I'm good."

"Be glad you didn't have to talk to the man for too long," Jeremy said. "His breath was like roadkill, and not the kind that was hit an hour ago. I'm talking the skunk-that-was-struck-by-a-semi-tractor-trailer-three-days-ago funk."

I gave an obligatory chuckle. He was trying to make me feel better, but I really wasn't in the mood.

"Speaking of roadkill. Your feet—why don't you put them dogs away? My eyes are starting to water."

I picked up my shoe and tossed it at him. It smacked the side of his arm and clunked to the ground. "Oh, shut up. My feet don't stink."

"Nah, I'm kidding." He tossed the shoe back at me. I ducked and it missed and hit the back cushion of the chair. "Your shoe smells like honeysuckle."

"Shut up, Nerd Boy!"

He raised his brows. "Oh, I know you ain't talkin' Candylicious. Wasn't that your skripper name?"

"Not even close, Barry Back Brace."

"Nasty Naomi."

"Forty-Year-Old Virgin."

"Fantasia Freak-a-Lot."

I looked at him. "Where did that one come from?"

He shrugged. "Ran out of names. Look, why don't you relax before you go out there and chop off someone else's head?" He stood up and headed toward the door. "Oh, yeah, I came back here to tell you the manager wants to see you in her office."

So much for relaxing. "Do you know what she wants?"

He shook his head. "Contrary to popular belief, I do not get into my aunt's affairs. I have to tell you, though, be prepared. Maybe dude with the big ears complained. Don't worry, I got your back on this one. Dude was straight ignorant."

I stood up and stepped into my shoes. "Might as well get this over with." I headed down the hall, toward the manager's office. I wasn't looking forward to this conversation, especially after being late a few times and my nasty attitude write-up, but hey, you never knew, miracles did happen. It might actually be some good news for a change.

As I walked down the corridor, I had a tough time believing that. And I was right.

DeShaun and Naomi

S omething had to give. He had been to four restaurants today and nothing. One wasn't hiring, the others took his application and told him they would call if something came up that fit his requirements. In restaurant speak that meant his application was going into the trash bin. He was a server applying to restaurants, not as the CEO to Fortune 500 companies—of course these spots had something that fit his requirements.

He had called a fifth and final time about that catering gig M.J. had mentioned, but they haven't gotten back to him. He wished people would stop being such assholes so he wouldn't waste his time.

He hadn't told Naomi yet, but the car people called and threatened repossession by the end of the week. He almost wanted them to take the damn car. It wasn't like they could afford gas prices anyway. Even if he found a job today, it would take at least two weeks before he got a paycheck. They would still have to play catch-up. A month ago, Naomi had started categorizing the bills; the *behind* stack and the *way behind* stack. Eventually, they all fell into one pile; the probably-never-getting-paid-and-getting-stuck-on-your-credit-report stack.

He reached into his pocket, pulled out his phone and dialed. It was cut off. "Dammit!" He had used his cell as the contact number for the job applications. He had also used the number as the contact for the catering gig. *Maybe they called.* He had to go under the assumption that they called so he made a quick decision to contact them one last time. If he didn't, he'd be thinking about this for the rest of his life.

When he got home, he burst through the door. Good, he beat Naomi home. He headed straight for the phone. No messages. He picked it up to dial. There was no dial tone.

Crap!

He had also left his e-mail address on the applications. Maybe when they realized they couldn't call to offer the job, they would send an e-mail. He ran to the computer but then remembered they stopped paying the Internet bill last month in order to make a partial car payment. He turned on the computer anyway. He had to try.

As predicted, the Internet was down.

He headed straight for the kitchen and opened the fridge. He pulled out a cold beer and demolished it in ten seconds flat. He grabbed another one as he tossed the empty can from the first one into the trash. *Now what?*

He took another swig. He thought about his father and what prompted him to get out of dodge, leaving him and his mother home alone to do the best they could. Did his father feel like DeShaun did at this very moment? He would never leave Mimi, but maybe his father felt overwhelmed. Regardless of the reasons, no way was DeShaun ever going to be that weak. He'd figure something out. What that something was, he had no idea.

Normally, he would have a delicious dinner waiting for Mimi when she came home, but not today. The only meat in the fridge was a frozen chicken and he wasn't in the mood to thaw out and fry chicken.

He took another gulp as he listened to the soles of his wife's heels click against the hardwood floor. He listened as she kicked off her shoes, her heels making a sharp clack as they landed against the floor. He polished off his second beer, listening to something sounding like a stack of magazines dropping to the floor. He heard her curse under her breath and then slap her keys down onto the foyer table. Apparently, she wasn't in a good mood either.

Eventually, the muted footsteps headed toward him. When she came into the kitchen, he glanced down at the stack of brand new bills in her hand. When she saw him, she greeted him with a tired "Hey."

"How was work today?" DeShaun opened up the refrigerator and grabbed the last beer. "Want it?'

"You wouldn't believe me if I told you."

"At this point, I'd believe anything."

"Not this."

"Try me."

"Okay, here it goes. Today I was fired from my crappy job at the bank. And do you want to know why?"

"Are you serious?"

"As a heart attack. Apparently, that guy, Jeremy, I thought was so cool, turned out to be an asshole. Surprise on me."

"What happened?"

"First, I was told I was being fired because I left work early to go on that interview I told you about."

"How did they find out about that?"

"Who knows? I'm guessing Jeremy. But that's not the best part. When I denied it, the manager came at me with another excuse—drinking at lunch."

"What? You were drinking at lunch? When?"

"That day I told you Jeremy and I went out to lunch. He bought us two—count 'em—two light beers. He had one, too."

"Really, Mimi? Drinking on the job?"

"I know you are not judging me. You were fired too, remember?"

"Not for drinking."

"Oh, no, just for stealing."

"For the last time, I wasn't stealing," DeShaun said, angrily.

"Then how did you get fired for stealing if you weren't stealing?"

"It was those bottles of wine I used to bring home for you."

"You were stealing those? I thought your boss gave them to you."

He shook his head. "Like you really thought Stiles would give anyone anything. I was bringing home the bottles but paying for them later. They were getting the money and then some. I wasn't even taking the discount when I paid for them."

"You got fired for that?"

"That old dude had it in for me a long time before that."

"So lemme get this straight; you're saying you paid them for the bottles of wine after the fact?"

"It was always the very next week."

"Why didn't you tell me that? More importantly, why didn't you tell *them* that?"

"I didn't think I had to tell you that." He pulled the tab on the last can of beer. It made a hissing sound. "And second." He took a long, drawn-out swig. "They don't care."

"I didn't ask you if they cared, I asked you if you told them that."

"What for? I hated that place. Besides, you hated me working there."

"It was a job, DeShaun. And even though I hated that job, you at least had a job. I wanted you to have a better position, not NO position."

"Look," DeShaun said, taking another sip. "What's done is done. I've been thinking. Maybe we need to hit up your parents again."

"There's no way that's gonna happen."

"We're desperate, Naomi. We've got to do something. You're standing there now with a shit load of bills in your hand."

"Why don't we hit up *your* parents for the money?"

"That's not funny, Naomi."

That was ignorant, I knew it. DeShaun's parents had divorced when he was six years old and he had only seen his father twice in his life, but I was only trying to make a point.

"Please don't remind me how your parents paid for our wedding, Naomi. And please don't give me the speech about how they put the down payment on the house and even loaned us money to purchase a car. Seriously, I can't hear that mess again."

"It's true. I'm simply saying my parents are not an option this time. We need to consider something else."

"Like what? We ran out of options when the power company threatened to turn off our electricity. Options sailed down the river when we received the car repossession letter in the mail yesterday."

"We got a letter yesterday?"

"Yeah. That, and a late notice from the credit card people, telling us that we are two months past due and that we are being charged fifty dollars a month in late fees."

"Oh, crap! I forgot about that."

"Ask your parents for a loan," he said. "We have to do something and quick."

"What I don't understand is why are my people always considered *your* go-to option first? Shouldn't that be my call? They're *my* family, not yours. Shouldn't I be the one to lean on them?"

"I have to be the first to suggest it because you won't."

"DeShaun, you know how my mother can be, especially about money."

"Exactly," he said, nodding. "Now imagine having to live with that when we can't make our mortgage payment."

"Stop running to my parents every time we get caught out there. Why don't you hurry up and get a job?"

He matched my gaze. "Why don't you?"

Our eyes locked. At first, we were dead serious, but then for some unknown reason, we burst out laughing at the exact same time. We must've been thinking the same thing.

"Can you imagine living with my mother and making out in her basement like teenagers?"

"You think that's funny," DeShaun said, "think about that ratty old bathrobe your pops wears. The one with the hole right in the crotch that he refuses to throw out. The man is a surgeon; he can afford a new robe."

"And what about that ugly brown scarf Mom ties on her head every night?"

"So that's where you get it from?"

"When she called me the other day, we only talked for a few minutes. She said she had to wrap her hair before bed and all I could picture was that ugly, holey scarf."

"So you want to go back to that, huh?"

"No."

"Will you ask for a loan then? We'll pay them back like we always do."

"I'll think about it."

"I'll tell you what," DeShaun said, scratching his chin. "Sleep on the idea."

"I will."

DeShaun thought a second. "Even after all this, there is a bright side."

"Really? And what in the world would that be?"

"We can both sleep in tomorrow."

"And how is that different for you? Even when you worked at the restaurant, you didn't go in until six in the evening."

"Yeah, but now you'll be with me." He placed a small peck on my cheek. "I love you, Mimi."

"I love you too."

That night, we made love. It was nice, but I wasn't into it as much as I had hoped. While he was inside of me, all I could think about was how in the hell were we going to ask to borrow money... again?

Naomi

The next morning, we didn't sleep in. DeShaun decided to get an early start and head downtown to see if any of those jobs had called. We had no way of knowing since our Internet and phone connections were cut off. It was a long shot, but what else could we do? I spent the morning in the kitchen, baking batches of cream cheese brownies while trying to get up enough courage to call my parents and ask for money. First, I needed to make a payment to have the phone turned back on. Otherwise, I'd have to beg in person. That was the last thing I needed.

I grabbed four blocks of unsweetened chocolate, placed them in a bowl and stuck the bowl inside the microwave. I set the timer for two minutes and watched until the chocolate melted into a heap of brown, sticky goo. When the microwave beeped, I opened it up and mixed in one cup of sugar along with one cup of flour and a stick of butter. I cracked two large eggs on the side of the mixing bowl, grabbed a spoon and started furiously mixing. I poured in a teaspoon of real vanilla and stirred. I stuck my pinky finger into the bowl for a taste. It needed more sugar.

We had decided to have DeShaun's phone turned on first. Restaurants he applied to may have been trying to contact him about a job. Since I hadn't started the job search yet, I didn't need my phone right away.

I poured the batter into a pan and then slathered on a layer of the cream cheese and sugar mixture I had prepared earlier. I reached into the kitchen drawer, pulled out a butter knife and marbled the cream cheese throughout. As soon as I stuck the glass pan into the pre-warmed oven, I grabbed my house keys from the coffee table and rushed out the door, locking the door behind me.

The sun's hot rays beat down onto my shoulders as I walked down the block to use the pay phone. I needed to call the cell company and make a payment with the credit card.

It was going to be another scorching summer day. It wasn't even noon yet, and I could already smell the heat bearing down on the cement sidewalk. As I continued down the road, the sun disappeared behind a swollen cloud, making the skies gray. Droplets of rain fell and bounced off my arms.

I was risking a big fat decline using the credit card for a cell phone payment. We hadn't even bothered to make a payment on any of the cards in months, even before we lost our jobs. Credit cards were one of those bills that fell in line after buying shoes and taking mini-vacations to Atlantic City. We were dangerously nearing a completely dried-up cash flow situation.

I hadn't been inside a pay phone since forever. The first one I stepped into didn't have a door for privacy, plus, it didn't work. Neither did the second or third. I had to walk another two blocks before finding one that actually took the coins jammed inside my pocket, in case they didn't accept toll-free charges.

I picked up the phone, carefully inspected it and then smashed and rubbed the receiver into the leg of my jeans, hoping to kill any surviving germs and bacteria. In my head, all I could hear was Chris Hansen from *Dateline* giving the results to germ tests on public property.

Fungus

E-coli

Fecal matter
Yuck!

I reached down into my pocket and grabbed the folded up envelope with the number to the cell phone company. As anticipated, *they didn't even have an 800 number to call, or at least I couldn't find it on the bill!*

I punched in the numbers and was immediately met with a recording, explaining I was being put on hold due to a high number of calls.

Thank goodness for the coin stash, I thought, while nervously shifting back and forth inside the cramped space.

Finally, a live customer service representative came on the line. The representative asked for my information. Annoyed, I gave the same information I had given to the automated system not two minutes ago.

When the girl said she was putting my card through for payment, I squeezed my eyes shut and silently prayed right there in that dirty, constricted, graffiti-ridden phone booth. Minutes later, the rep came back and said the payment had gone through and that the phone was pending activation in approximately ten minutes. My prayers had been answered. If only that worked for the pick six lottery.

I practically skipped all the way back to the house, with people in passing cars looking at me as if I was a crazy woman. When I got back to the house, I grabbed DeShaun's phone from the kitchen countertop and tried it. It was on.

I started dialing my parents' number and got to the last number, but for some reason, I hesitated pressing that final button. I took a deep breath. When I exhaled, I pressed the last digit at the same time. The phone only rang once before someone picked up.

"Hello?" It was my mother, sounding like I woke her up.

I took another quick breath, trying to muster up a little cheeriness. "Hi, Mom."

"Naomi, baby, how are you?" Her tone perked up when she heard my voice. A good sign.

"We've been great," I lied. I hit the speaker button and placed the phone back onto the kitchen counter. On speaker phone, I didn't feel as intimidated.

"I didn't recognize this number when it popped up," she said. "Did you get a new number?"

"This isn't my phone."

"Oh. So anyway," she continued, as if she was the one who had called me to shoot the breeze. "Your father is getting another award from the hospital. He's gotten so many, I lost count."

"That's great." My voice was beginning to crack like it always did when I was nervous. "Tell him we said, 'Congratulations.'"

She fell quiet. Anytime I referred to DeShaun, her pep zipped right out of her.

"So, how *is* your husband doing?" Mom asked.

I could not recall one time that I heard my mother say his name. I mean, I know she had before, she had to have, but it had been so long that I couldn't even remember. She always referred to DeShaun as *your husband* or *him*. When she felt like being really rude, she referred to him as *that guy*.

"DeShaun's fine. But listen, we may need to borrow some money." I decided jumping right in was the best approach. If we made too much idle chit-chat, I'd lose my nerve.

It fell quiet again.

"What happened this time?" She sighed. Not a good sign.

I bit my bottom lip. "We ran into a little trouble. It would only be for a short time. We'd pay you back in a couple of months."

"Let me guess, he lost his job," she said.

"What? No, he didn't lose his job." It annoyed me how intuitive she was. "We ran into some financial issues, that's all."

"That's what you said last time. You seem to run into quite a few financial issues lately, but that's to be expected when your husband is a waiter. He needs to go back to school and get his degree. Maybe then he can get a real job that pays real money instead of relying on the crumbs of customers. I believe in his world they call them tips. Speaking of which, why are you still working as a teller? I didn't spend all that money for you to get a degree and then not use it."

"I know, Mom. I'm just waiting until I find the right job."

"What's his excuse?"

It seemed like I spent every phone call with my mom defending our career choices. This call was no different. "He doesn't have the greatest job, I know, but it is a decent job."

At least *it was* a decent job.

"I told you not to marry him, didn't I?"

"He's a nice guy, Mom," I defended. "And he treats me well."

"Sure, he's a nice guy and he makes you dinner here and there, but that doesn't pay the bills. Face it; you married beneath you. Everyone thinks so—your aunt, your uncle, your cousins, every-one. The thing is, you know it, too." She paused. "The truth is, I don't feel comfortable loaning you money again. You both have to learn to stand on your own two feet and not call us every time you find yourself in trouble. If your father and I keep bailing you out, when will you learn to take care of yourselves? He needs to step up and— "

"Never mind, Mom. It's not that serious."

"Then why call in the first place and get me all upset? Your hus-band needs to learn how to provide for you."

I got quiet, attempting to figure out how to respond without getting into an argument. I understood where she was coming from, but DeShaun was my heart. Nothing I said would change her mind. If I continued to engage in this conversation, I'd be on the phone for hours.

"Hang up!"

I whipped around. DeShaun was standing at the front door with a combined look of defeat and anger—but mostly anger.

"How long were you standing there?" I asked.

"Long enough."

"Mom, I'll call you back." I hung up the phone, preparing for yet another argument.

DeShaun

He had pulled into the parking lot of the third restaurant he'd applied to. It was tiring, but he had to do what was needed. Naomi was home asking her parents for money and he had to do his part to help stay financially afloat.

He stepped into the first restaurant. When he inquired as to whether or not they had attempted to call him for a job, the first two restaurant managers looked at him as if they thought he was crazy. The young girl, whom he assumed was the hostess, simply said, "No," without so much as a glance in his direction. He had stood there, looking like an idiot as he tried to explain to the girl that his phone was out of order and that he may have missed the call. The girl smirked, as she told him, "No," once again and then followed it up with, "We're actually not hiring at this time." Then she added, "Even when we do start hiring, we'll be picking from the pool of resumes already on file."

Bitch! She didn't even know him and she was treating him like a dog.

The second restaurant was a little nicer, but still a no. The manager, the guy DeShaun had dropped off his application to, had come to the front and explained in a polite manner that he had a stack of resumes on his desk that he hadn't had the time to get to. He followed up his rejection with, "If there's a fit, we'll call."

In the parking lot of the third restaurant he had applied to, he took a deep breath as he prepared to step out of the car. He went to open the car door but couldn't bring himself to do it. He couldn't take any more rejections. He was sick and tired of begging for jobs, positions that a chimp could do.

He stuck the key back into the ignition, pulled out of the parking lot and headed home.

He turned onto Swedesford Drive, a backroad he often took when he wanted to think, and eased up on the accelerator. As he slowed, he spotted a tiny diner with a "For Sale" sign jammed into the corner of the front window. He swerved the car and pulled into the parking lot of the diner.

That was it! Why hadn't he thought of this idea a long time ago? Maybe this entire situation was God trying to tell them that they should open their own restaurant. He always thought about it, and even in the back of his mind, planned to do it someday. Maybe that someday was today. He was out of a job. Naomi was out of a job. This was the perfect time. The idea was so crazy, he might be able to pull it off. He grabbed a piece of tissue and a pen from the glove compartment and jotted down the phone number on the "For Sale" sign. He started the car and jumped back onto Swedesford Drive. As he drove along the winding road, he started crunching numbers in his head. Naomi was home asking her parents to borrow some money, but instead of asking for money to cover their bills for the next month or so, they could ask for a down payment to the restaurant. It wasn't like it had to be a loan either. He could bring her parents on as business investors.

He pulled over to the side of the road and grabbed his phone from the glove compartment. His fingers fumbled when he tried to dial, he was so excited. After three rings, she picked up.

"Hey, babe, I have a great idea," he said. "I think you're going to love it. It's something I should've thought about a long time ago…it doesn't matter, I've got the idea now."

She was silent on the other end for a moment. "What is it, DeShaun? I'm on the other line with my mother."

By the tone of her voice, their conversation wasn't going so well. It was even more reason to share his good, no great, idea that could end their money troubles. But before he could tell her, she said, "I've got to go. I'll see you when you get home." She hung up.

Never mind. This was something he wanted to tell her in person anyway. He stepped on the accelerator and turned off the back road and onto the main highway. It was faster. He couldn't wait to get home to tell Naomi about his business plan. This could really work.

He had to do this right, though. He had to get a presentation together first. Naomi could do that, she was good at creating graphs and charts and all that other stuff. Like a real business, he would present the numbers to her parents, the profit, the losses, expenses, everything. He'd detail how they could triple their money in less than five years. It would be tight in the beginning, but it could be done. It had to be done. When he looked into his wife's eyes, he saw the disappointment. Maybe he was being overly sensitive, but it felt that way. He didn't want to feel that way again.

He stepped on the gas, careful not to exceed the speed limit too much. This was the first time in years he felt excited about something and it felt good. He was going to give this restaurant idea his all. Her parents would then see that their daughter had married the right guy. It may have taken a little while, but he was going to show her parents that he was not some idiot waiter with no aspirations in life, like they thought. He needed the right opportunity and right now, he could not think of a better time.

When he had walked through the front door to give his wife the good news, he heard her talking to her mother on the speakerphone.

Apparently, the credit card charge had gone through. *Another sign?*

DeShaun had dropped his keys onto the foyer table and raced toward his wife's voice.

He was shocked at what he heard when he walked in on Naomi and her mother talking. Naomi was sitting on a stool at the kitchen counter, her back was toward him.

He heard Naomi's mother say, "Face it; you married beneath you. Everyone thinks so— your aunt, your uncle, your cousins, everyone."

His heart dropped to the floor as he listened at the entranceway. It was as if someone had taken a serrated knife and dug it deep into his heart and twisted as he listened to his mother-in-law continue.

The thing is, you know it too.

His mother-in-law's words stung, but what had socked him in the gut like a two-ton sledgehammer was what he *didn't* hear. Naomi had not stepped up to defend him. At that exact moment, his dream of owning a restaurant slowly deflated like a hot air balloon with a slow leak.

Naomi and DeShaun

DeShaun grabbed another beer from the fridge. "You want one?"

"Yup."

He grabbed two Kalik beer bottles from the fridge and handed one to me. He opened up the kitchen drawer and rifled through the utensils. "Have you seen the bottle opener?"

"It's not in there?"

He shook his head. "Nope." He checked the dish drainer and the drawer under the sink. Finally, he grabbed one of the bottles, lifted it to his mouth and bit down hard. Seconds later, I heard the *pfffft* of the bottle and off popped the cap. He lifted the next bottle to his mouth.

Pfffft.

He handed me one bottle and took a swig of the second one. "Problem solved."

"How in the world did you ever find Kalik beer in Pennsylvania?" I asked.

"Would you believe they sell them at the beer distributor in King of Prussia. A Bahamian beer in the Philly suburbs? The best part is that it was even less than the brand name beers here. I guess it's because no one was buying it. Maybe they mispriced it. Who knows? Had to buy a case before they realized their mistake." He took another big swig, leaving only an inch or so left inside the bottle. "You know what else I could really go for?"

"What?"

"A good hit."

"A joint? You must be kidding. I haven't done that since my college days." The one and only time I smoked a joint was with my college roommate and two guys she invited over, and even then I hadn't really smoked it. I pulled a Bill Clinton and didn't inhale. That was only because I had no idea how to inhale. Rod Bowie was the friend of the guy that my roommate was seeing and when they came over to our room, they were fully stocked with weed filled cigars and some sugary drink called Cisco that they had picked up in Delaware. I later learned Cisco was also referred to as liquid crack, which was something I found out the hard way.

"If I found one, would you smoke it with me?" he asked, grinning. With another Kalik in hand, he went into the living room and sat on the carpeted floor, in the space between the couch and the glass four-square coffee table.

"If you found one?" I asked. "Did you happen to remember you left a joint under your pillow?"

"Actually, yeah."

"What?"

"Not under the pillow, but remember that party I told you about where I worked for the Herjavecs' and Mrs. Herjavec tried to get all of us to smoke a joint with her that night? I didn't then, but she stuck it in my pocket. I forgot I brought that thing home and stuck it in the drawer. It's been there ever since."

"Seriously?"

"It's the good stuff, too. You know rich folk don't play around."

"Lemme see it," I said.

DeShaun jumped up from the carpet floor and dashed off to the bedroom. I heard him fumbling through the dresser drawers.

Minutes later, he returned with a lit joint dangling between his lips. "Man, this stuff is good. Try it."

He handed it to me. Slowly, I raised the joint to my lips. I took a deep breath and immediately, the smoke filled my lungs. I started coughing furiously.

"Take it easy," he said. "This ain't the cheap shit. This is quality weed here."

I lifted the joint and took a long, slow drag. I held the smoke in my mouth, but when I tried to inhale, I started choking again.

"I forgot you don't know how to smoke," he said.

"No, not really."

"Here, let me show you." He took the joint from my hands and took a puff. "Do it slow and easy, like this." He took another puff, held the smoke in his mouth and slowly inhaled. "Take your time." He handed it back to me.

I mimicked exactly what I thought he did. This time, I inhaled much slower. Almost immediately, I began feeling lightheaded, but not in a bad way, more like a loose limp piece-of-pasta way. I raised my head and looked over at DeShaun. He took a deep puff. I watched him inhale, thinking, *When did he take the joint from my hand?*

"It's good, isn't it?" He took another puff, sat back and rested his head against the couch cushion. "Why don't they make oxygen air like weed smoke?"

"I don't believe you make oxygen air, do you?" I asked.

"Seriously, think about it. Can you imagine how happy everyone would be if we walked around high all day?"

"Wouldn't that be a crackhead?"

He lifted his head and looked at me with a serious expression. Without warning, he burst out laughing so hard, tears rolled down his cheeks.

When I looked at him, I completely understood what he was laughing about. I started howling with him. He didn't have to say a word. I got it.

"We wouldn't have to worry about not having a job," he said. "And money? Screw money. Who needs it?"

"Yeah," I joined in. "We also wouldn't have to deal with people who were disappointed in us all the time. What were they called again....oh, yeah, parents."

This made him laugh even harder. "Yes! Your mother hates my guts, especially after she called me a loser on the phone yesterday."

"She doesn't hate you," I said. "She doesn't care for you very much. Now, there's a difference." Even before the full sentence escaped my lips, we started laughing. "And she doesn't think you're a loser, not really. She called all my boyfriends that."

"I'm not your boyfriend. I'm your husband and she does think I'm a loser. When she said it on the phone, you didn't even defend me."

"That's only because I couldn't get a word in edgewise. You know how she is, which reminds me, she declined us the loan."

DeShaun took another drag. "Another rejection, huh? That one can get in line with the rest."

I grabbed the joint from his hand. "Oh, what did you want to tell me when you called yesterday?"

"Nothing. I had an idea but it wouldn't work, especially now."

"Why not?"

"Because it involved your mother, you know, the woman who thinks I'm not good enough for her little darling because I can't keep her in the lifestyle she's accustomed to."

"No, no, you have to say it like this." I hoisted my nose in the air, lowered my pitch an octave and raised my hand above my head.

"Don't forget to stick out your teeny pinky." He choked back a laugh.

"Oh, yeah." I stuck out my pinky finger and in my best British accent, I said, "Son, you are not good enough for my daughter; you are a lowdown, dirty dog." I wagged my finger at him for added effect.

"Your mother's British?"

We laughed so hard, we rolled on the floor for a good five minutes. Still on the floor, he reached over and took the joint from my hand. He took another puff. "Seriously, babe, something has got to give."

"Yeah," I said. "You have *got to give* me that joint again."

He tried hard not to laugh. "I'm serious, Mimi. There has got to be something we can do to control the situation, instead of letting it control us like some damn puppets. What's that dude's name?" He hopped up from the floor. "Want another beer?"

"Sure, and what dude?"

"That little guy with the big nose?"

"What are you talking about?"

"You know who I'm talking about," he said, heading for the kitchen, while I took another puff. "Pinocchio!" He snapped his fingers. "That's his name! Anyway, we really need to come up with something to get out of this slump."

I heard what he was saying, but it wasn't registering. I was too busy watching the circle of smoke I was attempting to make, like I was some sort of weed smoking connoisseur. "How do you make rings?" I called in to the kitchen.

DeShaun came out of the kitchen with two Kaliks in hand. "It's like we're always on the defensive. We need to be on the offense and kick life's butt." With both beers in his hand, he crouched down into a football position. "We should be charging, instead of running in the other direction. Hike one! Hike two." He shot up, charging the air. The beers spilled down his white T-shirt. "Shit!"

I took another toke. "What do you think we should do about it?"

"Hey, take it easy with that." He handed me a beer and plopped back onto his spot on the carpet.

"I don't know what we should do."

"We could sell stuff on eBay," I offered.

"We don't have anything to sell. What about stripping?" he asked. "I bet you'd be real good at that, huh?"

"I would never strip again." As soon the words left my lips, I looked to DeShaun to see if he realized what I said. He didn't. "How about—" I couldn't even finish the sentence. I was out of ideas already. "Wait! I could sell my body," I joked.

He pulled at the hem of my khaki skirt. "That would bring us a buck fifty."

"Hey!"

"You know I'm only kidding. I would pay a million bucks for that ass." He got on all fours and crawled over to me. He playfully nuzzled his head in my lap and started whimpering like a puppy dog.

I patted his head. "Good boy."

He raised his head so that our faces were inches from each other. Slowly, he began softly kissing my neck. His lips worked down to my collarbone. He reached up and began fumbling with the buttons on my blouse. He got to the third button before getting impatient and ripping my shirt open. Buttons flew everywhere, but I didn't care. He reached around to the back of my skirt and unfastened the latch. His kisses were urgent and wet. I couldn't wait any longer. I hopped up and pulled off my blouse while he pulled his shirt over his head. I hiked up my skirt and went to pull down my panties before I realized I wasn't wearing any. He grabbed my waist and pulled me down to the carpet.

I threw back my head and enjoyed the ride.

DeShaun and Naomi

The next morning, I awoke before DeShaun. I felt like I had a big puff of ganja smoke, wafting around inside my head from last night. My body ached, as if I had run two marathons and completed a decathlon after that. I glanced over at DeShaun. He looked so peaceful when he slept. Looking at him right now, you couldn't tell we were three days from having our lights turned off, two days from having our car repossessed and one day from being evicted from our home.

I gently ran my fingertips up and down his arm. He stirred a bit but commenced snoring.

I loved him—I really did—but our financial situation seemed to keep overriding that love, causing us to neglect each other and focus all of our attention on the crisis at hand.

"Hey," he said, when he saw me looking at him. He sat up, rubbed his eyes and looked around the room, taking a mental survey of the situation. "What happened in here? Did a hurricane hit?"

"Yeah, Hurricane DeShaun. From what I remember, we were all over the place."

The bedroom looked like someone had broken in and junked the place, leaving articles of clothing everywhere.

I slightly recalled our frantic hunt for a condom. I had stopped taking the pill last month, until I got my prescription renewed, but now, with no insurance, we would have to continue relying on our old standby—Magnums, extra large.

Last night, DeShaun had pulled open the first drawer but couldn't find one. He yanked out the second and third drawers and eventually found a lone condom sitting at the bottom of the nightstand drawer.

I made a note to scrape together a few bucks and purchase some tomorrow.

I mentally calculated how much money was left in our joint account. After the last month's bills, we were left with a little over six hundred, but we still hadn't paid the water bill and one of the credit cards. The credit card we could skip, but the water bill was going in the mail this week. I wasn't supposed to get my last check from the bank until next week, but that money was already spent, going toward the mortgage we were already late on. DeShaun's checks hadn't been great, but the tips, which were often times more than his paycheck, went toward groceries. With that gone, I didn't know how we were going to eat this week.

I surveyed the bedroom, checking out the destruction of Hurricane DeShaun. In clichéd fashion, clothes were strewn all over the place. One of my bras was even dangling from the light fixture above the bed. *What the hell?*

"Last night was good." DeShaun kissed me on the cheek and swung his legs over the side of the bed. Nothing passionate, just a quick and what felt like an obligatory morning kiss.

He reached under the bed, pulled out his slippers and stepped into them. "Thanks to the joint, that was the first night in a long time that I didn't feel any pressure, thinking about money, the job or anything else for that matter."

I rolled over to his side of the bed. The covers slipped, exposing my bare upper body. "Do you think we'd be happy if we hit the lottery?"

He looked down at my bare breasts. "I already did. A few times last night."

"No, seriously," I said. "We have our health and we have each other. Is money really the only factor that's making us miserable?"

He shrugged. "Money doesn't make people miserable. It's *not* having money that keeps people strung out." He scooted over next to me on the bed. "Mimi, I've been thinking. What if we stopped working for people and did something on our own? It would be great. We could maybe own a business and make money for ourselves."

"DeShaun, we are in no position to even think about that right now. We can't even keep our bills current; how are we supposed to shell out thousands of dollars for a business?"

I waited for him to go the parents' route again. He didn't. He simply said, "Yeah, you're right," and dropped the subject.

"What do you suppose the Herjavecs are doing right now?" I asked.

He thought a moment. "I can tell you what they're not doing. They're not sitting here, stressing about money and talking about us."

"Yeah, but remember, the grass is always greener," I told him. "They probably have other issues. I watch *Snapped*."

"I can tell you one issue Mrs. Herjavec has," DeShaun said. "Her old man isn't putting it down like he used to on her. Every time I see her, she's complaining about not getting any. The sad thing is, it's really more than that. He never spends any time with her. He's always working. Oh, and did I tell you he's into young black guys?"

"Get out of here! Has he ever hit on you?"

"Hell no! I would kick his ass from here to Zimbabwe in a heartbeat. According to Mrs. Herjavec, I'm not young enough anyway. He likes 'em barely legal. She told me he gets them gifts in exchange for favors, if you know what I mean."

"As disgusting as that sounds, that is an idea," I said.

"What is?"

"To get a little something here and there in exchange for companionship."

"Let him hit it for some cash? Are you crazy? There ain't enough cash on the face of this earth to let that happen."

"Not him, you weirdo. I mean her. You say all she is really looking for is some companionship. You said so yourself, with her it's not all about sex. Hang out with her for a little bit, and I'd bet she'd be more than happy to pay a couple of these bills up in here."

"I'll ask you again." He reached over and playfully knocked the side of my head. "Are you crazy? You must still be high from last night. Didn't I tell you that was the good stuff?"

"Seriously." The question had started out as a hypothetical situation, but the more I formulated the entire scenario in my head, the more I could see it happening. "Take control of the situation, instead of letting the situation take control of you, right?" I said, scooting up alongside him and wrapping my arms around his neck. I softly pecked his cheek, a gesture he enjoyed. "Think about it, baby. It wouldn't be that bad. Take her to dinner, and, you know, hang out with her every once in awhile."

"Wouldn't that make me a male prostitute?"

"It doesn't have to be all about cash. You said so yourself. She's generous with gifts. You said so yourself. She will be so grateful to have someone around to talk to; she'll lavish you with a few little trinkets here and there. We'll sell 'em and pay off a few bills."

He shook his head. "I am not doing that."

I released my embrace and flopped back down onto the bed. "Yeah, I guess you're right. It was a stupid idea."

The more I thought about it, the more I realized how idiotic the idea was. I tried to rationalize the idea by believing that we'd be doing that poor little old lady, Mrs. Herjavec, a favor by providing someone for her to hang out with. DeShaun was right, it would never work.

DeShaun hopped out of bed and grabbed his boxers from the bed post. "Do you want some breakfast?" He stepped into his shorts. "You need some food in your body to fuel that brain of yours. You're talking crazy this morning."

"Nah, I'm not really hungry."

"Suit yourself, but I'm going to make me some grits and bacon."

"You hate grits."

"Not really."

"And you don't eat bacon like that either," I told him. "You think you are so slick."

He grinned. "I wanted you to eat something. Don't take this the wrong way, but you've been looking kind of beat down lately."

"Gee, how can I not take that wrong?"

He sat down next to me on the bed. "Are you feeling okay?" He reached over and placed the back of his hand on my forehead, like my mother used to do when I was a child, sick in bed.

"I'm fine," I reassured. "I'm a little tired. If I get hungry later, I'll grab something."

"Okay. You stay home and relax. I'm heading out to see if I can hook up a job someplace. I should only be a few hours. If you need anything, call."

"On what?" I asked.

"My phone's working, remember?"

"Yeah, but the house phone ain't."

"Shit! I forgot. I'll be back in a few hours. You should be good, right?"

"I guess I'll have to be."

We both laughed.

He reached for his jeans, hanging on the handle bars of the exercise bike neither of us used, and stepped into them. "Got anything planned for today?"

"I'm going to try to get in contact with McIntyre, Roth and Associates to find out if I got the job. I haven't heard from them yet."

"Good luck, baby. You need my phone?"

"Nah. I'll get my lazy butt up and call from around the corner again. Besides, they probably won't be in the office until nine, at the earliest."

He leaned down and kissed me. His lips lingered on my cheek for a few seconds and then, he looked at me with such intensity, I thought he was going to give me more bad news. Instead, the corners of his mouth turned slightly upward as he said, "I promise you, everything is going to be all right."

"I know."

He stood up and left, gently closing the door behind him.

I rolled over in bed, releasing a sigh of relief. It was a strange way to feel right now, but, through all of this, I was glad of one thing—we still had each other's backs. If being broke and a day short of homeless didn't break that, nothing could.

DeShaun

The clock on the dash read 11:27. The sun was high in the sky as he headed home. When he spotted the turn-off for his old restaurant, he thought about Stiles and how he would be there, unloading boxes of stock before the lunchtime rush.

During his job hunt this morning, the thought about asking Stiles for his job back crossed his mind at least a dozen times, but as soon as he considered it, he kicked the thought right out of his head. Stiles had fired him without a second thought. DeShaun hadn't even bothered explaining that the wine was paid for. At that time, he really didn't care. If he had not been fired, DeShaun probably would have ended up quitting that crap job eventually—but that wasn't the point. He should have left on his terms, not Stiles'.

It sucked even more because even with all of DeShaun's experience in the restaurant business, the reality was, he couldn't find a job.

So this was what it had come to? Him driving around, looking for decent restaurants to apply to? And it didn't matter whether or not there was a hiring sign in the window. He needed a job. This morning, he lied to Naomi, telling her that he had a few prospects in the works. She had looked so worn out and defeated, he wanted to give her some hope, false or not.

Then, when she started talking about the Herjavecs again, he realized that he had to get out of there early, before her hypothetical situation turned into reality. He needed to give her time to see how ridiculous of an idea that was.

Of course, when you thought about it, he was already taking a little extra from Mrs. Herjavec, who handed him an additional hundred or two on several occasions. But that was different. That was for his party services. What Naomi was speaking of was a whole other situation.

Why was he even still thinking about it?

There it was. Paoli Pike, the turn-off to his old restaurant. Maybe he'd pop in and see how the guys were doing. He started to turn his car onto the exit ramp, but couldn't do it. He stepped on the accelerator and kept straight. He was less than ten minutes from his house when his cell rang.

"Yo', man. How you doin'?"

It was M.J.

"I'm good, man," DeShaun said. "How you been?"

"Ah, man, you know Old Man Stiles. If it ain't one thing, it's another. He's yelling at everybody, accusing them of stealing."

"Still?"

"Yeah. He even fired Scott."

"You serious?"

"Yup, and you know Scott was the only guy that kissed that old fart's ass," M.J. said. "So, how's my girl, Mimi?"

"She's good."

"Did that catering gig work out for you?"

"It's in the works," DeShaun lied. He didn't want to tell him he had absolutely no prospects on the horizon.

"Good. Maybe when you get that job, you can hook me up."

"Sure."

"Oh, the reason I'm calling is because Fancy Nancy has been asking about you."

"Who?"

M.J. had a nickname for all the usual partygoers. Some lady with a big butt who flirted with everyone, male or female, M.J. called Apple Bottom Tart. There was a short, stocky guy with a bald head M.J. nicknamed "The Penguin." DeShaun had no idea who Fancy Nancy was.

"Jackie, Olivia, man, I forget her name," M.J. said. "It's that woman with the dark hair married to the gun dealer."

"Jenn Herjavec?"

"Yeah! That's her."

"What's she sayin'?"

"Every time she comes in here with Mr. Megabucks, she asks where you are. Now see, I could've picked up where you left off," M.J. said, laughing. "But, noooo, she only asks about you."

"Me? Why?"

"That's what I'd like to know. She gave me her number to give to you. She claims you're supposed to work a surprise party in her honor. My question is, if it's a surprise party, how she know about it?"

DeShaun completely forgot about the surprise party Mr. Herjavec had asked him to service. That would be a good gig for decent money. "She leave a number?"

"Five-five-five-three-four-five-three."

"You memorized her number?"

"Hey, Mrs. Megabucks is looking good lately. If you can't tap that, I wanted to be there to help out. "

DeShaun reached into the glove box, grabbed a worn napkin and a pen and wrote down the number. "And for your information I'm supposed to be working a party for them next week. No tapping here."

"An intimate party for two?"

"You always have to take it there, don't you?"

"Yes, I do," M.J. said proudly. "It's what I do."

Naomi

I woke up again at eleven o'clock in the morning. After DeShaun left, I went into the kitchen and whipped up a fresh batch of chocolate chunk cookie dough, but, by the time I was ready to pop them into the oven, I had lost the feeling. Instead, I stashed the bowl in the back of the fridge and headed upstairs for a quick nap.

That quick nap lasted three hours.

While still in bed, I reached up and extended my fingers and toes, stretching each limb to capacity. I felt like I had a bad hangover, the kind you got after mixing liquors all night long. My head ached, my body hurt, but mostly, my spirit was damaged. A month ago we were late on one or two bills simply because we hadn't gotten around to paying them. Now, we were late because we *couldn't* pay them.

DeShaun wasn't back yet, and I hadn't felt like making the hike down the few blocks needed to make the call to McIntyre and Roth and Associates to find out if I got the job. Part of me didn't want to make that call. If I didn't get the job, there went the last bit of hope I had left. On the other hand, if I did get the job, that meant DeShaun and I could stay afloat and stop this sinking ship from crashing to the bottom of the ocean. The best-case scenario; DeShaun would walk through the front door with a secured job and McIntyre and Roth would inform me I start early next week. That little bit of hope prompted me to roll out of bed and make that call.

I picked up the house phone, hoping for a tiny miracle. Nope. Still dead.

Earlier, before DeShaun had left, he kept reassuring me everything would be okay, stating, "We're smart people. Everything will work out." While lying in bed, I believed him. The minute I stepped out from the comfort of my bed sheets, that security blanket DeShaun fitted me with had been pulled off.

I went to the refrigerator and opened it up. Besides three Kaliks, a half crate of eggs and the cookie dough I'd stashed in the back earlier, the fridge was empty. I slammed it shut. My head was beginning to hurt again.

"You can do this," I told myself. "Something good will happen today." But they were only words I couldn't force myself to believe.

I lugged my body to the bathroom and opened up the medicine cabinet. I grabbed the bottle of aspirin, which may or may not have been expired. It took at least four tries before I was able to pry open the childproof cap. It was empty. I chucked it across the bathroom floor, where it bounced off the toilet and landed in the tub. I thought back to my senior year in college when I wrote a dissertation on the struggle and plights of African Americans in the United States. When I first started researching, I couldn't understand how people in the ghetto allowed themselves to live like that. My paper took the position that we are not a product of our circumstances and that we were the ones in control of our situation.

I didn't understand. I had never been in that position.

Most of those people I researched and wrote about, had great jobs one day, and the next day, found themselves slipping further into poverty. Once you reached the last rung on the ladder, you looked up and then down, realizing it was much less of a fight to hit the ground than it was to climb all those rungs to reach the top again. That's where I was—on that last rung, with one foot on the ground. What was my next move?

Early last week, I had taken the train into Philly and applied for food stamps. I had to admit, it was the most demoralizing thing I had ever gone through. After filling out tons of paperwork, I stood in a line a mile long. Two hours later, when I finally reached the clerk, who was smacking on her gum, she stamped my paperwork and told me, "We'll be in touch." I'd give them another day or two before I phoned them since the number I left was shut off.

Later that same day, I made the trek over to the unemployment office in downtown Philly. After giving them some information and filling out yet more forms, they too told me, "We'll be in touch." The office called later that week, when our phone was still on, telling me my application had been denied because of the reason for the termination.

I splashed a handful of cold water on my face and glanced up in the mirror. I had dark patches under my eyes and my skin had a dull, greenish tint to it. My hair hadn't been wrapped or combed in days and was a mess. Within the last week, I had lost some weight. Of course, I lost weight. We didn't have a crumb of food in the refrigerator!

At first, I didn't care that I got fired. I figured I would find another job right away.

Mistake number one.

My second blunder was not kicking the crap out of Jeremy for his big mouth, causing me to lose that bullshit job in the first place. If I ever saw him again, I would take my fist and jam it down his throat without hesitation. In fact, if I had a friggin' working phone, I would call him and cuss him out. I would go down there and slap him around a couple of times, him and his bitch auntie manager, who came up in that place smelling like fried catfish every day.

Screw wasting energy and calling McIntyre and Roth—a job I probably didn't get anyway. I decided to get dressed and go down to the bank. I was going to tell off all of those motherfuckers for trying to destroy my life over some crappy job. I was going down there all right, but first I had to take a shower. The last thing I wanted for them to see was me defeated and broken with stinky, mussed-up hair.

As I turned the faucet and stepped under the hot streaming water, I wondered if this was how those people that went postal at their jobs started their day.

Naomi

I was standing in front of the bank, but a funny thing happened on the bus ride down here. I wasn't angry anymore. This wasn't the right job for me. If I hadn't been fired, I probably would have stayed in that position, miserable, for the rest of my days. Jeremy did me a favor.

I turned around, about to leave, and bumped right into Jeremy. He stood there with several shopping bags in his hands, smiling at me.

Honestly, my first instinct was to slap the taste out of his mouth, and ten seconds ago, I probably would have. Instead, I cocked my head to the side and asked, "What are you doing here at this hour?" I looked down at his jeans and T-shirt. "And why are you dressed like that?"

"I tried to call you," he said. "When I heard you got fired, I was pissed."

"What do you mean? I thought you were the one who said something about my interview. And then you were the only one who saw me drink the beer—the beer that you gave me."

"I never said anything. I swear."

"How did your aunt find out then?"

He shrugged. "I don't know. It could've been anybody. You know people are always listening in on conversations in the back room. It could've been Deb from the Lower Merion branch—she was there."

"Come to think of it," I said, "She *was* at the restaurant with Bob from accounts, remember?"

"There you go."

"You never answered my question," I said.

"What question?"

"Why are you here now, dressed like that?"

"I quit. I was so sick of that place and then when you left—" His voice dropped off. "You were the only sane person in that hell hole."

"Thanks, I think."

"I'm here to pick up my last check."

"Oh."

He looked down at my jeans, T-shirt and studded flip-flops. "What about you?"

I couldn't tell him that I was down here to slap the crap out of him, so I opted for another story. "I was actually picking up my last check as well, but then, I remembered your aunt said it would be in the mail."

"Oh, okay. Did you get it?"

"The check?"

"The job," he said. "The interview you went on that got you fired?"

My gaze fell to a jagged chip on the concrete sidewalk. "Oh, that one. Yeah, I got it," I lied, kicking away a chipped piece of stone. "Yeah, it's an accounting-type thing, more money, closer to home."

"Congratulations."

"Thanks."

"Let's go to lunch to celebrate."

"I don't think—"

"Oh, come on. We're not going to be seeing each other anymore. You can at least have one last lunch with me."

I thought about the six dollars and change in my purse. "I really can't."

"It's my treat. One last time."

I checked my watch. It was after two. DeShaun probably wasn't home yet anyway, plus, I hadn't eaten anything today. My head wasn't pounding like it had been earlier, but I still had a droning stab in my temples. Hopefully, a quick bite would help.

We walked two blocks to the deli.

"I'm taking some time off from job hunting," he told me after we were seated. "It's not going to be easy, but I've got some money saved up so I decided to go back to school to get my engineering degree." He nodded toward the two brown bags he placed in the chair next to him. "That's what those are, school books. The bank was only supposed to be temporary anyway."

"Wow! That sounds great."

A server walked up to our table, placed two glasses of water in front of us and then, took a step back. She reached into the apron fastened around her waist and produced a pad and a half a pencil.

"Ready to order?" she asked, cheerily.

"We haven't gotten menus yet," Jeremy said.

"Oh, sorry." The server reached around and grabbed two menus from the table behind her. She handed one to me and slid one across the table to Jeremy. "I'll be back in a few minutes."

Jeremy looked up from his menu. "So tell me about your new job. Did you start yet? Is it a big company? What will you do in your new position?"

The waitress returned. "Ready to order yet?"

Jeremy gave me a quick glance. I pulled the menu up in front of my face to keep from laughing.

"I'll have the garden salad," I told the waitress.

She jotted that down. "What dressing?"

"Ranch."

"Would you like bread with that?"

"No, thank you."

Jeremy closed his menu and handed it back to the waitress. "And I'll have the BLT sandwich, extra mayo."

When she finished jotting down our orders, she turned and walked away.

Jeremy looked at me. "Why are you laughing?"

"You know why," I said. "The last time we ate here you were ready to ream into our server about being over eager. This one was kind of pushy and you kept it cool."

"I don't have time or energy to be letting these people get on my nerves anymore." He took a sip of his water. "So anyway, finish telling me about your job."

We were surprised when the waitress returned with our lunches so soon. She set the BLT in front of me and the salad in front of Jeremy. When she left, we traded plates.

"Anyway," he said, pulling up a slice of bread from his sandwich and sprinkling salt and pepper onto the plump beefsteak tomato. "Give me all the details about your new position. You're probably making more money and less crap work. And you don't have to deal with irate customers anymore." He took a huge bite. A glob of mayo dropped from the sandwich and landed in the middle of the pile of chips on his plate.

I took a small bite from my salad. "What would you like to know?" Good thing I wasn't all that hungry. The lettuce lay wilted on the plate and the ranch dressing tasted like straight mayonnaise. My stomach turned, but I couldn't tell if it was due to the unsavory salad or the fact that I had been feeling this way since leaving the house this morning. Maybe it was a combination of both.

"When do you start your new gig? What will you be doing?" He took another huge bite. There went half the sandwich. "Sorry to be so greedy, but I haven't eaten since yesterday and I'm starved." With his mouth full, he shoved in another bite. "Go ahead, finish what you were saying."

"Well," I began, "I start in about two weeks and—"

What the hell was I doing? Why was I lying?

I set down my fork. "I'm not starting in two weeks," I blurted out. "I don't even know if I got the stupid job. I haven't heard from the company."

"Really?"

If I was putting it out there, I might as well put it all on the table. "One more thing. I wasn't coming down here to pick up my check. I was headed down here to cuss you out."

"Me? What did I do?"

"I thought you were the one that got me fired," I said. "I thought it was you who told about the beer we *both* had. I also thought it was you who ran your big mouth about my interview."

He set down the rest of his sandwich and sat back in the chair. "You can't pin that mess on me. I didn't even know about your interview."

"I thought you eavesdropped and heard me talking about it on the phone in the back room and then ran to tell your auntie to get me fired."

"You were doing a lot of thinking, weren't you? And even if that was the case, why would I want to get you fired?"

I felt the heat rush up to my cheeks. I wished I hadn't said anything at all.

"I thought you were angry because I turned you down." There. I said it.

"You honestly thought I would do something like that because you wouldn't go out with me?"

"Let's be fair here. You were this jerk who wouldn't quit with the passes."

"I wasn't trying to get with you, not really. I knew you were married, so I didn't really expect anything. Besides, here's a little something you might not know," he leaned over the table and whispered, "I'm not into married women." He took a sip of his water. He looked me dead in the face and didn't cut his gaze once. "If you felt that way, I apologize. I obviously gave you the impression that I'm a douche."

He was being sincere and I appreciated that. "It's my fault, too. I guess I always assumed the worst about you, when, in actuality, you're not that bad."

"I gotta say," he began. "It still kind of hurts that you thought I would get you fired, and especially for something like that. Honestly, Naomi, I like you. You're cool people. Ever since you set me straight that day at lunch, I thought we were good. Guess I was wrong."

"It's not all your fault, Jeremy. I suppose I needed someone to blame for all this mess."

"What mess?"

I shook my head, not wanting to get into it again. "Let's just say I've had better days."

"Is there anything I can do?"

"Actually there is."

He raised his brow. "Yeah?"

"You're not working now, right?"

He nodded.

"So please tell me how are you making it, financially?"

"Well, there's just me. My one-bedroom apartment is only five-eighty a month. My car ain't great, but it's paid for. I don't have credit cards or student loans. Plus, when I worked at the bank, I was able to save money. I have six months' salary in my account.

No stress. I'll probably get a part-time job if I need it, but for now I'm good. Need to know anything else?"

"Nah. Sorry if I was being so nosy, but I was just wondering. I do appreciate the lunch, but I have to get home."

"No problem. You sure?"

I stood up from the table. "Yeah. Thanks again."

"Wait, take down my number and call if you need anything." He grabbed a pen from his shirt pocket and quickly scratched his number on a napkin.

"Okay." I turned to leave but my feet felt like cement and didn't move toward the door. It all happened so suddenly. My knees started to wobble and then gave out from under me. The last thing I remembered was somebody yelling, "Call nine-one-one!"

DeShaun

"Mimi!" DeShaun called, when he stepped into the house. He dropped the mail onto the foyer table. The new stack joined three other unopened piles of bills. "Yo, yo, yo, baby, you here?" he asked playfully. He listened for a minute and didn't hear anything. He was slightly irritated that she wasn't home. He was going to burst, if he didn't tell someone about the Herjavecs' party. The news may not have been as big as getting a full-time gig, but, with all that had happened lately, a piece of good news—no matter how small it was—should be celebrated.

He went over to the fridge and pulled out a cold Kalik. He popped it open with his teeth and took a swig. He reached into the fridge, pulled out a clear plastic container and yanked open the top.

Jackpot! Homemade chocolate chip cookie dough. The way he liked it too, cold.

He grabbed a handful and downed it in seconds. He grabbed some more and rammed that into his mouth. He lifted the Kalik bottle to his lips and washed down the dough with one large gulp. He went to grab more dough but realized that wasn't going to get it. He was hungry and needed something more substantial, a steak maybe.

He opened up the freezer and pulled out the next best thing, or at least the thing they could afford right now; hot dogs. He popped three dogs into the microwave and set it for two minutes.

He reached deep inside his pants pocket and pulled out the napkin with Mrs. Herjavec's number on it. He then reached into his back pocket and pulled out his phone. He dialed. The line on the other end rang three times before someone picked up.

"Hello?"

The voice sounded like Mrs. Herjavec, but he wasn't certain. He cleared his throat and then said, "Good afternoon. I'm looking for Mrs. Herjavec, please."

"This is Jenn."

"Hi, how are you?"

"Who is this?"

"DeShaun Knowles."

She was silent.

"DeShaun, from the restaurant."

When she still didn't say anything, he started to rethink his decision to contact her.

"The server," he added. He would have said something like, "The black waiter whose backside you grab every chance you get," but that probably would have included every restaurant within a sixty-mile radius.

"Oh, yes, yes," she said. "How are you? And please call me Jenn."

The way M.J. made it sound, Mrs. Herjavec had been to the restaurant several times looking for him. Talking to her on the phone, she didn't sound pressed at all.

He cleared his throat. "I'm calling to get some information about the party your husband is throwing for you."

He heard muffled commotion in the background on her line, as if she had covered the speaker with the palm of her hand. He waited patiently, listening to the garbled voices. He couldn't hear what she was saying but she sounded irritated.

"I'm sorry," she finally said. "What was I saying?"

"The party?"

"Oh, yes. It's next week, and we'll need about seven or eight waiters to service about one hundred and twenty-five people."

He rushed to the kitchen. "Okay." He pulled open several drawers, in search of a pen and paper to write down the information. He settled on a dull, chewed-down pencil and the corner of a recipe Naomi had cut from a Stove Top Box.

"We should meet up to discuss the plans," she said. "Are you available now?"

"Now?"

"If that's a problem, we can get together some other time. I just don't know when I'd be able to."

No way was he going to give her the chance to change her mind. "No, no," he said quickly. "Now's cool. Where should we meet?"

"You've been here before. Why don't we meet at my house?"

He had been to the Herjavecs once to drop off champagne glasses for a fundraiser they were having. It was way out in the boondocks, heading toward Drexel Hill, but a job was a job. "I can be there in an hour."

"Great. See you in an hour." She hung up.

He grabbed an envelope of an overdue bill, turned it over, and scribbled down a note for Naomi when she came in.

Had to meet with clients about a party next week. Be back soon.

He opened up the microwave and grabbed the hotdogs. He ate one bare, but dressed the other two with buns, mustard, ketchup and relish.

He skipped the onions.

With both hotdogs in hand, he grabbed his keys and dashed out the door.

"I am so glad you could come on such a short notice," Mrs. Herjavec said when she opened the front door. House was an understatement. Her spot was more like a palace.

She took a step back and opened the door wider, allowing him to enter. He hesitated, stepping onto the flawlessly polished marble floor. The first thing he spotted was a gigantic crystal chandelier hanging in the hallway. She had that tiny furniture that looked like it was for decoration as opposed to function. Set farther back down the foyer was a large staircase that curved around as it led to the top floor.

"Would you like something to drink? I have wine, vodka, juice."

"Um—"

"Wait. Let me guess," she said. "I seem to remember Berti mentioning you are from the islands. You grew up in Jamaica, right?"

"Bahamas," he corrected.

"Ahhh, the Bahamas. Berti and I try to visit the Turks and Caicos islands every chance we get. It's beautiful there. Is that where you're from? You barely have an accent."

"I was born and raised in Grand Bahama. I spent a lot of time in the States, which might explain the no-accent thing."

"Hmmmm. Don't think we've ever been to Grand Bahama. I bet it's beautiful, though."

"Yeah," DeShaun agreed. "I lived there for twenty-one years before moving to the States for good."

"You must drink Sands and Kalik beer then."

"You've heard of Kalik?" he asked, amazed. "Not too many people who aren't from the islands ever heard of it."

"When Berti and I travel, we like to pick up items native to the countries we visit. Berti was so fascinated with the taste of Kalik that we have it specially ordered and transported here. We also have a case of Red Stripe from a trip to Jamaica two months ago. Would you like a Kalik, DeShaun?"

"Sure, thanks."

"We only have Gold. Is that okay?"

"Even better."

Mrs. Herjavec headed toward the kitchen and he followed. Her platform heels clicked against the marble. He glanced down at her backside. This was the first time he had seen her from behind this close. Mrs. Herjavec wasn't skinny and frail like most of the other wives in her circle. While she did have a small waist, her thighs and backside clung for dear life to the white pants she wore, so much so, he could see that she hadn't bothered to put on any underwear this morning when she got dressed. Her white halter top hugged her breasts perfectly and accentuated her above average-sized chest.

"Here you go." She smiled as she handed him a beer.

He took it from her hand, feeling weird that she was serving him and not the other way around.

She kicked off her bone-colored heels and took a seat at the island counter in the kitchen. She patted the cushioned covered stool next to her. "Relax. Have a seat."

He walked over and sat across from her, instead.

She was watching him, studying his every move. "Is the beer good? I've never tried the stuff. Berti loves it."

"You're not drinking?" He tried not to sound too surprised.

"Maybe a taste."

He took another sip of beer before realizing she was waiting to try *his* beer. "Oh, you want to try this one?"

"If you don't mind. I don't really want a whole bottle."

He shrugged. "If you don't mind, I don't." He slid the beer over to her.

She wrapped her lips around the neck and took a small sip. "Not bad." She slid the bottle back over to him.

"Told you."

"I normally don't drink at home. The only reason I drink when I'm out is because these parties and functions bore me to tears."

"Really?" This revelation shocked him. "You always look like you're having a good time."

"That's because I'm drunk. If it wasn't for the wine, I don't know what I'd do. I can't believe how boring people who come from money are. It's ridiculous. All they want to talk is business and about how much money they can make."

DeShaun took another swig of beer. "Do you want to give me some information about the party so I know what I need in terms of service?"

She frowned. "Please, don't tell me you're in a hurry. You just got here."

He thought about Naomi. He hadn't seen her since this morning. He would have called home, but the house phone was still out. "I'm not in a hurry. I assumed you'd want to get down to business."

She looked down. Her dark hair tumbled around her face but he could still see her tanned cheeks turning crimson.

"Oh, no, I didn't mean that kind of business," he said. "I only meant—"

She laughed nervously. "I know. It just sounded weird the way you put it."

"Sorry."

"Don't be sorry. It was just…weird, I guess. I understood what you meant." She avoided eye contact, opting to trace imaginary circles on the granite countertop with her finger, instead.

She studied him earlier and now it was his turn. Tonight, she was behaving differently. It was refreshing to not spend the evening, fending off her advances. In this new light, she reminded him of Trisha Beck, a redhead little cutie he dated back in high school. Except for the hair color—and being like thirty years older— Mrs. Herjavec's features were the same, pronounced cheeks, long slender nose and captivating green eyes.

"Why are you grinning at me like that?" she asked.

He didn't even realize he was smiling. "You remind me of an ex-girlfriend from another lifetime, except she was a little more…quiet."

She nodded. "I get it. It's no secret that when I drink I become like this total whore who will hit on anything that moves. The honest truth is, I've never cheated on my husband."

"Really?" he asked, afraid he sounded a little too surprised again.

She shook her head. "Not even once."

"That's good." He couldn't come up with anything else to say so he finished off his bottle of beer.

"Have you ever cheated on your wife?"

He spotted a trashcan at the end of the island. He tossed his empty bottle into the garbage.

"Want another one?" She headed back to the fridge before he could even answer.

"No, thank you. I'm good," he said. "I don't like drinking alone."

"Fine." She flashed a smile. "You twisted my arm. I'll have one with you."

"Oh, no, I didn't mean it like that."

"Too late." She reached into the refrigerator, pulled out two bottles of Kalik and brought them over to the island. "What the hell did I do with that bottle opener? I had it a second ago."

He grabbed one bottle, brought it up to his lips and bit off the cap. He grabbed the next bottle and did the same.

"Ohmigod, I love it!" she exclaimed. "How in the world did you do that? You didn't break a tooth?"

"I used to do it all the time when I was younger."

"And you never broke a tooth?"

"Never."

She walked up to him. "I gotta see this." She cupped his chin in her palm and lifted his head. "You're right, no broken teeth. In fact, your teeth are perfect. Maybe I should start opening bottles with my teeth."

He laughed. "No, you don't want to do that."

She took a sip of her beer. "You never did answer my question."

"What question was that?"

"Have you ever cheated on your wife?"

He choked down the swig he just took. She handed him a napkin.

"Are you okay?" she asked.

DeShaun took the napkin and dabbed around his mouth. "I'm fine." He was more careful with his next swig. "So how many people are attending the party? I'll need to get a rough estimate so I know how many servers to bring with me."

"I don't know, one hundred or so."

"Do you have a pen and pad? I can write some of this down."

She reached behind her and pulled open a drawer. "Here you go." She slapped down a black pen and a notepad onto the island. "Tell me about your wife. What is she like?"

"My wife?"

"Yes, your wife." She leaned her elbows onto the island and rested her chin in the palms of her hands, ready to listen. "I bet she's pretty."

"She is."

"I can tell you what else she is."

"You can, huh?"

"Yes, I can. I'm part psychic, you know." Her eyes twinkled when she smiled.

"Okay, then," he said, playing along. "What else is she?"

"Lucky."

This time, DeShaun felt the heat rise to his face. The fact that Mrs. Herjavec could unnerve him made him uncomfortable. "You think so?"

"I know so. You seem like the type of guy that pays attention to his woman. You take her out, you show her a good time and then you romance her all night long. Am I right?"

"You'd have to ask my wife that."

"I bet she's young, too. She's pretty and young."

DeShaun shrugged. "She's about my age, a little older."

"I told you I'm part psychic. So you like older women?"

"I guess," he said. "Now, can I ask you a question?"

"You may."

"What did you mean when you said if you're not a young, black guy, your husband's not interested?"

Her smile faded. "When did I say that?"

"The other night at the party, when you cornered me in the kitchen."

She shook her head. "I am so sorry for that. I really don't remember too much."

"That's okay," he said. "I get that all the time."

"I bet you do." She took another sip.

"So, was it true?" DeShaun asked.

"What?"

"About your husband, liking young boys."

She thought a moment before she nodded. "Sure is."

"How did you find out?"

"Let's see." She took a deep breath. "I came home early from a charity event I was hosting. It was quiet so I assumed he wasn't home. In fact, he was supposed to be in China for this grand opening of something or another. I came into the kitchen, grabbed some leftovers and sat down and ate. I even went to the back patio to check out my roses. After that, I headed upstairs."

"He was up there the entire time?"

She made a noise that sounded something between a full out laugh and a chortle. "Yes and when I went to our bedroom, I found him and another guy engaging in sexual relations.

"Seriously?"

She nodded. "Unfortunately, yes. I will never forget it."

"What did he say?"

"Which one?"

"Either one, I guess."

"Absolutely nothing," she said. "They were so into it, they never even saw me. I grabbed my purse, and took off. I still have that image burned into my brain."

"How long ago was this?"

"About three weeks ago."

"He still doesn't know you saw him?"

"Nope."

"Have you told anyone?"

"Only you and my therapist."

"I'm sorry," DeShaun said. "I can't imagine having to live with a secret like that."

She shrugged. "It's all par for the course. I understood what I was getting into when I married Berti."

"You knew he was gay?"

"I knew he was eccentric," she said. "I had no idea to what extent. And I don't really consider it gay, more like he enjoys non-traditional activities of a sexual nature."

"Maybe we should get this done," DeShaun said. "I really do need to get home soon."

"How about this?" She tapped her index finger on her bottom

lip. "I really don't know all of the details yet. I'll have to talk to Berti. When I do, I'll e-mail you everything. How does that sound?"

"Sounds good."

"Great. I'll be in touch." She stood up. "Thank you for coming, DeShaun."

"Thank you for trusting me."

"You're welcome," she said with a warm smile. She grabbed his hand and squeezed. "And thank you."

He stood up to leave. "Take care."

Mrs. Herjavec saw him out the door. He hopped into his car and pulled off down the driveway. He couldn't wait to get home to his wife to tell her the good news about the party. Plus, after talking with Mrs. Herjavec, he'd found himself slightly aroused. Maybe it was the way she looked him in the eye when she spoke. It could've been the way she took a drink from his bottle or how easy it was for her to trust him with her secret. In any case, he felt the urge to go home and make love to his wife all night long.

Naomi and DeShaun

I heard DeShaun pull up to the house. It was well past 9:30.

"Mimi! You home?" He dropped the keys onto the hallway table and then I heard him head toward the kitchen. He flicked on the kitchen light.

"Mimi!" he called again.

He turned on the hall light and rushed up the steps. I listened as he took the steps, two at a time, and then went into the hall bathroom, searching for me.

"Mimi?" he called again.

"I'm in here."

DeShaun's footsteps got closer. A second later, he pushed open the bedroom door. "Hey, Babe, what are you doing in bed already? It's only nine-thirty. Why are you sitting in the dark?"

"Where have you been all day?"

DeShaun took off his shirt and tossed it into the hamper. "You didn't get my note?"

"No."

"I left it downstairs on the table."

"I didn't see it."

"It doesn't matter," DeShaun said. "I've got great news. I went to see the Herjavecs about a party they're having. I completely forgot about it, but when M.J. called this afternoon, he told me Mrs. Herjavec was looking for me. That should bring in some good money."

"When did you talk to M.J.?"

"What?" DeShaun flipped off his shoes and stepped out of his pants.

"I asked when you talked to M.J. today."

He walked into the bathroom and flicked on the light "I caught up to him on the road," he yelled from the bathroom. He turned on the shower, pulled the curtain back and stepped in.

After his shower, he exited the bathroom wearing nothing but a terrycloth towel wrapped around his waist. "Are you sleeping?" he whispered.

"No."

"Is everything okay, Mimi? You're acting strange. Why are you still sitting in the dark?"

"No, DeShaun, everything is not okay."

He quickly came over and sat on the edge of the bed. "What's wrong? What happened?"

"I went back to the bank today."

"Why would you do that?"

"Don't say anything, DeShaun. Listen, please. I went to the bank today. I was ready to cuss out Jeremy. Long story short, I found out he wasn't even the one who said anything. In fact, he even quit on my behalf."

"So who ratted you out?"

"You know what? It doesn't even matter at this point. I ended up going to lunch with Jeremy and—"

"Why the hell did you go to lunch with him?"

"Would you stop talking for a second and listen to what I'm trying to tell you? I felt sick and then before I knew it, I passed out. The ambulance came and…it was all such a mess."

"The ambulance? Are you okay? What happened, baby? Why didn't you tell me when I first came in?"

"The doctor said I probably had a panic attack due to stress. He ran some tests, all were negative so he sent me home."

"That's good," DeShaun said. "How do you feel now?"

"I don't know. Physically, I'm fine. Mentally, not so much. I saw the mail on the table. There were half a dozen overdue notices. Then, before I could even walk out the door, the nurse's station hit me with a bill for the ambulance for over eight-hundred dollars."

"Eight hundred!" DeShaun exclaimed. "What the hell? And damn, couldn't they at least wait until you got home safely first?"

"That's not even the worst part. Since losing our jobs, we have no insurance. The tests they ran were over a thousand dollars."

"Are you serious?"

"Does it look like I'm kidding? Something has got to give. We can't keep up like this. We're going to lose everything we worked for, DeShaun. I can't do that. We're getting notices about the house, we don't have enough money in the bank to get our phone turned on. Our credit cards are maxed out. We're broke, DeShaun. We are completely and utterly down and dirty broke. If we got jobs tomorrow with a million dollar salary, it'll take at least a month to catch up…and that's *if* we catch up before they take the house—our house. We're about to lose everything, DeShaun. Everything we spent years working to obtain, it's about to be gone. Poof! Just like that."

"Take it easy, baby," he said. "Don't get upset again."

"How can I take it easy? You may be okay with living on the streets, but me, I kind of like having a roof over my head. "

"Getting upset is not going to help things," he said.

"Stop it, please. I am not in the mood to be pacified with your don't-worry, be-happy, island speech. We're not in the islands where a tiki hut and a hot plate on the beach will suffice. We're in America, the real world."

"I got the gig with the Herjavecs," he said hopefully. "That'll bring some money in."

"Big deal. You got some gig, serving rich folk again. So what?"

Defeated, he turned away.

"Oh, baby, I'm sorry. I only meant that you are so much better than that. I know you're doing your best, but, right now, that's not enough."

"It's what I do," he said.

"I know, I know. It's just that…I don't know. I guess I'm upset that I didn't get that job at the law firm and we so needed it right now."

"Aw, man, Mimi. I'm sorry. When did you find out?"

"They never called, but you know how that goes. Don't call us, we'll call you."

"That's their loss."

"Their loss, DeShaun?" McIntyre and Roth probably ended up hiring some dim-witted moron. Here we are with no jobs, no health insurance and no prospects. So, if someone could explain the million-dollar question as to how it was *their* loss, I would be forever grateful because I can't see it."

"You're frustrated right now," DeShaun said. "I'll take care of everything."

"If you could have, you would've done so already. I would have, too. We're stuck. The sooner we come to that realization, the better off we'll be."

He sighed, shook his head and let his gaze drop to the floor, finally realizing it was the truth. Better to deal with the situation now as opposed to dealing with it after becoming homeless on Broad Street.

"DeShaun, baby, it's time we admit that we are officially desperate. We need to do something drastic and quickly."

"Like what?" he asked the question but, at this point, he knew the answer.

"It will only be temporary. Until we can get back on our feet."

"It's not a big deal, right?" DeShaun added. "She's an acquaintance and besides friends buy and do things for other friends. What's the big deal?"

"Exactly. And besides, she's one of those spoiled women who throws money around like it's nothing, right?"

"Right."

"It will only be temporary. Until at least one us of gets a job."

"Yeah," he agreed. "Temporary."

"This is the right thing for us to do under our circumstances. This is something that we have to do to stay afloat. We will be okay. You believe that, right?"

"Yeah."

He gently laid me down across the bed and pulled up the covers. "We'll definitely be all right." He lay down next to me on the bed, but spent the entire night tossing and turning almost as much as I did.

DeShaun

DeShaun put on his best pair of black pants, a long-sleeved white shirt and a red bow tie he bought especially for the occasion. He slung his white apron over the passenger side of the car so it wouldn't get wrinkled in travel.

Tonight was supposed to be the surprise party for Mrs. Herjavec, but when she found out about it, she ended up practically planning the entire event herself. The requests were a mix of simple to over-the-top extravagance. The plans included black and white balloons and high-end delicacies, such as baby octopus and foie gras. She also wanted fireworks to shoot off exactly at midnight. Luckily, the Herjavecs had a huge backyard and an even bigger budget. Jenn had hired a twelve-piece jazz band and planned to set up four separate bars, including a cigar and dessert bar surrounded by a champagne fountain. Rough estimation had them around the sixty-five thousand-dollar mark, and this was just for a surprise birthday party, which wasn't even a surprise anymore.

For the past week, DeShaun and Naomi managed to pay a few bills with the final check from the bank. Two days ago, Stiles surprised DeShaun by calling and telling him he had a check waiting for him at the restaurant. His former boss had been strangely friendly, asking how he was doing and if he had found a job yet. DeShaun had lied and told him he had, which wasn't too far from the truth. After all, he was working this party tonight.

Upon hearing this news, Stiles wished him well. Maybe his former boss felt remorse for firing him, then again, maybe he didn't. It didn't matter anymore. One reason he told Stiles he found another job was because if DeShaun was ever asked back, he probably wouldn't have the courage to turn Stiles down. A week ago, when he and Naomi decided to proceed with what they referred to as "The Plan," she had told him that he was better than the restaurant. Although it was good to hear her say it, he didn't need for her to tell him that—he knew he was, too.

He was doing this. He had to do what was needed to keep his family secure and intact.

He pulled up to the long, gravel-ridden driveway to the Drexel Hill estate. He spotted Mr. Herjavec's white Mercedes parked at the top of the winding drive. Mrs. Herjavec's silver Range Rover was inside the opened garage.

"DeShaun!" Mrs. Herjavec came running toward his car with a panicked look on her face. DeShaun did a double-take. She was wearing a short plush pink robe and a matching pair of slippers. That was it. She had her cell in her hand. "I am so glad you came early. These stupid caterers are not here yet and neither are the bottles of Dom I ordered last week."

"Did you call them?" DeShaun asked.

"Of course, I did," she said, shoving her cell in his face. "The stupid idiots didn't call me back. I tried to call Berti but he's still at work."

"Take it easy. Who's the caterer?"

"D'Antonio's."

DeShaun had dealt with the owner, Nicholas D'Antonio, several times. Two months ago, Nick held a private party for his business partner at Stiles' restaurant. Nick had attitude, but, if you showed him the same attitude back, he'd step up.

"Relax," DeShaun said. "I'll deal with that."

"Thank you." She slid the phone into the pocket of her pink robe. As she did, the robe tie came undone. Quickly, she pulled the tie together, but not before exposing a little too much.

DeShaun looked away. "You can go ahead and finish what you were doing. I'll take care of it."

Her face turned bright red. "I'm so embarrassed," she said, looking down at her outfit. "I rushed out here so quickly, I forgot I wasn't dressed." She scurried back inside. Before she shut the door, she yelled, "Oh, and thank you so so much."

"You're welcome."

"Dude, what is up?" M.J. walked out from around the side of the house. He came up and gave DeShaun a friendly pat on the back. "Good to see you again, my man. Thanks for pulling me along on this gig. You know rent is due tomorrow, next week it's the light bill. It seems like it never ends for a brutha."

"I hear you on that," DeShaun said. "Listen, can you hold things down here? I need to help out Mrs. Herjavec with something. I shouldn't be gone too long, but, if I'm not back in an hour, have the rest of the guys start setting up. Tell them to put ten chairs at each round table and fifteen at the long table, which should be in the front, closest to the patio doors. All the silverware, knives, forks, napkins, everything, is in Mark's van. Show the guys how to properly set up."

"No problem," M.J. said, grinning. "So, you gotta help out the missus, huh?" He nudged DeShaun in the shoulder. "Don't worry, I got you."

"Man, please. It's not even like that."

"Yeah, yeah, whatever. You go take care of that business and I'll keep it together here."

DeShaun tapped his temple with his index finger. "Something's wrong up there, you know that, right?"

M.J. nodded toward the front door. "It's not me you need to worry about. It's the man eater you should keep your eye on." He walked back around the side of the house and disappeared into the backyard.

Mrs. Herjavec came out of the front door, wearing a cream-colored casual jumper and matching pumps. Her long black hair was pulled up into a loose bun, high on top of her head. In that outfit, her tanned skin almost looked as dark as his. When she got closer, DeShaun noticed she wasn't wearing a bra.

"I changed as fast as I could," she said, out of breath. "The guests should be here in an hour, so we have to hurry."

"You don't need to go," DeShaun said, heading toward his car. "I can handle this."

She shook her head. "No, I want to go. I want to give that jerk a piece of my mind—in person."

DeShaun looked over at Jenn. Her expression was hardly angry. When she saw him watching her, she broke out in a smile.

"Okay, I'm not *that* angry," she admitted. "I wanted to get the hell away from all this chaos. I'm getting a headache."

"Let's go." DeShaun started walking toward his car but stopped, remembering he rode there on fumes. "We have to stop for gas, first. It'll only take a second."

She shook her head. "We don't have time. We'll take my truck." She made a beeline toward her Range Rover in the garage. He followed. She reached into her purse and produced a set of keys. "You drive. I have no idea where we're going." She tossed the keys to him.

They hopped into the truck. DeShaun looked down at all the gadgets and accessories. "Are you sure you want me to drive, Mrs. Herjavec?"

"I trust you," she said. "And I thought I told you to call me Jenn."

She reached over and pressed a button on the dash and the car started. "Is the place far?" She reached into her purse and pulled out her sunglasses. She also pulled out a cigarette and lit up.

DeShaun put the truck in reverse. "Not really." He studied her for a second, not realizing that she even smoked.

From the corner of his eye, he watched her put on the sunglasses, wondering why she even bothered, seeing as the dark clouds overhead covered the sun. Her hands trembled as she lit the cigarette and took a long drag.

He cautiously drove down the road, toward I-95 North. By the time they hit the highway, he felt completely comfortable behind the wheel.

"This truck totally suits you," Jenn said. "You should get one."

DeShaun laughed. "Okay. I'll get one next week."

"Is the smoke bothering you?" She took another puff. "I don't really smoke, only when my nerves are frazzled...oh, and when I drink sometimes."

"No, that's fine," DeShaun lied. He hated smoking, and with the windows up, the AC only blew the smoke around in the small confined space When he couldn't stand it any longer, he cracked the window some. She didn't seem to notice.

He was glad when she finished the last of the cigarette and put it out in an ashtray. He was glad until she reached into her purse and pulled out another one. "You sure it's okay I smoke?"

Once again, he nodded.

Speckles of rain hit the windshield. DeShaun stared at the road, concentrating on the cars in front of him while Jenn stared out of the window, puffing away on the cigarette. He stepped on the gas, the engine purred. It surprised him how easy it was to drive the truck.

He glanced over at Jenn, who continued staring out of the window, however, along with puffing away on the cigarette she had now started to wring and pick at a tattered tissue.

"Is everything all right?" he asked.

"Do I look *that* worried?" She took another puff. "I thought I was hiding it. Berti left this party up to me, and I don't want it to fall apart, especially where business is concerned."

Business? DeShaun thought this was a party for her birthday.

To make better time, he weaved in and out of traffic, careful to keep to the speed limit. No way did he want to get popped by the police while driving around in her Range Rover.

"Want to hear some music?" He was making an attempt to relax the tension-filled atmosphere.

"Sure." She reached into the glove compartment and shuffled through a handful of CDs. When she didn't find one she liked, she hit the satellite button on the dash. Bossa nova music filled the truck.

Mimi loved bossa nova.

Jenn pressed a few buttons and stopped on one station. DeShaun heard the start of a familiar beat.

"Are you serious?" he asked.

"What? You don't like Notorious B.I.G.?"

He was stunned. "You do?"

"An Armenian woman can't like rap?"

"I didn't say that," he began. "I just meant—" He paused. That's exactly what he meant.

"Truth? I only listen to it to bug Berti. He hates rap with a passion. It pisses him off every time we get into the car and I put this station on. Immature, I know, but it makes me smile when he fumes for miles. He never says anything, though. He doesn't want to give me the satisfaction. He gets even more upset when I start rapping to it."

"You rap to Biggie? Next, you're going to tell me you've been to a PAC concert."

"Ain't nuthin' but a gangsta party."

He laughed.

"You haven't seen anything yet," she said, holding her finger in the air. She listened for a second and then rapped in sync with Biggie, *"Nothing left to do but send her home to you, I'm through, can you sing the song for me, Boo?"*

DeShaun burst out laughing. "Wow! Just wow on that one."

"You should see how red Berti's face gets when I start rapping." She chuckled. "It's hilarious."

DeShaun shook his head. "I don't get it."

"Get what?"

"I don't understand your marriage."

She looked out the window and took another drag. "That makes two of us."

The rain started beating down harder. DeShaun flicked on the wipers. "Do you have the tent set up at the house already?" he asked. "That should've been done before I got there."

She nodded, still looking out the window. "Uh huh."

He glanced over at her. Somewhere on the expressway, between the Girard Avenue and Broad Street exits, she had taken off her sunglasses. He couldn't tell if it was sadness or fatigue in her eyes.

"We're almost there." He stepped on the gas, keeping an eye on the speedometer. He let up off the accelerator when he realized he was doing over eighty-five in the smooth ride.

"Can I tell you something?" Jenn asked.

"Yeah."

"Do you know how I found out about my own surprise party?"

DeShaun shook his head.

"Berti told me. That son of a bitch actually told me."

"Why?"

"Because my so-called surprise party was actually a client meet-up.

Supposedly, my birthday was the only day all his clients could get together. What bullshit! I was so pissed when that bastard came home from work one night and told me he needed my help to arrange everything. He had the nerve to disappear and leave me to handle all the crap. That takes some real balls."

DeShaun let out a sigh of relief when he pulled into D'Antonio's parking lot. "We're here."

Jenn rolled her eyes, opened the car door and stepped down onto the cemented driveway of the restaurant. "Speaking of dealing with assholes," she commented as she got out and slammed the door. "Shall I handle it or you?"

"I got this."

Naomi

I had started looking through the online want ads, but spent the last twenty minutes surfing through online gossip columns, starting with MediaTakout.com and TheYBF.com.

We had enough funds left over to pay either the water bill or the Internet service, but after that we were tapped out. We opted for Internet because that was due two days before the water bill. We figured in those two days, we would buy a few lottery tickets, hit the jackpot and then have money to pay the water bill and purchase an Escalade.

That's what happened when you were broke—you started living in the fantasy world until they shut off your water. Then you crashed back down to earth with a gigantic *splaaaaat* and shuffled around more bills to buy more time.

Before getting the bank job, I had worked at a telecommunications company for years before they laid me off. I forgot what it was like to have to search through endless classifieds, trying to find a job that fit my top three criteria; location, position type and salary. I started my search with jobs in close proximity. An hour later, that prerequisite was scratched off the list unless I wanted to become a dog groomer or a part-time mechanic. Two hours into my search, position type was a done deal, too. I was trying hard not to budge on my third criteria; salary. I needed to make a certain amount to break even. However, that amount kept getting lower and lower with each passing hour. By the time early afternoon hit, I was hovering dangerously close to the salary I made when I was babysitting in high school.

When the phone rang, I hopped up, thankful for the excuse to take a break.

"What are you doing today?" It was Jeremy. He sounded so upbeat, which was something I needed, especially after dealing with the dismal task of searching for a job. So far, I had e-mailed four resumes. One job had already e-mailed back, asking for an interview. Of course, it was the customer service job I was the least enthusiastic about, but, at this point, I was not about to get snooty about any position. "I was going to spend the day sending out resumes. Why?"

"I have a lead for you. A friend of mine downtown told me that her boss is looking for a new secretary."

"Where?"

"At the Millworks on Fifty-fifth and Chestnut. I told her about you and she said you should come down right away to meet them. They're looking to hire someone ASAP."

"I know where that is," I said. "But DeShaun has the car. Can they wait until tomorrow?"

"Nope. According to my friend, one of the big bosses is leaving tomorrow for vacation."

I rolled my eyes. "Of course, they are."

"I'm not doing anything. I can take you," Jeremy offered. "How long do you need to get ready?"

"Are you sure? I don't want to take you away from anything."

"Not at all," he said. "I spent the morning signing up for my core courses for grad school. I'm done for now. And before you ask, I received a partial scholarship and will have my loan deferred."

"I wasn't going to ask, but it's great that you have all this planned out. Congratulations."

"So, let me take you. It's no problem at all."

"Are you sure?"

"How long do you need to get ready?"

I checked the time. "Half-hour okay?"

"A half-hour? That better include a shower. I don't want you funkin' up my car."

"Shut up!" I laughed. "Just be here in a half."

"Cool. See you then."

I hung up the phone. *Yessss!* If I played my cards right, I may have a job as early as this afternoon.

"Wow. You look…professional," Jeremy said when I opened the door.

I had decided to go full out for this interview, busting out the flattening iron and going Halle Berry style, which was the reason I was running late. "I'll be just another minute." I ran upstairs to the bedroom to find my diamond studs, a college graduation gift from my parents.

"You showered, right?" Jeremy called from the front door.

"Shut up!"

When I went back out into the living room, Jeremy was sitting on the couch, flipping through an *Essence* magazine.

I held out my arms and twirled. "This look okay?" I dug in the back of my closet and found a crisp white blouse that was like new. I had only worn it twice. My pencil skirt hugged my curves in all the right places but wasn't too tight. I didn't mind Payless, but to be on the safe side, I picked out the one pair of black heels I'd bought from Nordstrom four years ago, when money wasn't as tight.

"You got a piece of string on your skirt."

I reached down and plucked off the string. "Now?"

"You look good." He grabbed my hand and pulled me toward the door. "Now come on. We're taking the train downtown. My friend says it's only two blocks away from the station and I'd probably spend more time trying to find parking."

I shrugged. "Sounds okay to me, but, if that's the case, I could have taken the train myself. You didn't have to come all the way up here."

"I know," he said. "I was trying to give you moral support."

"Aw, thanks."

"Plus, I figured I can get a free lunch out of you when the interview's done. I missed breakfast this morning trying to rush and get to you."

"You are a lie," I said. "You didn't call me until the afternoon, so if you missed breakfast that was on you."

"Whatever. It's the least you can do."

I smiled, feeling better than I had felt in a long time. Things seem to be finally falling into place. Two days ago, the phone was cut off and we had to decide between paying the credit cards or turning the phone back on. We made the right decision. Jeremy never would have been able to call me about this interview if we had decided to avoid a lousy late charge on the credit card. Besides, I never paid the credit cards on time when we did have jobs. Why start now?

I had been in such a hurry, I didn't have time to call DeShaun and let him know what was going on. "Hold on. I have to make a quick call." I wanted to see how his day was going.

Jeremy must've read my mind. He grabbed my arm and said, "You can call your husband from the car on the way to the station. We have ten minutes or we will officially be late."

He pulled me by the elbow and rushed me toward the door. I scrambled to grab my purse from the hallway table as he shuffled me out the door.

DeShaun

"Do you want to wait in the car?" DeShaun asked.

Jenn shook her head. "No. I want to see the bastard's face when I confront him." She narrowed her eyes and stood with her hands on her hips, trying her best to look ferocious. Instead, she looked like a little girl, mad at her best friend for stealing her favorite doll.

DeShaun laughed. "You are funny."

Jenn cracked a smile. "Seriously, I'm not going to let this idiot get away with trying to rip me off."

DeShaun shook his head. "Stay here. I'll be back." When he reached the door to D'Antonio's, he looked back at Jenn. She was fixing her hair and makeup in the rearview mirror. *So much for telling off D'Antonio*, he thought.

Several minutes later, DeShaun returned to the Range Rover. Jenn was meticulously filing her nails. When she saw DeShaun, she quickly shoved the file back into her purse. "What happened? What did the jerk say?"

"Call me the man. Not only did I get the price back down to what you agreed to, D'Antonio gave you a discount for future parties."

"Sqeeeeee!" She threw her arms around him and planted a big kiss on his cheek. "No way. Seriously?"

"Seriously."

"How'd you do that?"

"Nick D'Antonio is known for pulling crap like this. I'm surprised no one has taken him to court, or better yet, punched his lights out. He is one lucky son-of-a-bitch."

DeShaun purposely left out the part about him asking D'Antonio if he was hiring. It was embarrassing when Nick told him he would put his resume on file for future positions. Nick did look genuinely sorry when he told DeShaun he had just hired a guy. Eight months ago, Nick mentioned he had an opening at his restaurant. Back then, DeShaun had barely given it a second thought since he had a job.

The entire ride back, Jenn kept complimenting him, telling him how grateful she was and that she would have never been able to pull this off without him.

"I was at the point where I wanted to hide in my room for the rest of the evening," Jenn said. "What a great birthday, huh?"

DeShaun knew about disappointing birthdays. "On my eleventh birthday," he said, "my father promised to bring me a bike. It would've been cool if he actually came through."

"What happened?"

DeShaun shrugged. "He never showed up. Didn't see him for another few years after that. Not once did he ever mention the bike. Now *that's* a sucky birthday."

When they pulled up to the Herjavecs' front drive, the catering vans were already parked out front. DeShaun spotted M.J. directing the guys to bring the platters to the back yard.

"I don't know what you said to those jerks," Jenn said. "But whatever it was, it worked." She reached inside her purse and pulled out a stash of bills fastened together with a gold money clip. Her initials, *JiW*, were engraved on the front of the clip. The "i" was dotted with a tiny diamond.

"What's your middle name?" DeShaun asked.

Jenn looked puzzled. "Why would you ask me that?"

He nodded toward her money clip. "Your clip, there."

"Oh, that. My full name is Jennifer Ingrid Herjavec. Ingrid sounds like a little Dutch girl, doesn't it?"

"It sounds nice to me."

"What's your middle name?" Jenn asked.

"I don't tell anyone my middle name."

"Oh, c'mon, I told you mine."

"Nope."

"Please?"

The last time his middle name was mentioned, he was pummeling some kid in the fourth grade with his fists. "It's Ashton. You satisfied?"

"Really? You're lying."

"Seriously. It's Ashton."

"I like it."

"You're saying that now," DeShaun said. "But once you think about it, you're gonna laugh."

"It suits you."

"Thanks."

She reached down and pulled a one-hundred dollar bill from the money clip. "Take this for your troubles."

He didn't do this for the money. He was only trying to help out. "You don't have to do this."

"If it wasn't for you, I'd be serving cheese and crackers tonight."

DeShaun didn't want to take the money, but then he thought of Naomi. Technically, this is why he was here in the first place, *The Plan*. He took the money from her fingertips. "I appreciate it."

She hopped out of the truck. "Good. Now let's hurry and get this party over with. I want to go to bed."

DeShaun jumped down from the driver's side. "Oh, by the way, Happy Birthday."

Jenn grinned. "You know, you are the first person to tell me that today?"

"What about your hu—" DeShaun stopped mid-sentence, already realizing the answer to that question. "Sorry."

"Don't be. I don't care anymore. Apparently, he doesn't either."

DeShaun took the money and shoved it into his back pocket. He watched her disappear through the front door before he headed off in the opposite direction to the backyard to help set up.

Naomi

"Can I borrow your phone?" I asked, once Jeremy pulled out of the driveway.

He nodded toward the glove box. "It's in there."

I reached over and opened up the glove box. I found the phone, but that wasn't all I found. "Wow, what's this?" I held up a sealed condom. "And Magnum, too?"

"That's not mine."

"You guys are still using that line? Let me guess. It's your boy's and you were holding it for him."

Jeremy grinned. "Whatever."

"Hey, you're single. It's allowed," I said. "Speaking of which, whatever happened to that young girl from the Paoli branch? Last I heard, you two were hitting it off."

"That's just it. She's too young."

"So are you."

"You and I are the same age. Lilonique was like twenty."

"Lilonique?"

"Don't hate 'cause of her ghetto name."

"I'm not," I said. "It's not ghetto, really. It's…original."

"Yeah, and so is Chlamydia and Moët—and don't you have a call to make?"

I dialed DeShaun's number. "Yes, I do." The phone rang three times before his voicemail came on. I lowered my voice. "Hey, baby.

I just wanted to tell you that I am on my way to an interview, so even though I didn't talk to you, I know you're wishing me luck. Hope everything turns out okay for your party. Love you." I hung up.

"You two have been married for a while?" Jeremy asked.

"Four years."

"I would love to have had a few years of marriage under my belt by now."

"My suggestion to you is to take your time. Make sure you find the right person. Believe me, marriage isn't all that it's cracked up to be."

"I know all that," Jeremy said. "But you always have someone there to be with you."

I nodded. "That's true, but the downside of that is, you always have someone there to be with you."

"What does that mean?"

"They are *always* there. I left my parents' house and moved into a place by myself. I met DeShaun almost immediately and a year later, we got married. "

"Do you have any regrets about getting married?" Jeremy asked.

"Honestly, marriage sometimes feels like a job, only on this job, there are no long lunches, calling out sick or hiding at the vending machine when your boss gets on your last nerve.

"You must be referring to my aunt at the bank."

I grinned. "Maybe."

We pulled up to the train station. When we got to the ticket counter, he stepped before me and asked for two tickets downtown.

I reached into my purse. "You don't have to pay for me."

"I'll get this. After the interview—and when you get the job—you can pay for lunch."

"Heck no. Lunch costs more."

He turned back to the guy at the ticket counter. "One, please. She'll purchase her own."

I playfully smacked him on the back.

"Hey, if I'm paying for lunch, I'll have to save my money. You forget, I've seen you eat." He turned back to the guy at the counter. "I'm kidding. I'll have two tickets, please."

The guy handed Jeremy two tickets. "Better hurry up. The train is about to leave."

We rushed to the train, stepped on and took a seat. Within seconds, the doors closed and we were off.

The train ride seemed excruciatingly long. Between the Bryn Mawr and the Wynwood stops, I kept checking my watch. It was getting late. I didn't want the bosses to leave before I even had the chance to interview. By the time we reached 30th Street Station, I was fidgeting so badly, Jeremy pulled out his cell and offered to call his friend to let her know we were on the way.

"Would you?"

He dialed. I watched, hopefully, as he talked to his friend at the company. He was laughing and joking with her, so I assumed everything was okay. When he hung up, he turned to me. "Tanya said don't bother. They just left."

"Are you serious?" I asked, panicked. "Now what?"

"I'm kidding. Would you relax? If you don't you'll go into that interview nervous and sweaty. They're going to take one look at you and yell, 'NEXT!'" He yelled it so loud, a few people surrounding us on the train, looked at us.

I took a deep breath. "I know but I really need this to work out."

"Finances that bad, huh?"

I cocked my head to the side. "Why do you say that?"

"You asked me about my financial situation a couple of times."

"Really? I didn't realize. I'm sorry. I was curious, I guess."

"Don't worry about it. It's cool."

When we stepped off the commuter train, Jeremy led and I followed. We weren't running, but we kept up a fast pace as we skipped up the depot steps and out into the street. The day was beautiful. The beating sun was hot against our skin, but the cool summer breeze made the temperature just right. I wished I was spending the day shopping or leisurely heading to one of the cozy bookstores on Market Street. Instead the bright, beautiful day was overshadowed by fear and nervousness. I really wanted this job.

No, I *needed* this job.

We headed into the high-rise building and took the elevator to the twelfth floor. When he saw his friend, Tanya, at the front desk, his face lit up, and he smiled. "Hey! Long time no see."

Tanya was a cute girl that looked tiny, sitting behind the large oak desk. Her cropped hair had golden highlights running through it, just like mine.

"This is Naomi," Jeremy said.

"Hi." She gave a friendly smile. "The bosses are waiting for you. Good luck." She seemed nice enough.

"You got this," Jeremy reassured. "You look good. Now let the confidence shine through."

I turned and headed toward the large double doors. "I'll be back in a few minutes." My feet started sweating inside my Nordstrom black heels and my head started throbbing. I felt lightheaded, like I wanted to throw up. I struggled to take a deep breath. Those were definitely not good signs to have when going into an interview.

"How did it go?" Jeremy was standing at the exact spot he was when I walked into the interview—at his friend, Tanya's desk.

I shook my head. "I didn't get it."

"How do you know?" Tanya asked. "They normally have second and third interviews before deciding."

"Thanks for the information," I said shortly. "But I don't know you like that to be telling all my business."

Jeremy gave me a look, but said nothing. He turned to Tanya. "Sorry about that."

My head was spinning and my stomach was turning. "Can we go? I'm tired and not feeling well."

Jeremy turned back to Tanya. "I'll call you later."

"Okay."

We were a block from the train depot before either one of us said anything. "What the hell happened in there?" Jeremy finally asked. "And why were you so rude? Tanya was only trying to help."

I stopped walking and bent over, trying to catch my breath. "I know. When you talk to her apologize for me." I took in several deep breaths. "I seriously don't feel well. I need to sit down."

Jeremy grabbed my elbow and steered me over toward an empty bench. "Is it the same thing as last time?"

I nodded. I was seeing spots, my head was hurting, and it felt like I was gasping for breath.

Jeremy stood up, looking for someone. "I should get help."

I grabbed his arm and pulled him back down onto the bench. "No. I just need a second." I took in several more deep breaths. Eventually, the sharp pain in my head started to subside. I took in one last deep breath. I finally felt okay.

"Do you still want to go out to lunch?" he asked. "Maybe food will help."

I shook my head. I couldn't even think about eating right now. "I just want to go home."

"Okay."

We made our way down the last block to the train depot. "Do you have a second interview?"

I slowly shook my head, fighting back the tears. "It didn't work out."

I didn't want to admit that when I walked into the interview, I was a hot mess. Aside from feeling like crap, my confidence was shattered. Three men and a woman, dressed in pristine business attire, sat across from me at a long desk. I hadn't interviewed much since I only had two jobs in my lifetime, but, at the very least, I used to have confidence in my abilities. Today, I didn't. I felt like a loser who didn't deserve this job. Instead of encouraging me, my tiny inner voice kept repeating, *You aren't good enough, you aren't good enough.* When one of the men asked me a simple question, such as what qualified me for the position, I had no answer. Like them, I sat there, waiting for an answer to come, but it never did. I was surprised I even remembered my own name.

Before walking out of the office in shame, they graciously thanked me but told me that they were looking for someone with more skills in—whatever—I couldn't even remember the excuse they gave. Whatever it was, they were searching for in a qualified candidate, it wasn't on my resume. I sincerely hoped DeShaun was having a much better day.

DeShaun

"So, man, what do you think?" M.J. asked. "Should I go streaking through this party to give the ladies a little something to look at?"

"Yeah," DeShaun said. "I dare you."

M.J. brushed off his shoulder. "Don't think I won't. But these old women might go crazy."

"You need to stop," DeShaun said. "Seriously, what is wrong with you?" He looked out into the crowd at the party. There were over two hundred people in attendance, most of them fifty and over. He spotted Jenn in the crowd, standing alongside her husband while he chatted it up with another couple. When Jenn spotted him, she whispered something to her husband, politely nodded at the couple and then made her way over with an empty glass in her hand.

"Uh-oh," M.J. said. "Here comes the barracuda and she's on empty. Look out."

Jenn staggered over and smiled lazily at DeShaun. "Hi." She'd already had too much to drink.

"Hi," M.J. said, poking his head between the two of them.

Jenn looked at M.J. She leaned in and read his nametag. "Hello, Micah. I don't believe we've met."

"Call me M.J." He tipped the bottle and refilled her glass. "I've serviced several of your parties."

"Sorry, I don't remember, but nice to meet you anyway." She took a sip from her glass. "Do me a favor. See to it that the people under the canopy have a glass of champagne? It's running low over there."

"Yes, ma'am."

"Thank you."

"And you." She turned back to DeShaun. "Would you be so kind as to keep the wine flowing for us, especially the couple my husband is talking to? He's trying to make another business deal and feels as though getting them sloppy drunk is the best way to do it. It must work." Jenn shrugged. "That's how he got me to marry him."

M.J. laughed.

Jenn looked at M.J. "See? He thinks it's funny. Now, if you could take care of the guests under the canopy, that would be great."

"Yes, ma'am." M.J. disappeared into the kitchen for the champagne, but not before turning back to DeShaun and making a lewd gesture with his tongue behind her back.

Berti walked over to the both of them. "My good man." He grabbed DeShaun's hand and shook rigorously. "Glad to see you again."

"Same here, Sir."

Berti placed a hand on DeShaun's shoulder. "I'll let you in on a little secret. See that couple over there?" Berti nodded toward the older couple he was speaking to a minute ago. "They have a lot of money and are close to making a deal with my company. Here's what I need you to do. I need a good wine to help seal the deal. Any suggestions?"

"Well," DeShaun began, "I'd suggest a good Pinot. I can get a bottle right now, open it up, and let it breathe for ten minutes."

"Really?" Berti asked, impressed. "Why Pinot?"

"It's not pretentious. It's not as if you're trying so hard to impress.

However, its full-bodied taste will make an impression all on its own. And besides that, it's damn good."

Berti patted DeShaun on the back. "Bring it over in five minutes." He started back over to the couple but stopped abruptly and turned around. "You should be there, too, Jenn."

"I'll be there in a couple of minutes."

"Make it one minute." He leaned over and kissed her on her cheek. "This dress looks nice, but I prefer the red one." He walked away.

When he was out of earshot, Jenn mumbled, "That's why I wore this one."

DeShaun cleared his throat. "Well, I guess I'd better get that wine."

"Let me ask you a question? Do you believe Berti still loves me?"

Caught off-guard, in his head, DeShaun scrambled for an answer to the odd, yet inappropriate question.

"He's really not that bad," Jenn said, her slurring more pronounced. "He still loves me, but it's more like a business partner than a wife. We haven't had sex in over three months. And I've never once cheated on him."

He wanted to ask her if she actually wanted to have sex after witnessing him with some dude, but decided against it. "Two wrongs don't make a right." As soon as he said that stupid shit, he wanted to kick himself.

"See the guy over there." Jenn pointed to a crowd of servers, none of which DeShaun recognized. "The young guy with the braids in his hair—that's the one Berti has been fancying. He thinks I don't see him check these guys out. I see everything."

DeShaun looked over at the waiters. The one Jenn referred to was really young, like, barely legal young.

She finished off her glass of wine. "As soon as this party is over, he'll tell me he has to clean up a business deal at the office. Berti honestly believes I'm an idiot." She held up her empty glass and DeShaun filled it again.

"Maybe I should get you a glass of water, too," he offered.

"Water? I don't need water. I need for my husband to get off those young boys. Don't get me wrong; it's not that I care that he's screwing around, not really. I just don't want it to affect my finances. The more time he spends screwing, the less time he's in the office making million-dollar deals."

DeShaun was speechless. He guessed that answered the question as to whether or not she wanted to sleep with her husband after finding out about his extracurricular activities.

"Regardless, he will be tested before he even attempts to touch me again."

DeShaun took the glass from her hand. "Um, I'll get you some water."

"Don't bother. Didn't you hear my adoring husband? He needs me. I've got to go." With shaky legs, she stumbled back to her husband. DeShaun headed back into the kitchen to find that bottle of wine. After that conversation, he was the one that needed a drink.

At three in the morning, most of the guests had left except for a few stragglers who sat in lounge chairs by the pool. Although it wasn't his job, DeShaun stayed behind to help the caterers and his crew fold up the tables and clean the grounds. On the last table, he pulled out his phone and checked his messages. He had one, but didn't recognize the number. When he listened to the message, he heard Naomi's voice. She was going on an interview and was wishing him luck tonight. That was early afternoon. He wanted to call her but decided against it. It was too late and she was probably asleep.

"I have a message for you," Jenn said, walking up to him. She had changed out of her dress and wore a pair of jeans and a T-shirt. Her face was stripped of makeup and she was wearing her trademark casual hairstyle; a ponytail. She looked like she had sobered up some, too.

DeShaun folded up one of the tablecloths and placed it into a box labeled, *Supplies*. He grabbed another one. "Looks like you're feeling better."

She grabbed a corner from the tablecloth he was holding and connected it with his end. "You mean less drunk. Oh, and Berti says thanks for the tip. That bottle of wine you suggested was perfect. Mr. Reinhardt, the man he was speaking with, loved it. Berti gave him a bottle to take home."

"Did he seal the business deal?"

"Of course," Jenn said, grabbing another tablecloth. "He wouldn't have it any other way."

"Tell him I said, 'You're welcome,' and 'Congratulations.'"

"I would but he had to go to the office to handle some paperwork."

DeShaun wondered if Jenn had remembered what she told him about the waiter earlier. He quickly scanned the grounds and while most of the other waiters DeShaun had no affiliation with were still doing last minute clean up around the house, the young waiter with the braids was gone."

"Later this week, we're having a progressive party," Jenn said. "I'd love it if you'd be there."

Progressive parties were like a mobile party, in which each course was served at a different location, usually one of the attendees' houses. DeShaun had serviced a few and found it easy work. He made the same amount of money as a four-hour event, but in a third of the time since he would only be working one course.

"Which course are you doing?" he asked.

"I've been elected for the desserts."

"How many people? I'll need to know how many servers to bring."

"Oh, no," Jenn said, shaking her head. "I wasn't asking you to work the party. I was asking you to come along with me. Berti will be out of town and I hate going to these things alone. I need a buffer there to keep me from falling asleep…preferably, someone under the age of sixty and with a pulse."

"Um, I'm not sure about that."

"Of course you'd have to clear it with your wife first, but, look at it this way, you could make some great business contacts. You could pass out a card. These people are always having parties and looking for any excuse to throw around their money."

DeShaun found it amusing Jenn was describing these people exactly the way he and Naomi had described her.

He did like the idea. She may have actually been on to something. "I don't have business cards."

"You're so good at what you do, you need to really consider doing this full-time. You could make good money."

"Maybe."

"It was just an idea," she said with a shrug. "I just thought—"

"No, it's a good idea," he said. "Really."

"So you'll go with me?"

"I'll talk to Mimi and get back to you."

"Oh, by the way," she said. "Before I forget, here's the money for tonight."

She reached into her pocket and pulled out a couple of bills. She stuck the bills into DeShaun's shirt pocket. "Thanks again, DeShaun. And let me know what you decide about that party."

"I will."

When she left, DeShaun reached into his pocket and pulled out the money. He was shocked to see she had given him five, neatly folded, one-hundred-dollar bills. That was more than double his normal salary for working a gig like this.

Naomi

When Jeremy pulled onto the driveway, the house was completely dark. The outside lights weren't on so, as expected, I had beat DeShaun home. The time on the car dash read 9:37.

Jeremy and I were supposed to come straight home, but, after thinking about it on the way home, I made him stop at a restaurant to get something to eat. Along with my chicken salad sandwich, I chugged down an ice-cold beer—maybe not the best thing for me when I was feeling sick.

"Are you feeling better?" Jeremy asked, when he turned off the car. "I can take you to the hospital, if you want."

I shook my head. "I'm fine, thanks."

I wasn't fine. I was the furthest I had ever been from fine. I felt tired all the time, and, according to the doctor, it was mostly stress related. However, the stress was there because of life. Unless you rolled over and died, how could you just stop living your life?

"Do you want me to come in with you?"

"No. DeShaun should be home soon."

Jeremy looked at me and took my hand. "Please, don't get all worked up. Everything will work out. It's not as bad as it seems."

"I know it's not," I lied, trying to get out of another "Everything-Happens-For-A-Reason" speech. When I was younger, my mother kicked that line to me every single time something went wrong. I fell off my brand-new bike and busted my knee. When I wailed all the way back to my house, Mom inspected the gash and told me, "Oh, please. It's not the end of the world." You'd think a psychologist would have a better method of comfort for a child.

It may not have been the end of the world, but that mile long scrape running down my leg hurt like hell. That's what I was feeling now; that mile long scrape of life that never seemed to find any relief. I'd get over it; I always did. But hearing another lecture wouldn't help.

"Call if you need anything," Jeremy said. "I'll keep my eyes open for more jobs."

Before I got out of the car, I reached into my purse and found my keys. "Thanks." I stepped out of the car and headed toward the front door. Before I opened the door, I turned around. Jeremy was watching me, waiting until I got into the house, like a parent did.

When I went to open the door, I noticed it was slightly ajar.

Was DeShaun home already? I pushed open the door and reached for the light switch. When I turned on the light, the air rushed right out of me. I thought this day could not have gotten any worse…. I was dead wrong.

The entire front room was trashed, as if someone had a party and forgot to clean it up. If only that were the case.

Chairs were overturned, papers scattered on the floor and the kitchen drawers ransacked. Surprisingly, the bedrooms were practically left untouched; only a few small missing items.

"We'll file this police report and let you know if anything comes up," a portly officer with red hair said. "I don't see evidence of forced entry. Does anyone else have a key?"

"Just my husband."

Jeremy stepped between the officer and me. "When will we hear something?"

"You the husband?" the officer asked.

"No."

"You'll hear from us when we find out something. That may be tomorrow, it may be next week."

"And it may not be at all," Jeremy said, irritated. "What the hell kind of scam are you guys running around here?"

The officer raised his brow. "I understand you're upset, sir—"

"Upset nothing. In case you don't understand, this is a robbery and well, gee, I assumed you were supposed to catch, I don't know, say, THE ROBBERS!"

"Relax," I told him. "It's not their fault. I'm the idiot that didn't make sure the door was locked when I left."

The officer cut his eyes from Jeremy and spoke to me. "Like I said, ma'am, we will be in touch when we hear something. You've listed everything that's missing, correct?" .

I nodded. Other than a few jewelry items and the laptop, everything else was in place. The officer had suggested it was probably a last minute robbery because of the few smaller items taken.

"Do you have someplace to stay?" the officer asked.

The officer's question was direct, but what I heard was, *I wouldn't stay here if I were you in case they decided to come back and finish what they started.*

"My husband should be home soon."

The officer cleared his throat and handed me a card. "There have been a string of robberies in this area over the past several weeks. I strongly suggest you change your locks. If you do not feel comfortable staying alone—when your husband is not here—have friends stay with you. Do you have any questions?"

I shook my head and took his card. "Thank you."

Stay with friends? I haven't had a good friend in years, since getting married. Aside from DeShaun, and I guess now Jeremy, I kept to myself. I had acquaintances when I worked at the bank, but as for friends I confided in, that wasn't really my taste.

"Do you have someone that can stay with you until your husband returns?" the officer asked.

"I can stay with her until then," Jeremy offered.

The officer apologized again for the situation and handed me another business card. As he gathered up the other officers to leave, I looked down at his card.

J.M. & Sons
Specializing in Locks for:
Homes
Business
Tool Sheds
We Have the Lock for All Your Needs!

"Great. Another cost I can't afford."

After the police officers left, Jeremy turned to me. "This must be the worst day for you. I'm really sorry."

"Actually, it's not." I said. "In third grade, Jalil Henderson didn't ask me to be his partner for the square dance showdown. He asked Penelope Miller, this freckle-faced, orange-haired little brat instead."

Jeremy stared at me, trying to figure out what I was talking about.

"But then Penelope told Jalil no, and don't you know the little shit came back and asked me."

"You said, no, right?"

"The hell I did. We square-danced for two hours straight. He stepped on my toes the entire time, but the important thing was I got him, even if by default."

"Is there a point to that story?"

"Nope."

He looked at me for a second and then chuckled. I joined him. "What do you need me for?" he asked. "You can amuse yourself."

"I have no idea what made me think of that." I thought a moment. "Oh, wait. It was that pudgy police officer with the red hair."

"Which one?"

"The one that dusted for fingerprints and gave me the card."

"Oh."

"I'm so tired, Jeremy. I don't even know which way is up anymore."

Jeremy reached over and gave me a hug. It was awkward at first, but as I took a deep breath and relaxed, it felt more natural, comforting even. "Hang in there. It really does get better, I promise."

Maybe it was going to get better someday, but today was not that day.

DeShaun barged through the front door. He looked at me and Jeremy. "What the hell is going on in here?"

Naomi and DeShaun

"Why did I see the police leaving? Are you okay?" DeShaun shot a look at Jeremy.

"I got home from the interview and someone had broken in."

"While you were here?" DeShaun asked, stunned. "Are you okay?'

I shook my head. "No, while I was at the interview. I'm all right."

DeShaun looked around, as if he still couldn't believe what he was seeing. "How the hell did that happen?"

Jeremy stepped up. "It happens. The cop even said there were a string of robberies in the area."

"Who are you?" DeShaun asked.

"This is Jeremy," I told DeShaun.

"Who?"

"Jeremy. From the bank."

DeShaun quickly gave Jeremy the once over, sizing him up from top to bottom. He then turned back to me. "So what exactly happened?"

"Somebody broke in," Jeremy said. "They only got away with a few small items."

DeShaun whipped back around to Jeremy. "I'm not talkin' to you, man." He turned back to me. "As a matter of fact, I'm still trying to figure out why he's here in the first place."

Jeremy took a step toward DeShaun. "I'm here because you weren't."

DeShaun, in turn, stepped toward Jeremy. "What?"

I stood in between the both of them. "He's here because he's the one that gave me the information about the interview. He took me there."

DeShaun looked around again. "I hope you got the job. You do know we let our insurance lapse. I'm still trying to figure out how this happened."

"I left the door open. I'm sorry, DeShaun. I thought I locked it but— "

"Ah, man, Mimi. You did what?"

"I'm so sorry. I ran out of here so quickly, I don't think I locked the door. The police said there was no forced entry."

DeShaun took a deep breath. He opened his mouth to say something but stopped. He took another deep breath. "I don't believe this shit! I don't believe you! I am busting my butt, and it's like you're trying to sabotage everything we have—or should I say everything we *don't* have."

"That's not true," I said, feeling hurt. "It was a mistake."

"How many more mistakes can we afford to make, Naomi? Maybe you should've left everything on the front lawn to make it easier for the thieves."

"Hey, man," Jeremy interjected. "It was a mistake. It happens."

"Why are you still standing in my living room, flapping your gums?"

I turned to Jeremy. "Thanks, but you can go."

"Call if you need anything," Jeremy said. He turned to DeShaun. "It really was a mistake that plenty people make."

DeShaun shot him a warning look.

I grabbed Jeremy's elbow and started shuffling him toward the front door. "Thanks," I whispered. When I got him out the door, I made sure to lock it.

I took a deep breath before turning back to DeShaun. "I'm sorry, baby."

Then he did something I did not expect.

He grabbed hold of my wrist and pulled me to him, holding me close.

"Baby, I know you're sorry," he said. "I'm glad you're okay. These are only things. It's not a big deal. It just seems like everything is getting so hard lately. Bills piling up, losing our jobs, everything. I hate the fact that I spend all my time, worrying about our next move."

"Me too," I said. "The good news is that whoever it was only took the smaller items. The police officer said it was probably a last minute thing."

"If there was a bright side to this mess, that'd be it," DeShaun said. "Don't worry. Everything will be fine."

"How was the party?" If that rich lady popped him off a few extra bills, now would be the perfect time.

"It went okay."

"Well?"

"Well, what?"

"Do you feel comfortable befriending her? You know, The Plan?" I asked. "The way you described her, I pictured this little old lady who felt entitled to everything, including you."

He shrugged. "She's actually not that bad or that old."

"Really?"

"At those parties, she was drunk most of the time, which was why she acted like she did."

"Did she hit on you again?"

He shook his head. "Not this time."

"Of course, she doesn't throw herself at your feet when we need her to," I jokingly commented.

"She had issues with the caterer. I spent half the afternoon, hooking her up with a good price for the food. You remember D'Antonio's?"

"That's good. You saved the day. She should be thankful for that, *real thankful.*"

"She was," DeShaun said. "At the end of the night, she gave me five hundred dollars." He reached into his pocket and pulled out four one-hundred-dollar bills and two twenty-dollar bills.

"What happened to the rest?"

"Oh, yeah." He stepped into the foyer. Seconds later, he returned with two dozen brilliant red roses.

"Where did you get those at this hour?" I asked. "They're beautiful."

"Thank goodness for all-night gas stations. I wanted to do something for you to make you feel better."

"Thank you." I gave him a peck on his lips. I took the roses upstairs with me to the bedroom. He followed.

He kicked off his shoes and headed into the bathroom for a quick shower. While he took his shower, I inspected the roses. For gas station roses, they were quite exquisite. When I heard the shower turn off, I yelled into the bathroom. "What's our next move?"

DeShaun exited the bathroom, along with a cloud of steam. His dripping wet body was wrapped only in a towel. "We'll play it by ear, I guess."

"Are you really okay with this, DeShaun?" A little piece inside wanted him to not be all right with what was basically being a male escort, sans the sex. But we'd exhausted all other resources. What else could we do?

He shrugged and then nodded. He whipped off the towel and put on a pair of boxers and a white tee. He jumped into bed next to me and then rolled over and flicked off the light. "G'night," he said with his back to me.

After giving me those beautiful roses, I had expected him to want a little intimate time. After the day I had, I needed a little extra attention. Suffice it to say, I was a little disappointed when he turned to his side and pulled the sheets up to his chin.

"Oh, by the way," DeShaun said, with his back still toward me. "Jenn asked me to service a progressive party for her."

"That's great. I don't know what a progressive party is, but as long as money is flowing, I'm good with it."

"She also had a pretty good suggestion." His back was still to me.

"Yeah? What was that?"

"She thought now would be a good time to start a service business. I'm basically doing that now. I'll need some business cards. Other than that, I'm set. I don't need any advertising. With businesses like this, word-of-mouth is the best way to go."

"Do you think that's a good idea at this time," I said. "Starting a business is for when you've established yourself and have savings. You know, something to fall back on, just in case."

"This is the perfect time. If not now, then when?"

Why was his back still to me?

"I'm just sayin'—"

"You know what? Maybe you're right," he said. "Good night."

I rolled over in bed and laid my head on the pillow. He must have been exhausted; within ten minutes, I heard snoring. I was up for another three hours, staring into the darkness, thinking about the strange but brief conversation I'd had with the back of my husband's head.

DeShaun

DeShaun stood in the Herjavecs' doorway. He hesitated a moment before knocking. He felt guilty about having to lie to Naomi to get out of the house, but she would not have understood why he needed to attend the party to put out feelers for a possible business that she didn't even want him to start in the first place. Naomi couldn't see the long-term positives of starting this business. She only saw the money not filtering in right away. According to the business draft he and Jenn briefly discussed, starting his own business was more practical than continuing to work for someone else. He would be doing something he loved. The money would eventually roll in.

He stepped onto the porch and rang the bell. He looked down at his suit and straightened his tie. Jenn never told him how to dress for the party, but he had worked a few progressive parties before and most of those functions were semi-formal.

He stared down at his polished black shoes. Maybe he overdid it a bit.

When Jenn opened the door, she was wearing a white, sleeveless cotton summer dress. Her dark hair hung loosely in wavy curls below her shoulders. She wore minimal makeup, just enough to soften and highlight her already beautiful features. "Wow!" she exclaimed, giving DeShaun the once-over. "Aren't you burning up in that suit? Is that a vest?"

"Too much, huh?"

"Just a bit."

DeShaun felt the heat rise to his cheeks.

"No, no, I mean you look good, but it's just so—so hot."

"I could run home and change."

He thought about how much explaining he had already done to get out of the house in his suit in the first place. He told Naomi that the party was formal, saying that he was supervising the other service people so he needed to dress professionally to distinguish himself from the other workers.

He was in the clear when Naomi simply said, "My baby is the supervisor? Good for you." She'd kissed him on the cheek and wished him luck. On the ride over, he felt guilty, but the last thing he needed was another argument. How could he go back now and explain changing into another outfit?

"No worries," Jenn said, grabbing him by the hand. "I have a surprise for you." She rushed him up the steps and steered him down a plush carpeted hall and toward a back room. He had never seen the upstairs of her house.

"Where is everybody?" he asked.

"Everybody like who? Berti is on a business trip and I'm here."

"What about the servants?"

"What servants? I don't have any servants."

"The people who are always here, cleaning, when you have a party."

"We use them for the evening, like we do service people. They don't actually work here. No way could I stand having somebody in my house all day long. Besides, I like walking around nude. The only time I put on clothes in my own home is when the cleaning people come twice a week."

She pulled him into the bedroom. It wasn't as elaborate as ex-

pected. It looked clean and comfortable, but no hanging chandeliers or gold-plated walls as he envisioned. The paint colors on the
wall were a light tan and peach. Not at all a room he pictured Mr.
Herjavec sleeping in.

"Like my room?"

He nodded, not questioning why she called it *her* room, instead
of *their* room.

She went to her closet and reached up to the top shelf. She
pulled down a large rectangular box. "This is for you."

DeShaun took the box and opened it. Inside was a tan casual
suit with silver buttons.

"It's Armani," she said excitedly. "Take a look."

Before DeShaun could, Jenn pulled out the casual button down
shirt and held it up to him. "Try it on in the bathroom, over there.
I want to see if I guessed your size correctly."

When DeShaun came out of the bathroom, he was surprised to
see the suit fit perfectly. "How did you know my size?"

"I was a tailor's assistant when I was in college. He taught me
how to size up someone's inseam with one look. "

"You worked before?" DeShaun said. "And went to college?"

"Don't sound so surprised. I had to. My parents were piss-poor.
I worked my way through four years of college and came out with
a bachelor's degree in liberal arts."

"Is that where you met Mr. Herjavec?"

"My last summer at the tailoring shop, he came in, wanting a suit."

"Did you know *his* size at one glance?"

"Believe it or not, he was huge back then. Berti has always been
a larger man. He just watches what he eats now. He spends tons
of money on nutritionists, dietitians and trainers."

"Sounds like he enjoys spending money on things that keep him
in shape," DeShaun said. "There's nothing wrong with that."

"Aside from that, he's cheap," Jenn said. "We were so in love back then, but, I guess the love has turned into more of a mutual respect for one another. Sometimes barely that."

DeShaun thought of Naomi. "It's good that you both have respect for each other."

"The only thing I didn't like back then was that Berti never understood I *wanted* to work. I wanted to make my own money. Do you know what it's like to have someone not value what you do? "

He decided to plead the fifth on that one. He knew exactly what it felt like.

"*C'est la vie,*" Jenn said. "It's not like I didn't come out on top."

"Are you happy, though?"

"Happiness? That's secondary. I'm just trying to win this race with a slow and steady pace. You know, take one day at a time." She grabbed DeShaun's shoulders, turned him around and steered him toward the full-length mirror. "You have got to see how good you look this. Berti could work out seven days a week, ten hours a day, and still not look as good as you.

He checked out his reflection. He had to admit, the suit looked good. The material of the pants, hung loosely on him and the shirt felt like silk against his chest. She was right. The clothes fit perfectly. He looked like a completely different man.

Jenn pulled open the top drawer of her dresser. "I've got one more thing for you." DeShaun caught a glimpse of several pairs of silky, colorful panties and bras. She handed a black box to him. "You must accept this. I insist."

DeShaun opened up the box. It was a brand-new men's watch. It looked expensive; it didn't have any numbers on the face, and a tiny diamond was in the place of the twelve. "I can't accept this." He had a hard time taking his eyes off the sparkling piece of jewelry.

"You most certainly can," she urged. "It goes perfectly with the suit."

He thought of Naomi again. "I really shouldn't." For some reason, he kept forgetting the fact that, yeah, he really should. This jewel on his wrist was worth a car payment.

"Please. I want you to have it."

He secured the watch around his wrist, lifted his arm and then inspected every inch of it. "Thank you."

"Your wife wouldn't mind if I gave you a tiny kiss, would she?"

He shrugged. "No, I guess not."

"Good." Jenn leaned up and placed a small peck on his cheek. "You like it, don't you?"

"I love it. Thanks."

"Now, for my final gift."

"Another one? You've already done so much. I can't accept one more thing from you."

"Yes, you can. Besides, this one is cheap, but it will make you a million bucks some day."

She dropped to her knees and looked up at him suggestively. "Can you guess what my last surprise is?"

He was getting nervous. "What are you doing?"

"You'll see." She bent down, reached under the bed and pulled out a brown box. "This is for you."

He opened up the box. Inside were three rows of green and white business cards with a gold trim. DeShaun picked out one.

Service Specialist
Providing all your service needs for:
Intimate gatherings
Weddings
And other social functions.

At the bottom of the card was contact information; his name and phone number.

"What is this?" he asked.

"What do you think it is? It's your business card. Do you like it?"

"It's great." He was slightly confused. "But how—when?"

"I had them made up the first time we talked about you doing this. I put a rush on them since I knew you'd need them for tonight."

"I don't know what to say—"

"How about thank you?"

"Thank you."

She took him by the hand. "We'd better go. And bring a few cards with you to pass around." She grabbed the keys from the dresser and handed them to DeShaun. "You don't mind driving the Mercedes tonight, do you? I plan to get drunk beyond belief."

Still speechless, DeShaun shook his head. Apparently, he was now the owner of a brand-new business and his wife had no idea. Just another secret he was keeping from Naomi. He suddenly realized lying was a habit that he didn't much care for.

DeShaun

"Who do we say I am?" DeShaun asked when they walked into the party. He scanned the scene and quickly surmised that, as expected, he was the only brother in the house—as a guest. There were plenty of black guys walking around in aprons and bow ties with trays in their hands.

"Tell them you're DeShaun, the Service Specialist," Jenn said.

"They're not going to question why I'm with you?"

Jenn shrugged. "Why would they? And even if they do, it's none of their business. I bring escorts to these boring soirees all the time."

"You do?"

"They're mostly my friends that they already know," Jenn admitted. "This will be the first time I bring a gorgeous black man to the party."

DeShaun took a deep breath, not knowing if he felt up to dealing with the stares and whispers of snobby, rich people. Everything was cool as long as he was providing them with drinks, but tonight, he felt out of his element. He decided to have a drink. He grabbed a glass of wine off the table and chugged it. One or two more glasses and he might be able to stomach the inquisitive stares.

They walked through the immaculate house, past the kitchen and straight for the outside back patio. Jenn swished open the double glass doors and made a beeline to a small table with two older couples, enjoying a bottle of wine.

"Skip and Barbara. How nice to see you again," Jenn said, as she gave each person at the table a double kiss on the cheek.

They exchanged small talk for several minutes. Both older couples had grandchildren in their thirties. One was a doctor, another a lawyer, blah, blah, blah. It was pretty much what DeShaun guessed rich people conversed about at these parties. Eventually, the couple looked past Jenn and directly at him. "And whom do we have here?"

"This is DeShaun Knowles," Jenn said. "DeShaun, these are the Ayersons and the Yorks."

The couples waited for a more detailed explanation. When they received none, one of the women asked Jenn, "So, how do you know Mr. Knowles?"

"He's a Service Specialist."

"A Service Specialist?" one of the men questioned. The two women exchanged sly grins, which even Stevie Wonder could have seen.

"What does a Service Specialist do exactly?" the oldest-looking of the two women asked.

DeShaun looked at the men and hated the fact that he felt intimidated. They weren't any better than him; they just had more money.

"I'm glad you asked," Jenn said. "A Service Specialist supplies the necessary five hundred servers that it requires to handle one of your boisterous parties, Skip."

When everyone laughed, DeShaun felt more at ease.

"Interesting," the other man said, "I normally don't handle those things. I had no idea there was a company that provides such a service."

"We do," DeShaun said. "For instance, those five-hundred service people that Jenn referred to for the Ayerson party would need to coordinate with the caterers so that the hot food is served hot and the chilled food remains cold for the guests."

"I suppose that is true. I never thought about that," Barbara Ayerson commented.

"The food should be served in a methodical manner in order to do this. It's my job to make sure everyone has received the appetizer before even one person receives the main course. It's a simple case of coordinating. Every second counts. Champagne glasses should always be filled and, if there's a special item needed, it's my job to provide you with it or have the appropriate person get it to you."

"Answer me this," the other gentleman at the table began. "Don't most caterers supply a serving staff?"

"Some do. However, the main job of the caterer is to prepare good food. Service is secondary for them. For me, service is job one." He looked down at the bottle of wine sitting at the center of the table. "For instance, you tell me you prefer a dark, smooth and racy vintage wine. I, in turn, offer you a bottle of Chateau Margaux circa 1995. This tasty wine contains passionate fragrances of blackberry and cassis. It hails from a vineyard that goes back a thousand years. The best part; at four hundred dollars a bottle, it's not too pricey for its eloquent taste."

The entire table fell quiet, including Jenn.

"Wow," one of the men said. "That's remarkable. How did you retain all of that information?"

"That's my job."

"My wife and I are planning on having a party in the next month or so. Do you have a business card?"

DeShaun looked at Jenn. She was holding back a smile, but in her eyes, he saw a big, *I told you so.*

"That, I do." DeShaun reached into his pocket and produced one of the business cards.

The man inspected the card, nodded and stuck it in his shirt pocket. "This will most certainly come in handy."

"Great," DeShaun said. "I look forward to hearing from you."

DeShaun drove the Mercedes up the Herjavecs' driveway. When he pushed the gear into park, Jenn woke up.

"Are we back?" she asked sleepily.

"We sure are."

She straightened up in the passenger-side seat. "What time is it?" DeShaun checked the dashboard clock. "Wow, it's past two o'clock." After the party tonight, he was so excited, he wanted to go out and celebrate, but he decided against it when he thought about that forty-five-minute ride he had back to his house. "I'd better hurry and get home."

"You really handled yourself well tonight, DeShaun. I realized you were smart, but if I can be honest, I thought your confidence level would be the thing to do you in. I keep trying to figure out why you haven't done something like this before. You know your stuff. You could be so successful at it."

"It never really occurred to me," DeShaun said. "I mean, I thought about opening a restaurant, but that wasn't really my thing. This is, and for pulling that out of me, I thank you so much."

Jenn smiled through sleepy eyes. "No thank-yous needed here. I simply gave a suggestion and you ran with it."

She reached over and placed her hand on top of DeShaun's, whose hands were tightly gripping the steering wheel. Their eyes lingered on each other for several seconds.

"I really should get home," he said.

"Don't forget your cards. I don't know when I'm going to get to see you again so you'd better get them now." Her hand was still on top of his. His grip on the steering wheel tightened.

"Yeah," DeShaun agreed. "I don't know when I'm going to see you again."

He released the steering wheel and pulled his hands from under hers. He hopped out of the car and raced over toward the passenger side to open the door. When he did, she stepped out the car. They were dangerously close and he wanted to move away, but his feet were two cement blocks. While staring him in the eyes, she reached down, took his hand, and guided him toward the front door. She released him for a second to unlock the front door. With her shoulder, she nudged open the door. She then reached down and grabbed his hand once again. Without saying a word, she led him straight to her bedroom.

Naomi

I lay in bed in complete darkness, wondering where DeShaun was. It was past three in the morning and, while he had been known to roll in late from the parties he serviced, this was the latest he had ever come home. I thought of him hurt in a terrible accident or worse. Maybe that piece of junk car finally broke down, leaving him stranded.

But, he had his phone. He would call.

I decided to give him another half hour before calling the police. Maybe he was laying in a ditch somewhere and couldn't get to his phone. My mind raced with all sorts of gory thoughts until finally, I flicked on the light and called him again. But yet again, his voice-mail came on. On my final attempt, the automated voice told me the phone message mechanism was filled to capacity.

A half hour later, I let out a sigh of relief when I heard the key to the front door jiggle in the lock. I hopped out of bed, grabbed my robe and shot off down the steps, but not before glancing at the clock. It was after five.

"Are you okay?" I asked when he walked through the front door.

"What are you doing up? I thought you'd be asleep."

"You're kidding, right? How can I sleep when I hadn't heard from you all night? Why are you so late? What happened?" I shot off question after question and didn't even notice the unfamiliar tan suit he was wearing.

"I called you," he said.

"No you didn't."

"I called twice."

"You're lying. I've been sitting by this phone all night. You did not call."

"I called your cell."

"Why would you call my cell when you know it's not on?"

"I thought we turned it on. Isn't that what you told me a few days ago?"

"No," I said. "I told you I turned on the house phone. You know that because unlike tonight, you called the house phone several times."

"Oh, my fault. I thought you said you turned both phones back on. I guess I forgot."

He went to the refrigerator, grabbed a cold beer and then slammed the fridge shut. He bit off the cap and took a drink. Why are you watching me?"

"I'm not watching you. I'm looking at you."

"Well then stop *looking* at me." He took another drink. "It's annoying."

I turned and headed for the living room. I plopped down onto the couch, expecting him to follow. When he didn't, I yelled back into the kitchen. "How was the party? Did you make good tips tonight?" He didn't answer so I went back into the kitchen. He was gone. When I reached the top of the steps, I heard the running shower. I glanced down at the crumpled up tan suit he left next to the bed. I picked up the shirt, checked out the designer label and then held the shirt up and took a whiff. It smelled like a combination of perfume and smoke. When the shower shut off, I dropped the shirt and hopped back into bed. DeShaun fumbled around in the bathroom for another five minutes and when he finally emerged,

I shut my eyes, pretending to be asleep. He jumped into bed next to me and pulled up the covers. Two minutes later, he was snoring.

I sat awake for over an hour before deciding to nudge him. He stirred but kept on snoring.

"DeShaun?" I whispered.

"What?" He sounded annoyed.

"What is wrong with you tonight?"

"I'm sleeping, Mimi, that's what's wrong. The sun is about to come up and you're poking me like you're ringing a dang doorbell."

"That's my point. You roll in here *this morning* and with attitude to boot."

"So? I'm tired."

"Was the party that bad?"

He rolled over. "Can we please talk about this tomorrow?"

"It is tomorrow!"

He sighed. "I'm going to sleep. When I get up, I'll give you every single little detail you want about the party." He flopped down onto his pillow and pulled up the covers.

"I tried calling you…*yesterday*, when you went to work. You left your apron."

He was quiet for a second. "They had extra."

"Lucky you."

"Yeah, lucky me. Now if you don't mind, I'm going to get some sleep.

Naomi

Early the next morning, I had planned to ask DeShaun about the party again, but when I woke up he was gone. The suit was gone, too, but I spotted something on the floor, halfway under the bed. I reached down and picked it up. It was a business card. DeShaun usually had a few business cards from prospective clients, but this wasn't one of their cards. His name and phone number was on this card as the owner. I slipped on my robe and headed downstairs to the kitchen. Dishes were piled in the sink and the coffee maker hadn't been touched. DeShaun always drank at least one cup of black coffee in the morning. I went to the refrigerator. He left a note stuck on the outside of the fridge with an apple magnet.

Had to go out
Be back soon.
Love
-D

I crumpled up the note and tossed it into the trashcan. I carefully laid out the business card onto the dining room table—in full view. He had started a business without my consent, which could've been the reason he was acting so strangely lately. It wasn't as if I didn't want him to go forward with the idea. It was more like now was not the best time. Apparently, he didn't agree. No matter what the case was, a serious talk was long overdue. I was so deep in thought about my husband, I didn't hear the phone ring.

"Hello?"

"Hey?"

"Who is this?" I asked.

"I know we don't work together anymore but, jeez, you forgot about me already?"

"Jeremy?"

"That'd be me. How the hell are ya?"

"Good. How are you?"

"Just chillin'," he said. "I start grad school in another few weeks. The Dean wants to meet with me about a possible job on the main campus. He wants me to drop by tomorrow to discuss things."

"Good." I was only half-paying attention. "That's great."

"Yeah, I'm excited," he said. "Did the cops ever get back to you about your stuff?"

"No."

"I figured."

Jeremy rambled on about the cops for a few minutes and then told me about some story he saw in the newspaper about corruption on the police force. I wasn't really listening because my mind was elsewhere.

"You okay?"

"What? Yeah. I'm fine."

He started to say something else, but the other line buzzed. I checked the number but didn't recognize it. "Gotta go." Before I clicked over, I heard him rush in the words, "Call me later."

"Hello?"

"Ms. Knowles, please."

I didn't recognize the voice, probably another bill collector. "This is Ms. Knowles."

"Good morning. I'm calling from McIntyre, Roth and Associates.

We would like to extend a formal offer for the administrative position you interviewed for."

My heart pounded through my chest. I hadn't heard from them in at least a month. I assumed I didn't get the job. This was great news.

"You'll need to come in and fill out some paperwork. It shouldn't take too long," the lady on the other end told me.

"When do I start?" I hoped I didn't sound too eager.

"You'll need to submit to a drug test. Providing all is in order, the training class will be held in two weeks, contingent of course on the mandatory test and the necessary paperwork. We will send you the information to the address you provided on the application form. We will also e-mail you a copy for your records. Have the paperwork returned to us as soon as possible so we can begin the process."

"Thank you. I'll have the paperwork to you early next week."

Just as I hung up, DeShaun walked through the door.

Naomi

I sat on the edge of the bed, fuming. "Where were you?"

"Running errands."

"We never finished our discussion last night." I tried to contain the anger, but his nonchalant attitude was starting to really piss me off.

He sighed. "I don't feel like going there again." He went into the bathroom. When the toilet flushed, I stood up and went to the door.

"And what's with the designer suit?"

He didn't answer so I shot off question number two. "And why didn't you bother to tell me about the company that you're apparently the owner of."

"I have a question," he said. "Why are you going through my shit?"

Was he serious? "You're mad at me because I found out some information you were trying to hide?"

Again, he didn't offer an answer, so I continued. "For your information, you left your new suit crumpled by the bed when you strolled in last night. Oh, I'm sorry, I meant *this morning* when you strolled in at nearly five o'clock. And when you went to *hide* your brand new suit, the business card must've dropped out of it." I folded my arms across my chest and cocked my head to the side. "There. I answered your question. Answer mine."

"It's no big deal. I decided to start the company without telling you. I wanted to wait until I had some clients before I said anything."

"And the suit?"

"The suit was a gift."

"From?"

"Who do you think?"

"The rich bitch? Why is she buying your clothes? Am I going to go upstairs in your drawer to find boxers with hearts on them that she bought you, too?"

"You tell me," he said, angrily. "You're the one that likes to snoop."

He wasn't getting off that easily. I squared off my shoulder and stared him in the eyes. I couldn't figure out which was worse, him going behind my back or him having the balls to be defensive about it.

Finally, he said, "She took me to a party to get clients for the business and I needed a suit. That's all." He picked up the crumpled clothes he left on the bedroom floor and began hanging them up in the closet. He never picked up his junk. He was doing this to get away from my questions. That only made me even more curious.

"I'm confused. She knows about your brand-new business before your wife does?"

"It was Jenn's idea in the first place."

"It was Jenn's idea? Does Jenn have any other ideas, like maybe tripping and falling onto my husband's erect penis? I bet she came up with that idea too, or was that idea yours?"

"What are you trying to say?"

"I'm not trying—I'm saying," I told him. "Are you sleeping with her?"

"Are you serious?"

"Dead serious. It's not a difficult question. Are. You. Sleeping. With. The. Bitch?"

"No, I'm not sleeping with her. Why are you even asking me this?"

"I'm not an idiot, DeShaun. It's not adding up. The new clothes, the business, coming in at five in the morning. Something's not right."

"Your conscience is finally getting to you, huh?"

"What's that supposed to mean?"

"That means you basically told me to get out there and get all I can from her. Now I'm out here trying to do just that and you don't like it. I was the one that didn't like the idea from jump, remember?"

"And now you do?"

"Would you listen for a change?" He borderline shouted. "I'm trying to tell you that you never once asked me how I felt about this whole thing. I'm the one that has to go out there, using people, while you sit back and reap the rewards. How do you think that makes me feel?"

"Why didn't you say something then?"

"I did!" he yelled. "But you weren't trying to hear that. How do you think it makes me feel to know that you don't consider me good enough for you?"

"I never once said you weren't good enough for me."

"You didn't have to. You left that up to your mother, Miss Perfect, to say it. Remember that conversation over the phone, the one where you didn't even bother to defend me when Mommy Dearest called me a loser?"

"Are we back to that again?" I took a deep breath. "Look, DeShaun. All I'm saying is that the idea was to only do this until one of us secured a job, right?"

DeShaun nodded. "Yeah."

"Right before you came home, I got that call."

"What call?"

"That law firm I interviewed for ended up offering me the job today. I've accepted."

"That's good," DeShaun said.

"Good? It's great. You don't have to do this anymore. You don't have to see that woman. You don't have to go forth with this business idea. I can bring in some money while you continue to look for a job."

"I have a job."

"Are you seriously going to pursue this business of yours? Don't you believe we need to have two steady incomes to get back on our feet before we even consider something like that?"

"I'm still working parties," he said. "In fact, I have one tonight."

"You didn't say anything about a party tonight? Where?"

"You didn't give me a chance." He balled up his socks and tossed them into the hamper. "It's for one of the clients I met at the last function. He's throwing a surprise party for his wife and is paying top dollar for me to coordinate the service with the caterers."

"What time?" I was disappointed and didn't bother hiding it. "I wanted to celebrate with you tonight. It's been so long since we've had a special night together."

"It's going to be late," he said. "But I should be home by two at the latest."

"Is *she* going to be there?"

"Who?"

"You know who I'm talking about."

He shook his head. "As far as I know, she went out of town with her husband for the next few weeks." He turned and headed back into the bathroom. "I'm going to take a shower."

I watched after him. Something definitely wasn't right.

Naomi

I spent the day cleaning the house, starting with the upstairs, working my way downstairs and ending the cleaning fest with mopping the kitchen floors. I hated cleaning, but surprisingly, it was cleaning that burned off my recent burst of excess energy. By the time I finished the entire house, including the garage, I was too exhausted to think about DeShaun and our earlier argument.

Early afternoon, the phone rang. I picked it up, hoping it was DeShaun. It wasn't.

"Are you busy?" Jeremy asked.

"Just doing some cleaning. What's up?"

"I'm calling to find out if you want to hang out and grab a drink tonight?"

A drink? I could've really gone for a drink, or two, or three, but I wasn't really in the mood to socialize. Grabbing a bottle of wine and parking my butt on the couch was a better option. "I can't. I'm doing some major cleaning and by the time I finish, I will be beat down and ready to hop in the shower and go to bed. Thanks for the offer, though."

"Aw, c'mon," Jeremy said, apparently not ready to surrender. "One drink and then you can go home and put your feet up. It won't be for long. I'm meeting the Dean at seven. Just meet me for one drink at six."

Another time I would have seriously considered it, but I couldn't bring myself up to hanging out this evening. "Not tonight, Jeremy."

"Okay," he said, finally giving up. "We'll do it another time." I heard the disappointment in his voice.

"Another time," I agreed.

I hung up the phone and finished cleaning out the kitchen. An hour later, DeShaun still wasn't home and he didn't call. At one point, I feared the phone was cut off again, so I checked the line. It was still on.

I hopped into the bathtub and washed my hair. After my bubble bath, still wrapped in my bathrobe, I plopped down onto the bed and fell asleep.

I awoke two hours later to the sound of the running shower. I jumped off the bed and softly knocked on the closed bathroom door. "DeShaun?"

"I'll be out in a minute."

Thirty minutes later, he stepped out of the bathroom with a white towel around his waist. "Hey," he said, buzzing around the room. First, he went to his top dresser drawer and pulled out a pair of boxers. He reached into the second drawer and pulled out a balled up pair of black socks. After that, he headed back to the bathroom and brushed his teeth. I watched him splash some cologne on his face with a scent I didn't recognize.

"Where are you going?"

"I told you I'm working that party tonight, remember?" He pulled up his slacks and then buttoned up his crisp, white shirt. "Seen my belt?"

"Hanging in the closet."

He shuffled over to the closet, sifting through the hanging clothes. "Ah, there it is."

"You're wearing that to service a party?"

He sat on the edge of the bed and put on the black socks. He reached under the bed and pulled out a pair of shiny black shoes. "They have specific uniforms they want us to put on when we get there."

"So you're getting dressed up now to change into a uniform when you get there?"

He rolled his eyes and sighed. "Why are you always hounding me? First off, this is not dressed up. Second, I can't show up in a pair of ripped jeans for a formal function. You've seen me dress like this a million times before."

Actually, I hadn't, but if I said something, it would start another argument, so I kept my thoughts to myself. Instead, I asked, "I thought we were going to talk tonight? I think I know why we've been arguing so much lately."

"Can't now, Mimi. I'm late. Besides, I've been home for about an hour, but you were asleep."

"Why didn't you wake me?"

"You looked so peaceful, I didn't want to bother you."

Did he honestly think I was an idiot? He didn't wake me because he didn't want to continue our conversation.

He went over to the closet and grabbed his gym bag. "I'll be home late."

"This morning you said no later than two," I reminded.

"I can't predict when I'm going to be home. Sometimes these things run over, but I promise you this, I'll try to be home by two, okay?"

I was dissatisfied with that answer, but I nodded anyway. What else could I do?

He bent down and gave me a peck on the lips. "Have a good night."

"You too."

"I love you."

"Love you, too."

He grabbed his wallet from the dresser and left. As soon as he pulled out of the driveway, I picked up the phone and called Jeremy. "You still want to go out?"

Naomi

I checked my reflection in the mirror. Jeans and a form-fitting tee were the perfect look for a casual evening. We were only going for a drink, so there was no need to get all dolled up. I brushed my short, cropped hair out of my face and laid it nicely. I never thought I'd see the day Jeremy and I would become friends. While working at the bank, he seemed creepy to me. Now, he's okay.

"You look gorgeous," he said when I opened the door.

"Oh, please. I'm wearing jeans and a shirt and I barely have any makeup on."

"You look best that way—natural," he said. "You don't wear a ton of makeup and that works for you."

"What are you, my stylist now?"

He laughed. "Yeah, and later on, I'm going to need you and your sexy body to try on a few nightgowns."

A few weeks ago, him saying that to me would've made me cringe. Tonight, it was actually kind of funny and I enjoyed the compliment—something I was lacking lately.

When we pulled into the parking lot of the bar, Jeremy surprised me by hopping out of the car and whipping around to open the passenger-side door. I couldn't remember the last time DeShaun did that for me.

The bar didn't quite look like one of those seedy ghetto bars you saw on television, but it wasn't an upscale one either. I wouldn't expect to see any of my old, snobby co-workers hanging around here, thank goodness. Through the glass door entrance, I spotted pool tables in the back and an old-school jukebox situated in the corner. When Jeremy opened the entrance door, current R&B hits rolled out into the streets.

"You don't have to be all formal and open the door for me," I told him. "This is not a date. We're simply hanging out."

He sucked his teeth. "Now see, if I didn't open the door, you'd be talkin' about me like a dog."

"You have my permission to cut that crap out tonight. Treat me like one of your boys."

"It's like that?"

"It's like that."

"How come you don't go out with any girlfriends?" he asked. "No sisters, close cousins?"

"I have an older sister but we don't talk at all. I had one or two close friends but since getting married, I've lost touch. I guess DeShaun became like my best friend. But now—"

"Okay," Jeremy said. "Let's make a deal. No gloom and doom tonight. I'll be your girlfriend, well, you know what I mean. We're going to have some fun. Agreed?"

"Agreed."

We walked through the smoke-filled bar and I Immediately smelled the stench of alcohol, peanuts and something that smelled like chitterlings and pig's feet put together. So much for not being that stereotypical ghetto bar. "What kind of dive did you bring me to?" I half expected a shoot-out to break out at any moment.

It was only five-thirty, but most of the patrons looked as though they had been there for hours. One guy was even passed out on the bar, with his head resting on the countertop.

"This place didn't look that bad outside," I said.

Jeremy flagged over the waiter. "It may not be the Ritz, but this place has the best Long Island Iced Teas."

"No drinking for me," I said. "The last time you ordered me a drink, I got fired. I don't know what'll happen this time."

We both laughed.

"Speaking of which, did you hear from anyone about a job yet?"

"Actually, I did," I said. "Remember that law firm I told you about? They called back and offered me the job."

The bartender returned and dropped down two humungous glasses in front of us. "I'm supposed to drink all this?" I dipped my finger in the glass and tasted it. It tasted like straight alcohol.

"Think of it as a congratulations drink," Jeremy said. "We need a celebration shot to go along with this. Bartender!"

I shook my head. "Not for me."

"Oh, c'mon, just one. I can't get too drunk anyway. I have to meet the Dean tonight, remember?"

"I forgot. We could've hung out some other night."

The bartender placed two shots in front of us. Jeremy picked up both and handed me one. "We'll do one shot, grab a beer and then head out."

Jeremy raised his shot high in the air. "Here's to getting that job."

I raised my glass. "And to your grad school."

"May we both be successful in life," he said.

"Here, here."

We clinked our shot glasses together and downed the drink. The room temperature liquid burned down my throat, leaving a heat sensation. "What the hell is this?"

"Beats me. I told the bartender to give us his most potent stuff."

"So much for not getting drunk."

"I'm kidding. It's Jägermeister. I used to drink it in college."

We clinked our glasses together and took another drink.

"I brought Tanya here last week," he said. "You remember her, the one whose head you bit off after the interview."

"I felt so bad about that," I said. "Was she really mad? I know she thought I was a bitch."

"Nah. She's cool. Speaking of which, I'm assuming you're feeling better."

"Haven't been back to the doctor, but I still get nauseous from time to time."

"You know what will fix that?"

"Lemme guess," I said. "Another shot."

"Exactly!" He waived his hand. "Bartender, another."

"This is my last one. And this should be your last one too. Remember your meeting."

He handed me the second shot glass. "I know."

We took the shot and then he turned back to the bartender. "One six-pack of Corona to go, please."

The bartender reached into the refrigerator behind the counter and pulled out a six-pack. Jeremy paid for it and we left.

He held up the pack of beer. "This will give me something to do tonight after I drop you off."

As soon as we got into the car, I checked my watch. "What time did you say your meeting was?"

"Seven."

"You do know it's six-forty-five?"

"Are you serious? Shit! I'm gonna be late."

"How far does he live?"

"About ten minutes from here, but I have to take you back first and that's going to put me back another twenty-minutes. I knew something like this would happen! Do you know how stupid I'll look, going up there late?"

"Take it easy," I told him. "We'll go to your meeting first. I'll wait in the car."

"You sure?"

I nodded. "Let's go."

"I really appreciate this." He reached into his pocket and pulled out a pack of mints. He popped two into his mouth and then started the car. "I won't be long, I promise." He pulled off the lot and down the road toward the expressway.

Naomi

The ride seemed to take forever. By the time we turned into the Deans' driveway, I began to feel a slight buzz.

We drove toward a large colonial-style home. Several cars were parked out front. As we got closer, I heard music playing. "Are we going to a party? Oh God, please don't tell me this is a college party."

"Not that I know of." Jeremy pulled over the car, reached into the glove box and pulled out a crumpled up piece of paper. He turned on the car light and attempted to focus on what was written on the paper. "This is the right address."

He pulled up closer to the house. There was no way this was a function for college kids. The guests entering were dressed in fancy suits and gowns as opposed to stumbling through the front door in jeans and tank tops. The valet guys took turns parking luxury cars and SUVs. When Jeremy pulled up in his Honda, the valet gave it the once-over before asking for his invitation.

"I don't have one," Jeremy said.

The guy shrugged and nodded his head, motioning toward a patch of grass farther down. "Park it over there then."

Jeremy pulled up to the spot where the guy indicated. "Are you coming?"

"Not really dressed for a formal party," I said. "I'll wait for you in the car."

"Okay. I should be no more than twenty minutes. Wish me luck."

He reached into his pocket, pulled out another mint and popped it into his mouth. "Can't be too careful."

"Good luck."

Jeremy got out the car and headed toward the colossal two-story house. He turned around, saw me watching him and waved. I waved back. I was glad I had the chance to get out of the house. If I wasn't out, I'd be sitting around, thinking about my argument with DeShaun, which would have been depressing.

I closed my eyes and listened to the loud music blaring from the house. It sounded like a mixture of jazz and blues tunes. Every so often, I checked the rearview mirror to see if Jeremy was headed back to the car. He had been gone for over thirty minutes. I'd give it another five minutes before trekking up to the large house.

Fifteen minutes later, I hopped out the car and made my way toward the house. I walked up to the door, figuring I would be stopped in my tracks, especially dressed like I was, but instead, I walked right in without so much as a second glance. The first thing that captured my attention was the huge crystal vase sitting out on a table in the hallway. The hardwood floors led straight to the back patio, where most of the guests were gathered.

When I walked through the patio doors, the back of the house was even more extravagant than both the front and the inside put together. The Olympic-size lavish pool was lit with bright, fluorescent lights and was surrounded with men dressed in crisp, starched tuxedos and women dressed in colorful sparkling gowns. Men and women in plum-colored tuxedos and black bow ties walked through the party, holding up serving trays with cocktails on them.

I lost myself for a moment, picturing these types of parties being the very same parties that my parents had attended years ago. Between the ages of seven to eleven, I remembered my father donned a black tux, while Mom usually wore floor-length ball gowns. She would kiss me on the forehead and leave me with the babysitter, telling me that she was going to the Cinderella ball and that she would be back before midnight. I went to bed, picturing myself attending those fairytale balls, wearing a poufy white gown with diamonds running down the sides and red shimmering shoes. Not sure why I pictured red shoes, though. It may have had something to do with *The Wizard of Oz* being my favorite movie.

I would picture a handsome Prince Charming and when I first met DeShaun, he reminded me of that prince I envisioned as a child. What I failed to realize was that fairytales didn't always have happy endings.

I glanced out over the crowd. Almost everyone—younger, older, coupled up or single—had a glass of champagne in their hands. That was the life I would've killed for.

I searched for Jeremy, but there was no sign of him. It wasn't too hard to spot the black faces throughout the crowd. Most of the black people wore the maroon tuxedoes. I did spot one black man in the crowd. His back was to me, but even from the back, I could see he had a nice physique, tall and broad. He stood by the pool with a well-dressed, dark-haired woman and another couple.

The woman he was with was pretty. She had an exotic Middle Eastern look to her. *At least the only brother in here wasn't with a blonde.* Her white dress hugged her curves and was simple yet elegant. She wore a pair of diamond stud earrings and a matching bracelet, but no necklace.

I searched the crowd again for Jeremy. I was ready to go. I was sick of watching people flaunt their wealth in front of each other, but especially in front of broke me. My gaze drifted back to the mixed couple, but this time, the guy turned around. My heart leapt up to my throat and my knees buckled from under me. I grabbed on to the post next to me to steady myself. I couldn't take my eyes off of the black Prince Charming, *my* Prince Charming. The only difference was, I wasn't the Cinderella who was tightly holding his hand.

Naomi

I couldn't take my eyes off DeShaun. He looked so happy, chatting it up with those people. He said something and everyone in the group laughed. I especially took note when the woman he was with, in the tight white dress, looked up at him and playfully smacked him on the shoulder. The longer I watched, the more it felt like the air was rushing out of me.

"You've decided to come in," Jeremy said, walking up behind me. "I apologize it took so song, but Dean Freitag told me he wants me to enter his enrichment program as an intern. Can you believe that? He actually asked me to personally intern for him."

I couldn't take my eyes off my husband. "What is this a party for?"

DeShaun reached over and grabbed two glasses of champagne from one of the guys in the maroon suits. He handed a glass to the woman and they clinked their glasses together. She must be Jenn! She was hardly what I pictured. I had assumed the woman DeShaun always spoke about was at least sixty years old. This woman with DeShaun didn't look a day over thirty-five.

"Dean Freitag said something about a surprise party for his wife. Nice, isn't it?"

I nodded. "Very."

"Are you okay?"

I turned around and headed back toward the front door. "No. I'm ready to go."

Confused, Jeremy followed my fast pace. "What's wrong?"

"Let's go, please."

When we got to the front door, I did a quick jog back to Jeremy's Honda, still sitting on the grassy knoll. When I reached the car, I bent over and stopped to catch my breath.

"What's wrong? What happened back there?"

"Nothing." Feeling as though I was going to get sick, I bent over and took several deep breaths. "I guess I wasn't feeling well and needed to get out of there."

"Do you want me to take you to the hospital?"

I shook my head. "It passed. I'm good."

"Okay," he said skeptically. He went around to the passenger side of the car and unlocked the door. "I know you said not to open up the door for you, being Miss Independent and all, but—"

I slammed the door shut and backed him up against the car. I wrapped my arms around his neck and kissed him. I used my tongue to prod open his lips and force my tongue down his throat. He didn't resist.

"Oh, God, Naomi," he said, breathless. "I've waited for this moment for so long. I know it's wrong, with you being married and all, but I'm so attracted to you. I can't help myself."

I took a step backward, trying to put a little distance between us, but he took a step toward me and grabbed me by my waist. He pulled me to him and kissed me hard. His fingertips ran up and down my back as he continued kissing me. This time he was the one that inserted his tongue into my mouth. His lips were slightly dry, but it still felt good.

"Do you want to go somewhere?" he asked.

I shook my head. "We can stay right here."

He glanced over my shoulder. The traffic was far enough down the driveway that you couldn't see us in the dark. The only way we were visible is if someone rolled up on us. "Get in the car," he said.

He rushed back over to the driver's side and I got in on the passenger side, but the heat between us had cooled down some. We both sat, looking out the window, not sure of what to say or do.

"Want a beer?" he offered.

I nodded.

He reached into the backseat and produced two warm beers. He handed me one while he popped open the other. I quickly pulled the tab on the can and chugged down half the beer without a pause. When we finished those, he reached back and grabbed two more. With the drinks we had earlier, I was beginning to feel more relaxed. His hand reached over and started rubbing my thigh. He was beginning to feel more comfortable, too.

"Are you sure you want to do this?" he asked.

I reached over and placed my hand between his legs. I gently started to massage. I felt it becoming engorged. He rolled down the window and tossed his beer can out onto the grass. I had his full attention now. "Is the backseat okay?" he asked.

The backseat was littered with clothes and books and other stuff I couldn't see in the dark. With one swoop of his arm, the junk was pushed to the floor.

He climbed into the backseat first. I followed.

He kissed me again, this one was a little wetter than the first. When he felt no resistance, he got bolder and gently outlined my lips with the tip of his tongue, eventually pushing my lips open with his tongue and hungrily exploring.

"Let me ask you something," I said, in between his wet kisses.

"What's that?" he said, still probing my body with his tongue.

"I thought being married was a deal breaker for you."

He sat up and looked at me. "You're throwing that back in my face right now?" He leaned down and went in for my neck, running the tip of his tongue up and down.

I tried relaxing by leaning against the backseat. I felt something stick me in my back, so I tried adjusting my position. It was difficult since his body was pushed up against mine. This time, the sticky thing poked my side. Jeremy sat up and pulled off his shirt. His chiseled chest was completely bare except for a thin line of dark hair that trailed from his belly button and ended well below the waist of his jeans.

He smiled, exposing perfectly white teeth. He was trying to make me feel comfortable. I forced a smile back.

He leaned down and kissed me again, but this time it was much softer. His hands rubbed up and down my body, eventually settling on the small of my back. This was a good time to take off my clothes so I slipped out of my shirt, and then my pink lace bra. I unfastened my jeans, exposing my matching pink and white cotton panties. It was awkward at first, but eventually we fell into a groove. He moved to the right so I had more elbow room and I slid back so his butt wouldn't grind into the gears of the car.

Headlights from a car sped toward us, but it swerved and continued down the road. Without skipping a beat, Jeremy continued on, pounding up and down inside of me. It felt good, but I kept thinking about my husband as I stared up into the dark, starless sky. I closed my eyes, but all I could see was DeShaun's face.

What I didn't think about, which I should have, was a condom.

Jeremy opened his eyes long enough to look down at me. I must've had a look other than ecstasy on my face because he said, "Don't worry, it's okay. I'll pull out."

Thoughts of DeShaun and that woman in white kept running through my head. I kept seeing his face at that party and how happy he looked. I hadn't seen that smile in a long time.

That charmed life I had wanted for us for so long— he was living it. To make matters worse, he was living it without me.

DeShaun

This was the fifth party DeShaun attended with Jenn. Each time it got a little easier to fit in, thanks to Jenn's generous gifts of designer outfits and diamond cufflinks. He even felt comfortable engaging in conversation, whether it was about business, politics or vacation preferences. People were starting to recognize him and Jenn together. When she first introduced him to her friends, she referred to DeShaun as her business associate. More recently, he was still introduced as a business colleague, but Jenn had since added "dear" to his friend label. At the party before last, she had even called him her "special friend." The fact that her circle started trusting him allowed him to secure more gigs. Next week, he was doing a party for the Herjavecs' accountant and the week after that, he was servicing a bris for her lawyer.

He felt terrible about lying to Naomi regarding where he was going, but she wouldn't understand. If she had it her way, his business would never get off the ground. If he had to lie a little to get ahead, he was willing to do so.

Tonight, they were at some Dean's house, who was throwing a big surprise birthday bash for his wife. As soon as they walked in, they spotted Misty and Liam Connery. DeShaun had met them both at a party for a mutual friend of Jenn's.

"We have to say hello to Liam," Jenn whispered. "He recently closed another deal with Berti worth millions. I'm sure he'll want to celebrate in a big way. Seal this deal and you will make big bucks. Just follow my lead and I'll work you in."

DeShaun squared back his shoulders and held his chin high. He was as good as any of these people and tonight he was going to prove it. Not only was he planning to persuade Mr. Connery into throwing the biggest bash this year, he was going to charge him through the roof. DeShaun was trying to make deals while, at the same time, taking mental notes for preferences for prospective future engagements. Mr. Connery was the type who didn't give a damn about spending money. As long as the service was good, Liam and Misty Connery would be willing to blow one-hundred grand, easy. From that take, DeShaun stood to make $7,000, maybe $8,000.

Jenn broke the ice with a hug and a peck on the cheek for the couple. "Liam, Misty," she exclaimed. "So glad to see you here. You remember my good friend and business associate, DeShaun Knowles?"

They both nodded. Mr. Connery extended his hand. "Good to see you again."

"Same here, sir," DeShaun told him.

Mr. Connery turned back to Jenn. "Is Berti coming this evening? I missed him at the last party."

"He couldn't make it. Now that he received that Japanese account, he spends a lot of time over there."

"Oh, he did get it!" Misty exclaimed. "How wonderful. Does this mean you're finally going to take that step and move to Tokyo? You've been talking about it for years."

DeShaun looked at Jenn, but she remained focused on the couple. She put on a wide smile. "Not sure what I'm going to do. I suppose I'll have to discuss it with Berti sooner or later. But if I do decide to go," she continued, "I should hope DeShaun would service my farewell party. You know, make the send-off as extravagant as humanly possible."

"You never said anything about moving," DeShaun said.

Jenn smiled. "Like I said, I'm not sure, but if I did, you most certainly better have the best servers there to make my party a huge success."

"When will you be sure?"

Her smile faded but she quickly regained composure. "I'll let you know as soon as I do. I'm going to need the biggest send-off possible. Since you know so much about wines, I'll expect the best."

"You know wine?" Mrs. Connery asked. "I love wine. In fact, we have a vineyard in California."

"I know a little," DeShaun answered and then turned back to Jenn. "When were you going to tell me?"

Mr. and Mrs. Connery snuck a quick glance at one another. "Perhaps we'll discuss it later," Mr. Connery said. He took his wife by the elbow and escorted her through the crowd.

As soon as the Connerys disappeared into the mob of glitz and glam, Jenn turned to DeShaun. "You do know you just let the richest couple at this party slip through your fingers."

"I got that," DeShaun said. "But what I don't understand is that you're moving and didn't say anything?"

Jenn took DeShaun by the arm and guided him over to the side of the house, away from prying eyes. "I wanted to tell you, DeShaun, but I didn't know how. Besides, it's not definite. Berti mentioned it, that's all. I didn't realize it would be such an issue for you."

DeShaun looked down. He didn't know it would be such a problem for him either. Over the past months, Jenn showed him a world he only dreamt about. He was here, right now, experiencing the same champagne and caviar he only served to people like her.

She was the first one to accept him. If she left, who would keep him abreast of the inner workings of the social circle?

But it was more than that.

He enjoyed spending time with her. Jenn was the type that could mingle with the wealthy older people, but also hang with him on a level that even Naomi couldn't. He hated to admit it but lately, it felt like Naomi was that nine-to-five job he dreaded going to every day while Jenn was the seven-day vacation to Hawaii. DeShaun had history with Naomi. He got that. He loved Naomi like no other, but what if their relationship had run its course? He needed to go home and talk to his wife. He loved her and wanted Mimi to be his seven day vacation to Hawaii—not another woman.

"I have to go," DeShaun said.

"What about the party? There are so many people here that can elevate your career. You don't want to blow this, DeShaun."

"I'm sorry. I have to go. I have something more important to do."

DeShaun ran all the way to his car and hopped in. He sped down the driveway and past a parked, out-of-the-way car on a grassy knoll on the property. He was so fixated on rushing home to his wife, he never saw the couple in the car.

Naomi

When Jeremy pulled up my driveway, I reached into the backseat and grabbed my heels.

It was slightly awkward at first; neither of us said anything. When I was finally able to look at him, he was staring at me with a smile on his face.

"I know I should feel guilty," he said, still grinning. "But I don't."

"Jeremy—"

"Don't say anything. I want to remember you like this. I want to remember *us* like this."

I shook my head. "This shouldn't have happened."

His smile faded. "It was meant to be, Naomi. I always knew this would someday happen. It had to, it's fate."

"It's not fate, Jeremy. I shouldn't have done it. I'm sorry."

Jeremy's gaze dropped. I felt so badly for hurting him. I was hurt, watching my husband with another woman, and now I transferred that hurt onto an innocent person that had been nothing but cool with me. It felt bad—really bad.

I pushed the car door open. "I have to go."

"Can I still call you?"

I wanted to tell him, "No, don't ever call me again." He was a mistake that should have never happened, but I already hurt him enough. I simply nodded and quietly mumbled, "Sure."

He took my hand. He didn't seem to notice me jerking my head away as he attempted to kiss me.

"Goodnight, Naomi."

I got out of the car and made the slow walk to the front door. I stood on the porch until his headlights disappeared.

I dropped the keys onto the hallway table. I passed through the hallway without so much as a glance into the antique mirror hanging on the wall. I could only imagine how I looked. All I wanted to do was take a long, hot shower and forget the night ever happened. I wanted to forget seeing DeShaun with *her*. I wanted to forget that first feeling of hurt that stung my heart and stopped my breath. Most of all, I wanted to forget Jeremy and the seventeen minutes he spent pounding into me like a sledgehammer.

"Where were you?"

I practically jumped out of my shoes when I looked up the steps and saw DeShaun standing at the top. "DeShaun? What are you doing here?"

"I finished early. Where were you?"

I slowly made my way to the top of the steps, thankful he hadn't turned on the lights. "I went out with friends."

"You didn't tell me you were going out tonight."

That makes us even, I thought. There were plenty of things he neglected to tell me as well.

I made a beeline straight for the shower. He stood in the bedroom doorway, his eyes watching my back. I softly shut and locked the bathroom door. When I turned on the shower, I heard a soft tap on the other side of the door. "I need to tell you something, Mimi."

I ignored him and jumped into the shower, scrubbing every part of my body from head to toe, paying special attention to the inside of my leg, which was sticky from Jeremy. I spent thirty-minutes in the shower, hoping DeShaun was asleep by the time I finished.

He wasn't.

When I turned off the shower, he knocked on the door again.

"Are you finished? I need to talk to you."

I came out of the bathroom wrapped in a towel. I sat on the edge of the bed, whipped off the towel and gently patted the wet spots dry.

He waited for me to finish before he said, "Things between us haven't been the same lately."

I walked past him and grabbed a pair of panties from my top drawer. I opened the second drawer, pulled out a white T-shirt and pulled it over my head. "I suppose you think I'm to blame for that?"

"No, of course you aren't to blame."

"How was your party tonight?"

"Fine, I guess."

"You work hard?"

"Sure."

"Liar!" I blurted out. "You're looking straight in my face and lying."

"What are you talking about?"

"Stop it, DeShaun. This morning, you looked me in the eye and told me you were working a party tonight. You were working it all right. You worked it big time in your designer suit with *her!*"

He was speechless, but I didn't need his words, which were probably more lies. His eyes said it all.

"This is what it has come to?" I said. "You can look me in the face and lie."

"How did you— "

"Does it matter?"

"I am so sorry, baby." He went to grab my arm but I pulled away. "I only told you I was working the party because you wouldn't understand."

"And the business?" I asked. "You're continuing the business, aren't you?"

"It's going to work, I promise."

"You told me you were going to look for a job and forget this service business thing."

"I know, but it's really going well." He pulled out several business cards from his pocket. "See? These are clients. Rich clients who will pay top dollar for quality service. I don't need to work for someone. I can do this myself. I need you to trust me, Mimi. I cannot do this without you."

"You've been doing a great job without me so far."

"It's not like that."

"And what about her?" I asked. "How long have you been sleeping with her?"

"Jenn?"

"Is there more than one rich bitch you're sleeping with?"

"I never slept with her. We've been hanging out, that's all. She introduced me to some high profile clients, but that's it."

"I saw you, DeShaun. You both looked so comfortable together."

"How did you— "

"I'm still trying to figure out when exactly this whole thing crossed over into the bedroom."

"I told you, I didn't sleep with her. I swear it."

I looked at him and shook my head. "Remember the last time you swore to me? In my eyes, that no longer holds too much weight."

"That was a mistake," he said. "It was at the bachelor party. It was only one night and I told you what happened."

"Yes, you told me that *after* you swore you never slept with that stripper."

"You've never gotten over that. You told the marriage counselor that you forgave me for that. So, you lied?"

"I did forgive you. What I didn't do was forget. You're not the same person anymore, DeShaun."

He looked at me with a blank stare. "What is that supposed to mean?"

"You lied about taking the wine. You could be lying about this."

"I told you what happened with the wine!"

"Sure you did, *after* you got fired for it."

"I did it for you," he said. "You are the one who loves all this fancy shit."

"Are you blaming *me?*"

"I'm just saying, you liked the wine and I got it for you."

"I can't believe this shit. You're telling me you stole the wine for me?"

"I DIDN'T STEAL THE WINE!"

"Fine!" I screamed. "If you didn't *borrow* the wine—for me—you would have never gotten fired and we wouldn't been in this position in the first place. Is that what you're telling me?"

"Maybe we wouldn't have. And maybe if you didn't insist that I go against my morals and take another human being for all she's worth, then maybe I wouldn't have caught some feelings for her."

My heart sank. My legs gave from under me. I had to sit down on the bed. "You're in love with her?"

"No." He shook his head. "I mean, it's not like that. I just don't want to see her hurt in all of this."

"What about me? Don't I matter anymore?"

"Of course you matter, Mimi. It's just that—"

There was no possible way for him to finish that sentence without it feeling as if a knife had stabbed me in the gut. A single tear stung the corner of my eye. "It doesn't even matter anymore, De-Shaun."

"What do you mean?"

I was close to admitting what happened between Jeremy and me. I opened my mouth to tell him, but DeShaun spoke first.

"I swear to you, I'll stop seeing her," he said. "You're the one I want to be with. Give me another chance and I will make it up to you. If you want me to get a real job, then that's what I'll do. I'm not giving up on you, Mimi. I'm not giving up on us."

I couldn't even look him in the eye when I said, "You might feel differently when you hear what I have to say."

DeShaun

DeShaun twirled Mrs. Jordan around, then he dipped her. Her peach ball gown flowed with her every move.

"You are my favorite server; you know how to dance," the older woman said.

DeShaun was well into his third drink and although the party had ended hours ago, he stayed behind to help clean. The only people left were Mr. and Mrs. Jordan, a banker named Neil Garret and The Countess and her latest boy toy, José. The D.J. had long since gone, so the remaining few were relaxing in the living room, listening to jazz on Internet radio.

"Have some more wine," Mrs. Jordan said, handing a glass to DeShaun and one to M.J. "You've worked hard, you deserve it."

M.J. took the glass but DeShaun declined. He wanted to get paid for the evening so he could get out of there and go home to bed. It was already past one in the morning and Naomi would be waiting up. She waited up for him every night, even though she pretended not to. When he pulled up the driveway after work, he'd see the flickering light from the television quickly go out.

DeShaun sighed. The Countess should have paid him for his services hours ago, but she was busy twirling around in the living room, dancing to old disco tunes while sipping from her glass of brandy. That woman could drink. Eventually, she stumbled toward the patio double doors.

"DeShaun," one of the servers he hired called from the kitchen. "Should we start packing the glasses? They're not completely dry."

Before he had the chance to answer, he heard a big crash coming from the patio. DeShaun looked outside in time to see the Countess tumble over into the pool. He heard a loud splash and she was gone.

DeShaun and several of the guests rushed out to the patio. Instinct kicked in and DeShaun dove into the pool and swam toward the bottom. The Countess' limp body was sprawled out, her eyes half open and no bubbles coming from her mouth. He grabbed her waist and scooped her up to the top. He struggled as he pulled the Countess to the side of the pool, where Mr. Jordan and M.J. pulled her out of the water. Immediately, Mr. Jordan bent down and began performing CPR. DeShaun yelled out to a server standing in the patio doorway. "Call nine-one-one now!"

Naomi

I flipped through channels, taking a second to check out the clock on the television counter. It was after three in the morning and DeShaun wasn't home yet. I thought about calling him, but didn't want to look like I was checking up on him, even though I was. I hated feeling this way, but lately, I couldn't trust anything he said.

I picked up the phone and dialed, but quickly hung up. I refused to check on him. I would rather lie here watching television in the dark, pretending to be interested in an infomercial on a hair styling product.

At 3:10, I hopped out of bed and rifled through his dresser drawers, telling myself I needed to spy in order to keep my marriage intact. I rummaged through his closets but didn't find designer clothes I hadn't already seen. I went over to the nightstand but stopped short of pulling it open and going through his underwear.

What was I doing? What would this prove? I was officially one of *those* wives.

Weeks ago, I was so close to telling him the truth about Jeremy and me, but decided against it, especially after he told me he would never see *her* again. DeShaun found employment with a local store downtown to help pay bills and assured me that he wouldn't service any more parties. He even promised to forget about his service business for a while.

I sat on top of the bed, wanting desperately to get under the covers and go to sleep, but I couldn't. I was dead tired, but I needed to know what was going on and where he was tonight.

I thought of my mother, the psychologist, and what she would say about a woman that rifled through her husband's personal belongings.

If you don't trust your husband, the marriage is already in trouble.

Instead of going through his underwear, I went to the closet, opened it up and looked down at the row of shoes on the carpeted closet floor. I didn't recognize the brown leather pair. I reached inside the shoe and felt around. I reached further, into the toe of the shoe, and pulled out a sparkling silver watch with a tiny diamond on the face. I reached down into the matching shoe and felt around. From the toe, I pulled out a wad of bills held together with a rubber band. The wad contained one-hundred and five-hundred dollar bills. Quick calculations said I was holding more than $7,000.

DeShaun pull up to the driveway at 3:33. I hopped back into bed, turned off the television and then flicked off the nightstand lamp. I listened for the key in the doorway.

It was quiet.

The refrigerator motor kicked in, a dog barked down the road, but still no key in the lock.

I got out of bed and went to the window. I looked down at his car parked on the driveway. He was inside the car, shuffling around. I couldn't see what he was doing until he reached into the backseat and grabbed a pile of clothes. Before getting out the car, he took each piece of clothing—a rumpled white shirt, a pair of black socks and a vest—and wrung them out.

Why were his clothes wet? More importantly, why was he wearing his serving uniform if he was loading boxes at the store?

When I heard the front door key jiggle inside the lock, I hopped back into bed and pulled up the covers. DeShaun dropped his keys onto the kitchen table, the clatter echoed down the hall. The refrigerator motor cut off as he opened it up. I heard the cap of a Kalik beer bottle pop off.

By the time I heard his heavy footsteps heading up to the bedroom, I was ready to do battle. This was the last time he made a fool out of me.

Naomi and DeShaun

I charged as soon as he walked through the bedroom door. "Do you honestly think I'm an idiot?"

He walked past me and to the bathroom, quietly shutting the door.

"Did you hear me?" I yelled. "I am so sick of you treating me like a fucking doormat."

The shower came on, but there was still no response.

I marched up to the bathroom door and pounded my fists as hard as I could. I kicked the door, hit it again and when that didn't work, I used my shoulder to try to force my way in. When I finally barged in, DeShaun was calmly drying himself off with a towel.

"Are you crazy?" he asked, staring at me.

I stepped up, right in his face. "Are you?"

"I don't want to fight tonight. I'm tired."

"You're tired? What about me? I'm tired of being played for a fool while you do your dirt with Miss Rich Bitch!"

He shook his head. "Do you ever give it a rest, Naomi? Seriously."

"How can I give it a rest when you're hiding seven-thousand dollars from your wife? And don't forget about the diamond-encrusted watch."

"You're going through my shit again?"

"I sure am. You can best believe that money is mine."

"I'm saving that money for my business," he said. "When will you understand that I'm doing all this for you?"

"You're sleeping with the Rich Bitch for me? How noble of you, DeShaun."

"I need that money."

"I don't care. And I need you to *not* cheat on me. I need you to stop lying to me. I need you to stop hiding money from me. That's what I need! I don't care about your needs anymore."

"Like you ever did."

"Is this the part where you tell me how it was my fault you cheated?"

A tiny, throbbing bluish-green vein popped out in the center of his forehead. "I can't believe you!"

"And then you have the nerve to ride up the driveway at four in the morning, hiding in the car while wringing out wet clothes. Why the hell are your clothes wet, DeShaun? What the hell were you doing?"

"For your information, I saved a lady's life tonight. She fell into the pool and I jumped in to get her. She could've drowned."

"Are you seriously kicking this lie to me? You expect me to believe that my husband is a hero and saved some lady at a party that he claims he wasn't at in the first place. Oh, please. You can come better than that. Respect me enough to at least get a *good* lie together."

"I don't give a damn what you believe anymore."

"Mom was right," I spat. "You are a loser. I can do much better."

"If that's what you truly believe, maybe you should go out there and try."

"Maybe I should. Maybe I should find a guy that doesn't lie to me all the time about where he's been."

"And maybe I should find a woman I don't *have* to lie to."

"You don't have to lie to anyone, DeShaun. Be a man and handle yours. Stop tiptoeing around here like a bitch!"

He narrowed his eyes and balled up his fists. I thought he was going to hit me. Instead, he took a second, drew in a deep breath and dropped his head. "I don't know what to do anymore. I give up. I tried to include you in on my plans for our life and you didn't want to hear it. It's like you can't stand me being happy."

"What the hell is that supposed to mean? Of course, I want you to be happy. I want the both of us to be happy. I just don't want you to go out there and fall on your face. Your failures are my failures, too."

"Why does it always have to be a failure? Why can't it be success?"

"Good question. Why can't it be a success? Why can't it ever be a success with you?"

DeShaun pulled back and I saw the hurt in his eyes. I saw that look quite frequently lately. I imagined he saw the same in mine.

"You know what's funny?" he asked. "You keep referring to Jenn as 'The Bitch,' when it was her who did *your* job and supported me with my business."

My contained anger resurfaced, but I kept my tone even. "Of course, she did. She had nothing to lose and everything to gain, especially that big black dick of yours."

"It doesn't matter!" he yelled. "You are my wife! She isn't! You're supposed to support me. Instead, she's the one acting like my wife while you are acting like 'The Bitch!'"

The words stung like an open-handed slap right across the cheek. What hurt even more was that even when he realized what he said, there was no remorse in his eyes. He stared me down like he was daring me to come back at him. I had to force my hands by my side to keep from slapping the taste out of his mouth. A slap would only last a second. I wanted to hurt him much deeper than that.

I knew just how to do it.

"Funny you say that," I began. "I felt the exact same way when Jeremy was acting like my husband while fucking me all night."

This time it was my turn to stare him down. "Now who's The Bitch?"

Naomi

DeShaun gathered up his belongings, one by one, and stuck them in the oversized leather suitcase he'd bought two years ago for our vacation to the Bahamas.

That trip seemed like a lifetime ago.

My anger had subsided and I didn't want him to leave, but it was too late. Too much had already been said and done. This marriage was over.

While he finished packing, I went to the kitchen, pretending to fix a sandwich while acting like I didn't care that he was leaving, but really, I bit down on a towel and sulked in the corner, silently crying. As soon as I heard the front door shut, I slumped down onto the cold kitchen tile and cried for two hours. This time I didn't have to worry about being quiet. I was alone.

Approximately an hour later, at five in the morning, I was startled to hear DeShaun's key in the lock. I was sitting in the living room with the television on, watching a reality show about two girls who joined a rock band. I turned the volume down and listened to him jostle about in the foyer. I figured he forgot something but then I heard his footsteps approaching. When he came into the living room, he saw me. His face was expressionless. We stared at each other for an eternity before he came rushing at me, like he was on the attack. At first, I began fighting him off, but after a minute, I realized he wasn't assaulting me. His hands wandered all over my body. He grabbed my breasts, my butt, my hips. His hands probed everywhere. He pulled up my nightgown with such fervor, he practically shredded it to pieces. He pulled my underwear to the side, opened up his zipper and started thrusting himself inside of me. He did all of this while sucking hard on my erect nipples. I had never been so excited before in my life.

When he was through, he quietly stood up, zipped up his pants and stealthily made his way out the door and back into the darkness. He never said a word.

The door shut behind him and that was the last I heard from him.

When he came to me that night, I believed he was no longer angry. If anything, I felt his hurt. I couldn't say anything either; I was just as damaged. Our marriage had died in the arms of deceit and infidelity and I didn't know how to get over it.

Part II

Naomi

Days were getting colder as the sweltering heat of summer passed. In its place was the early morning chill of fall. The trees began sporting yellow, orange and brown leaves, with most falling to the ground and crunching beneath the feet of pedestrians.

The sun shone its rays directly through my bedroom window, providing life in an otherwise dreary home. In other circumstances, this would have been a welcomed cozy fall morning.

For me, today was no different than any other day since DeShaun left. His business must have been going well. The only time I heard from him was when he sent a check in the mail to cover the mortgage and a few other expenses.

For the past few days, I had been going to bed late and waking up early. This particular morning, I woke up earlier than usual with a sick feeling in my gut. I took every pill in the medicine cabinet, including an antacid and a painkiller, but I still couldn't get rid of the pain.

With DeShaun gone, everything became a chore: getting up, brushing my teeth, everything. I hadn't slept alone in over four years. Every night I fell asleep crying. The first few days he was gone, I bawled like a baby for hours at a time, until I finally fell asleep. It hurt and it hurt bad. Losing DeShaun was akin to losing a limb.

Today, I felt lightheaded so I decided to make an appointment with the clinic. The appointment was for 9:30, so I had about an hour to get ready, but the way I felt, I needed at least twice the time.

I jumped in the shower, hoping the warm water would wake me up.

It didn't.

After my shower, I headed downstairs and grabbed a yogurt from the fridge. Maybe lack of food was why I felt that way.

It wasn't.

In fact, the first spoonful of the yogurt turned my stomach. I checked my watch, grabbed my car keys and headed out the front door, hoping I wouldn't have another dizzy spell before reaching the doctor's office.

The doctor listened to my heartbeat through the stethoscope. "How long have you been experiencing these symptoms?"

It all started around the time DeShaun and I lost our jobs. "About two months ago."

The doctor listened intently and then pulled the stethoscope from his ears. "Your heart rate is slightly high."

"Is that a problem?"

"Not really. However, higher heart rates normally signify other issues. It may be stress. Have you felt stressed lately?"

That was the understatement of the year. "Maybe some."

A few weeks back I was supposed to start the job at McIntyre and Roth but that was around the time DeShaun had walked out. I had completely forgotten about the drug test. When I called to make it up, the secretary informed me that since they hadn't heard from me, the position was offered to someone else. I was so depressed, I couldn't even get angry with myself for being so stupid.

"We're going to perform some tests. To get a clearer picture, we'll do an ultrasound too. By your symptoms, I'm thinking you may have high blood pressure."

Oh, great, I thought. *That's the last thing I needed to deal with right now.*

"Relax a moment," the doctor said. "I'll have the nurse come in and take some blood. It'll only take a few minutes."

"How long for the results?"

"A week, two tops, for most of the tests. We can give you the results of the ultrasound today. We'll call if the tests come back positive for disease or other issues, otherwise, if you don't hear from us, consider your health good. If the dizziness persists, make another appointment." He grabbed his medical chart and started for the door. "Stress affects the body in different ways. I suggest you take it easy. Think about taking a vacay and relaxing. It'll do you good."

I wished.

What I wanted and needed to do was to take a long puff from a fat blunt, the poor man's vacation, ghetto-style. The good news was that I wouldn't have to worry about taking sick or personal time from a job. The bad news: I didn't have that job to take sick or personal time from. My husband had left me and I didn't have an income. What the hell was I supposed to do now?

After the nurse finished sticking me and after the ultrasound, she escorted me to the waiting room.

The nurse returned ten minutes later. "Ms. Knowles, the tests show you do have slightly elevated pressure, but we can easily take care of that."

At least one problem was solved.

"However," the nurse continued. "Another test indicates that you're pregnant."

My jaw dropped to the ground. "Are you sure?"

The nurse nodded. "Not only that, but we saw two heartbeats. You're pregnant with twins. We determined you're approximately six weeks along."

For the second time in the last two minutes, my heart dropped, but I had to admit; with the direction my life was headed, I wasn't surprised. I did the mental calculation and realized it had been exactly six weeks since I had been with Jeremy. It was only a few days later, DeShaun and I got together. I couldn't imagine the situation getting any worse.

Naomi

After returning from the doctor, I thought about calling De-Shaun. But what would I say? *I'm pregnant and you might be the daddy, but I'll have to get back to you on that.*

Besides, how could I put my tail between my legs and call him? He cheated on *me*, the one woman he vowed to remain faithful to. He may have denied it, but I knew the truth. I felt the truth. DeShaun didn't have to come out and confess his infidelity, the answer was there.

But I had cheated too. Then again, that was only after his indiscretions. But two wrongs don't make a right.

I went back and forth like that for an hour.

I eventually made the decision not to tell him about the babies inside of me. He'd come back to me out of obligation or pity and I didn't want that. He needed to return to me on his own volition. He loved me and couldn't breathe without me, like I couldn't without him.

I headed toward the kitchen for a snack when the phone rang. I didn't want to get excited, but I couldn't help it. Maybe it was DeShaun. It had to be! He'd admit his wrongdoing, I'd apologize for mine and we'd go to therapy. Our marriage was going to be stronger than ever. We were going to be okay. I knew it.

My heart dropped when I looked at the caller ID and it read: Miriam Archer.

In no mood to speak to my mother, I let it ring. I didn't feel like telling her about the past few weeks and if I talked to her now, I would. Even if I didn't confess, she'd be able to tell. It's what she did for a living.

The phone rang until going to voicemail.

Guilt took over and I went over to the phone to call her back, but before I could, there was a knock at the door. My first thought was DeShaun.

Still gripping the phone, I headed toward the door but the phone rang again. It was my mother. I chucked the phone across the room, where it landed on the couch.

I peeked through the peephole. It was Jeremy.

I hadn't spoken to him since that night we had sex in his car. *What did he want?*

I stood with my back against the door, like I was barricading him from entering—and maybe I was. I had nothing to say to him.

"I see your shadow under the door." He hesitated. "Look, I'm sorry for showing up without phoning first, but I was afraid you wouldn't take my calls."

I kept quiet, still hoping he'd go way.

"I only want to check on you to make sure everything is okay. If you need me you can call—anytime."

I took a deep breath and pulled the door open. "Thanks."

He smiled, sighing in relief at the same time. "Wow. I didn't think you'd actually open the door."

"Then why did you come over?"

He shrugged. "I don't know. I guess there's always hope."

His curly hair had gotten bigger and bushier, and black sticky stubble was beginning to peek out from his chin. He was a little thinner too.

"DeShaun left me," I said, not quite sure why I'd even told him, other than it felt good to finally be able to tell someone. I didn't want to say anything to my parents yet and I didn't have any true girlfriends. My sister, the one I hadn't seen in years, was out of the question, so he was my only option. "He packed up and left."

"I'm sorry."

I felt his sincerity. "Thank you. I appreciate that." That was the response I would have never gotten from my mother.

That reminded me. I had to call her back before she went downtown for her Saturday ritual; hair appointment, facial and a mani and pedi combo.

I took a step back, allowing Jeremy to come in. "I have to make a quick call, but you can wait if you like."

"Don't get mad," he said. "But is it me or have you put on some weight?"

"Maybe a few." I avoided eye contact and grabbed for the phone on the couch. "This call should only take a second."

"It looks good on you. The weight, that is. It suits you."

"Oh, thanks." I started dialing, but then remembered Mom's message. I pressed the voicemail button on my phone and listened.

"Are you okay?" Jeremy asked. "You just turned completely white."

I let the phone drop from my hands. Most of the message was incoherent. Mom was sobbing uncontrollably, but I was still able to make out the last thing she said.

"Your father's dead, baby. He's gone."

DeShaun

The night he left Naomi, he had driven around in his car, trying to decide where to go. Jenn kept popping up in his mind. Berti was out of town and she would let him stay with her temporarily. But he didn't want to go there.

That evening, he ended up calling M.J. and practically begging him to stay at his place for awhile, only until he could get his bearings and decide on a long-term move. Unfortunately, M.J. lived in a one-bedroom apartment that he shared with his dog, and, unbeknownst to DeShaun, M.J. had picked that particular evening to entertain a lady friend. That night DeShaun had the distinct pleasure of lying on his buddy's couch while listening to lovemaking noises that, from DeShaun's standpoint, sounded painful.

Two days later, after having sex with Naomi, DeShaun had sent her a curt text, telling her he was all right and that he'd be coming by sometime soon for the rest of his things. That was weeks ago. Aside from dropping her money from a few of his gigs for the mortgage, he hadn't contacted her again.

"Well, hello there. Fancy meeting you at this party."

DeShaun turned around. Jenn stood there in a coral pink-and-white, strapless gown. He hadn't seen or talked to her since the night of Dean Freitag's party, the same night Naomi somehow saw him there with Jenn. The same night he promised his wife that he would stay away from Jenn and forget the business.

He had secured a few lucrative jobs and tonight was one of them. DeShaun had scheduled the party for Berti's and Jenn's attorney, but hadn't expected to see her there since last he heard, she was out of the country.

"How are you?" he asked.

"I'm good," she said with a smile. "In fact, Berti and I just came back from a mini-vacation in Italy. A little relaxation trip before heading to Japan."

"You look good," DeShaun said. "So, you're still planning on moving to Japan?"

She nodded. "That's the plan. It's supposed to be within the next two weeks. It keeps getting pushed back. If I had my way, I'd push it back forever." They stood in uncomfortable silence for a minute. "I almost forgot. A friend of mine is planning a party in a week and I'm sure she would love for you to service it for her. Would you be able to do that? I know it's late notice, but it's sort of a last-minute thing."

"I can do that."

"Good."

She reached up and rubbed his arm. "I have to be honest. I've missed you."

"Me too," he admitted. "No one could rap Biggie better than you."

She laughed. "Please call sometime, DeShaun. If it's okay with your wife, maybe we can hang out again."

His smile faded. "Yeah. I will definitely do that."

She turned and headed back into the crowd. Before she disappeared, DeShaun called out. "Wait, Jenn!"

She turned around. "Yes?"

"Doing anything tonight?"

"It's almost one o'clock in the morning."

"That a problem?"

She winked. "Not for me. For you?"

"I'm good."

"I'll see you after the party then." She turned and disappeared into the crowd.

DeShaun

He used a rag to rinse off the last of the glasses, giving special attention to the water spots. When each glass was properly dried, he placed them back into the box resting on the countertop. Since buying amenities such as glasses, napkins and silverware, he was able to charge double his normal rate. Tonight, he made good money—no—great money. He had six parties lined up in the next few weeks and several more around the bend. He was finally enjoying what he was doing and actually making money at it.

Too bad it had come at a cost.

As he carefully placed the final glass back into the box, he thought of Naomi. On a night like this, he used to go home and tell her all about the evening, including the money he made. They would sit back with a glass of wine and have a good laugh about all his Countess Vargas stories, and he had plenty of them tonight.

Those days were over.

"Hi, DeShaun." Jenn came up behind him. "I thought you left."

"Hey. I'll be done here in twenty minutes."

"Are we still on tonight?"

"Of course."

"Great," she said. "I'll wait for you by the pool. Come and get me when you're ready."

DeShaun watched her as she walked out the French doors and onto the patio. Her dress was clinging in all the right places. He felt a slight sensation inside his pants. It had been such a long time since he felt so much excitement for another woman besides his wife, but Jenn was one woman who did it for him.

"What are you doing?" M.J. came up behind DeShaun and placed two more dirty champagne glasses onto the countertop. "With that one, you're playing with fire."

DeShaun rolled his eyes. "Man, what are you going on about now? 'We're just friends."

"That may be so," M.J. said. "But I ain't stupid. I've seen the way you look at her."

"Nothing happened, so you might as well stop right there."

"Yeah, okay and I'm Bobo the Clown."

"You said it, not me."

"Man, shut up!" M.J. smacked him on his shoulder. "Seriously, though, her old man is an arms dealer. Did you forget that part?"

"Nothing is going on."

"And on the honest tip, Jenn looks good. I'll give you that," M.J. admitted. "But there's one big difference between her and Mimi."

"And what's that?"

"I have never seen you look at Jenn the way you looked at your wife."

DeShaun sighed. "I ain't got time for that."

"And before you go and get all ig'nant," M.J. said, "you asked for my opinion, remember?"

"Who did? I have never asked for your opinion in the past and you can best believe, I won't in the future, either."

M.J. punched him on the arm. "You know you were dying for my expert knowledge. That's what we do. We offer opinions, whether or not they're wanted."

"Man, get outta here."

M.J. reached around and unstrapped the strings to his stained apron. "I'm done. You comin'?"

DeShaun ran cool water over the remaining glasses in the sink. "Nah, I'm gonna hang around for a few."

M.J. raised a skeptical brow. "You sure about this, man?"

"You got one more time to get in my business," DeShaun said with a hint of a grin. "After that, it's you and me."

"If you're good, I'm good. Take it easy."

DeShaun sealed the box with tape and brought the glasses out to his car. Balancing the box with one hand, he reached into his pocket and pulled out his keys. *Damn, which key was it?* The box wobbled back and forth as he fumbled around with the key in the lock.

"Let me get that for you." Jenn grabbed the box from DeShaun's hands. "You weren't leaving without me, were you?"

"Of course not."

Jenn grabbed hold of his arm and leaned up to kiss him on the lips. "I'm sorry," she said. "We shouldn't be doing this. What about your wife?"

"Naomi and I split up."

The look on her face said she was genuinely surprised. "What happened?"

"Life happened," he said. "Don't feel guilty about my situation. If anything, you need to consider your situation." He opened the car door, took the box and carefully set it on the back seat.

"New car?" Jenn asked.

"Rental."

"Nice."

"Thanks."

"Follow me home tonight."

He wanted to resist her, he really did, but he couldn't. And why should he? He was single, almost. "Okay."

She reached up and placed her hand on the back of his head. She pulled him close and planted a warm, passionate kiss square on his mouth. "Good." She let go and headed over to her Range Rover. DeShaun hopped into his car and followed her for twenty minutes down the road, until they reached her house.

DeShaun

After Jenn disappeared up the steps, DeShaun pulled out his cell, thinking he wanted to hear Naomi's voice, no, he *needed* to hear her voice. He fought with every ounce of his being not to dial the number, but an uncontrollable force took over. He dialed the first six numbers of her cell, his finger resting on the seventh number. He took a deep breath and pressed the last number.

One ring.

Two rings.

Three rings.

"Hello?" Someone picked up on the fourth ring, but it wasn't Naomi. It was a dude.

DeShaun looked down at the number displayed on his phone to be sure he dialed correctly. He lowered his tone and asked, "Is Naomi there?"

"Nah, who's calling?"

"Who's this?" DeShaun asked.

"Who's this?"

DeShaun hung up. He wasn't about to get into it with some dude, frontin' with his wife's—or rather, soon-to-be ex-wife's phone.

His stared down at his phone. Screw the bitch! It had only been a few weeks since he moved out, but dang, from what it seemed like, she couldn't wait to have the next dude laying all up in his spot. *Screw her for being such a slut!*

"I made up the guest bed for you," Jenn said when she returned. "In case you don't feel comfortable with this yet." She had taken off her dress and was wearing a pair of curve-hugging jeans and a form-fitting silk blouse with the top two buttons undone. Her long, dark hair was fastened into a ponytail high on the top of her head and she had washed off her makeup, exposing tanned flawless skin.

DeShaun grabbed the bottle sitting on the bar and two wine glasses. "I don't need the bed in the guest room." He walked up to Jenn and kissed her. "You don't mind if I stay in the bedroom with you tonight, do you?"

Jenn looked up at DeShaun, as if she was trying to read him. He stared back, letting her know that he was serious about this. When she was satisfied that he meant business, she reached down, gently grabbed his hand and quietly led him up the steps.

Naomi and Jeremy

I walked up the steps, taking two at a time, just as I did when I was nine years old. The house was almost the same as the day I left for college years ago. The walls were still painted lime-green with tan trim. The pictures that hung on the walls were even the same; my fifth-grade school picture with me dressed in my red-and-white striped sweater, looking like *Where's Waldo?* Next to that picture was the one of my mother and grandmother on the day of Mom's wedding.

I remembered loving that picture as a kid, staring at it for hours, wishing that was me in my wedding dress with my mother adjusting my veil. When I had opened my old bedroom door, I was surprised that the bed had been removed and was replaced with a cherrywood desk and chair set with a closed laptop resting on top of the desk. The plush fuchsia carpet I had played dolls on had been ripped out and in its place was hardwood flooring.

"We made a few changes since you left," Mom said. "Couldn't keep it the same forever, now could I?" A single tear ran from the corner of her eye.

After hearing the news about my father's death, I hopped in the car and made the trek back to Alpharetta, a ritzy Georgia suburb where I had spent my childhood. Driving sixty miles an hour, it had still been a twenty-four-hour ride.

I took a seat next to my mother on the loveseat, where my bed used to be. She scooted over, making room for me, and then slung her arm through mine. Gently, she laid her head onto my shoulder.

"Do you know what you're going to do?" I asked.

She shrugged. "I don't know, baby. I'm considering selling the house."

"No, Mom. Why?"

"It's time. Besides, your dad and I were talking about selling before."

A stream of tears ran down her cheek. I reached inside my purse and handed her a travel pack of unopened tissues. She fumbled with the pack, eventually ripping it apart to open it up. Tissues flew everywhere. "I don't get why they make these things damn near impossible to open!" She dabbed at her tear stained cheek, looked at me and then burst out crying. "Oh, God, I'm so sorry," she said, taking one of the flyaway tissues and dabbing at the corner of her eye. She put her head down and cried into my shoulder. It hurt to see her this way. In all my years on this earth, I had never seen my mother cry—not even when my grandmother, her mother, passed away.

"I told myself that I wouldn't do this in front of you," Mom said, still blotting her eyes. "You know what this is?"

"What is?"

She blew her nose into a tissue. "It's displaced aggression. I'm taking out my impulses on a less threatening target." She held up the ripped packet of tissues. "And by the looks of it, I had plenty of impulses."

We laughed together. Leave it to my mother to incorporate her work into a moment like this.

"I used to hate it when your daddy always reminded me that I had displaced aggressions. I remember this one time I had a bad day at my office and I arrived home, ready to start a fight. I didn't know I wanted to start a fight, it was imbedded in my subconscious to do so. So that's what I did. I walked in the front door, looking for anything to complain about. But your father," she said, smiling, "your father was perfect. I came home to a spotless house and when I walked through the foyer, I could smell his rack of lamb in oven. There had to be dirty dishes in the sink, so I prepared myself to nitpick at that. When I walked into the kitchen, not only were the dishes done, he had mopped the kitchen floor like I said I was going to do. The bathrooms were clean; the bedroom was spotless. I had nothing to complain about."

"So what happened?" I asked.

"I walked straight up to him, looked into his face and told him his moustache had to go. I hated that thing. It always tickled when he kissed me and I was sick of looking at it."

"You told him that?"

"I sure did. And do you know what he said?"

"What?"

"He looked at me, kissed me with that moustache and told me he loved me.

I shook my head. "You know that's corny, right?"

"Maybe, but that's why I loved him."

"Would you ladies like some lunch?" Jeremy called from the bottom of the steps. When my mother saw him, she quickly lifted her head off my shoulder and wiped her eyes dry.

I was thankful Jeremy was able to come home with me. Otherwise, it would've made for a long, sad trip. Instead, I was treated to his corny jokes and off-tune singing, which was actually a nice diversion from the sadness.

"I'm sorry," he said. "I didn't mean to interrupt. I thought you two might be hungry."

"That would be nice, uh—" Mom paused and looked at me.

"It's Jeremy," I whispered.

"That would be nice, Jeremy." After he went to the kitchen, she turned back to me. "You both got in so late last night, we didn't really have time to talk, but you can expect that I have questions about this man.

"He's a nice guy."

She gave me the side eye. "That may be true, but you showed up on my doorstep with this man I have never met, or even heard about before. You can rest assure I have questions. You don't have to stay at the hotel. You can stay here."

When I first told my mother I was coming, she offered for me to stay at the house. Even before I knew Jeremy was coming, I declined. I felt it would be best to get a room at the hotel in case I needed a quick getaway from my relatives, who could sometimes be a little overbearing.

"Jeremy's a friend, that's all." I hoped to leave it at that, but I knew better.

"What kind of friend? And where is DeShaun?"

The name DeShaun sounded strange coming out of her mouth. I could count on one hand the number of times she mentioned him in our four-and-a-half years of marriage.

"DeShaun and I aren't together anymore, Mom."

"When did this happen? And are you sleeping with this new guy?"

"A few weeks ago, and no, me and Jeremy aren't sleeping to-gether." I didn't really lie. We had *slept* together once, so techni-cally I wasn't sleeping with him. "I'll tell you everything after the funeral. In the meantime, we need to start planning. Did you order the flowers and call the caterer?"

"Your aunt Joyce is taking care of all that. Your father's attorney wants to meet with me this afternoon regarding your dad's will."

"Do you need me to go with you?"

She shook her head. "No, baby. You stay here with Jerome. I'll deal with it."

"Jeremy," I corrected.

"Sorry," Mom said. "I have so much on my mind right now, I can barely remember my own name. Besides, your sister is coming with me. She'll be at the house tomorrow."

"Cara's coming?" I hadn't heard from or about my sister in years. When Grandma passed, she didn't even bother to come to the funeral. I kind of expected her to show up for Dad, but with her, who knew?

"The family is coming by the house tomorrow afternoon after the funeral," Mom said. "I feel like I haven't done anything to get this house in order."

"Don't worry about that. I'll handle it."

Mom raised a suspicious brow. "Since when do you clean? In that respect, you and your sister are just alike."

I tried hard not to roll my eyes. I didn't want to make my mother more upset, but being compared to my sister was something I didn't take lightly. "For your information, I wouldn't be cleaning. I would call a service to do it."

She hugged me. "Now that's the Naomi I know." She gently cupped my chin inside the palm of her hand. "I'm really glad you're here. I've missed you." She kissed my cheek and headed down the steps.

As soon as she grabbed her keys and walked out the door, I dropped to the ground and started crying—not gently sobbing, but bawling with the ugly face and all. Jeremy heard me and came bolting out of the kitchen and up the steps.

"Baby, baby, are you okay?" he asked, throwing his arms around me.

"My daddy is gone," I cried. "He's never coming back. I don't know what to say around my mother, my marriage is over, I'm alone, I don't have any money, I don't know how I'm going to support myself, I don't know— " I took a deep breath, almost mentioning the twins I was carrying, but I held my tongue. "I don't know anything anymore. What am I going to do, Jeremy?"

He squeezed tighter. "It's going to be okay. I'm here and I will always be here for as long as you need me. I promise."

Naomi and Jeremy

F or the past few hours, since arriving on my parents' door-step, I thought about the little details about my father, like his ability to come in from a hard day at the hospital and still have time to tuck me into bed and read me a story. I thought about the last time I talked to him. I had complained about my marriage and how unhappy I was. He had listened to me over the phone and offered up one simple suggestion: "Tell him how you feel. You only think he knows, but speaking from experience with your mother, he has absolutely no idea."

I wished I had listened to his suggestion.

"You hungry? Want a sandwich?" Jeremy asked. Since we had gotten here, he had been nothing short of helpful. He woke up early this morning and did the stack of dishes my mother had left in the sink. Even when she complained that the saucers were in the wrong cabinet, without saying a word, he simply moved them to the correct cabinet and asked if she needed anything else done around the house.

"I'm not really hungry," I said, fishing through my purse. "Have you seen my phone?"

"Yeah. It fell out of your purse last night when we were driving so I just hung on to it. I'll go get it." He dashed off and seconds later, returned with my phone. "Here ya go."

I scrolled through the caller ID. I had three toll-free calls, probably from solicitors. I scrolled down further and saw DeShaun's number. According to the caller ID, he called me at 2:28 in the morning. I immediately hit the "call" button to dial him back. Even though we weren't together, I thought he would want to hear the news about my father since they got along somewhat.

He picked up on the first ring.

"It's me," I said. "How are you?"

"Fine." His answer was curt and somewhat off-putting.

"I saw you called me early this morning," I said.

No response.

"So I thought I'd call you back to find out what you needed."

"It doesn't matter what I needed because you were never willing to give it to me. The good news is that you've found someone new so maybe you can satisfy his needs."

"What are you talking about? What is wrong with you? You called me, remember?"

"And what a mistake that was," he said. "Oh, before I forget, I contacted a lawyer. He's drafting the divorce papers as we speak. Make sure you're home next week so the papers can be hand delivered to you. I wouldn't want you to say you never got them. I want this done as quickly as possible."

He hung up, leaving me staring dumbfounded at my cell.

"What happened?" Jeremy asked. "Who was that?"

"That was that asshole I mistakenly married. Do you know he had the nerve to have attitude with me for no reason?"

"Maybe he's still hurt that you've moved on."

"Like he hasn't," I said. "In fact, he seemed to have moved on while we were together, the son of a bitch. I was simply trying to be nice and give him a call to tell him about my father when he jumped down my throat."

"You both are still hurt about what happened," Jeremy said.

"Stuff like that takes time to get over." Jeremy hesitated, as if there was more he wanted to say.

"But?" I asked.

"You're making the first move to be cordial to him, and it's a shame he's still carrying a grudge like this. It's as if he's miserable and wants to continue making your life just as miserable."

"You think so?"

"Let me put it this way. If I lost you, I would be devastated too. You are beautiful, smart and you have a heart of gold. I would never even think about being with another woman. Honestly, he should be the one here supporting you instead of me."

"I'm sorry to drag you down here," I said. "I just didn't want to make this trip alone."

"Don't get me wrong. I'm glad I can be here for you if he can't."

"And about the other women," I began. "He claims that never happened."

Jeremy laughed. "Oh, come on. You don't believe that, do you? Of course he's going to say that. He's trying to make you feel responsible for the breakup. The truth is, he messed up first, but he wants you to bear all the guilt."

I reached over and grabbed Jeremy's can of soda. "Do you mind?"

He shook his head. "Go right ahead."

With the can in hand, I hopped up from the chair and headed straight for the liquor cabinet my parents always kept stocked for parties and social gatherings. I poured in a shot—or two or three— of my father's old favorite, brandy. I wanted to take a huge gulp and let all the feelings of anger, guilt and sorrow wash over me, but I was pregnant. I handed the can to Jeremy, who looked at me from the corner of his eye. "You go ahead," I told him. "I'm not really thirsty right now." I was going to have to deal with this difficult week without the help of liquor. *Crap!*

Naomi and Jeremy

The day of the funeral was cloudy and dismal. As soon as the sun started peeking through the clouds, attempting to dry up the wet asphalt, tiny sprinkles of rain began to fall. During the wake, the rain poured down so hard, we could hear it beating against the side of the church. A couple of times, the lights inside the church flickered, but never went off.

I sat next to my mother and hugged her close throughout the service. She cried the entire time, but I didn't shed one tear. I had to be strong for Mom. Jeremy sat a few pews behind me. During the eulogy, I looked back at him. He gave a warm smile that brightened up the dreary day.

I appreciated him being here. He helped me stay strong and composed when all my cousins, aunts, uncles and other relatives I hadn't seen in years, showed up to our house yesterday evening before the funeral for a get together. Jeremy had even smiled through the barrage of questions from distant relatives, whose faces I couldn't even remember.

"Where was DeShaun?" they asked. "How come you don't have any kids yet?" A few of the nosier relatives forged on with the follow-up question: "What happened? "

The funeral service lasted forever. The prayer seemed extra long and during the doxology, Aunt Helena nodded off, her snoring echoing throughout the church. After the service, my mother, one of my aunts and three of my cousins hopped into the limousine, preparing to head down to the cemetery.

As Jeremy came out of the church, Mom flagged him over. "Come with us."

"You sure?" he asked, looking at me.

"Of course, we're sure." Mom said. "You've been such a great help."

He was as shocked as I was. "Okay, then." He got into the limo, squeezing in next to me, and one of my cousins.

The limo pulled off but then stopped suddenly. A woman in a black dress, dark shades and a large hat with a veil frantically waved toward the limo.

"Oh, brother, here comes Cara," my cousin said, with a roll of her eyes. "Nice of her to finally show up."

Cara pulled the door open and hopped in. "I know ya'll weren't going to leave without me." With a twitch of her hips, she smashed into the car seat. "Ya'll knew I was going to be late. You could've waited." She took off her hat and flopped it into the seat next to her. "I can't believe how beautiful the service was. There were so many people there. I hope there are that many people there for my funeral. Of course, I'd never know if there weren't."

After chuckling at her own joke, she pulled out a handkerchief from her purse and began blotting her forehead. "I forgot how muggy and warm it can be in Georgia, even well into the fall season. What a day to have a funeral, huh?" Her cheery voice was in deep contrast to the solemn silence from everyone else in the limousine. "I should have cut my hair like yours," she said, reaching over three people and patting down the sides of my hair. I jerked my head back.

Jeremy leaned over and whispered, "Who is she?"

"That's Cara," I told him, "my older sister."

Me and a few of my cousins I hadn't seen in years stood around, talking. It felt good to finally come home and reminisce about the good ol' days, even if under dismal circumstances.

"Remember when we got beat for sneaking out to meet Marshall Cummings?" Sarita, my father's sister's daughter, said. Cousin Sarita was five years older than me, but she had treated me like a little sister more so than my real sister ever had. "I'll never forget that day with good ol' Marshall."

"Those were good times," Cara said in between bites of her decrusted tuna tea sandwich. She reached down and grabbed a napkin, not one, but several, and daintily dabbed around her mouth, like she was having tea at the royal palace. The clump of napkins was full of pink, smudged lipstick, which for some reason bothered me.

"How would you even know about Marshall?" I asked. "You weren't there."

She took another bite. With her mouth full, she said, "I heard you getting the switch. It was so funny." She laughed to herself at the memory. "Unlike you, I never snuck around behind Mom's and Dad's backs."

I cut my eyes at her. "I can name at least one time you did."

"Oh, yeah," Cara said. "I forgot about that time. I suppose I was a sinner in the past like you. However, unlike you, that was in the past."

"You don't know anything about me now."

"I'm going to say hello to Aunt Denise," Sarita said, quickly making her exit.

"I forgot Naomi even had a sister until today," Jeremy said to Cara. "You two resemble one another."

"She's a little thicker," Lena, our second cousin, said.

"Yes, I am," Cara agreed. "The Lord doesn't mind a little extra meat on my bones and neither should you. Besides, we have different fathers. All the girls on my daddy's side are a little thicker." She turned back to Jeremy. "Fair warning, new guy. You'd better watch my sis. She keeps tons of secrets. My advice to you, find out her secrets before you get involved."

"Half sister," I corrected. "And why don't you shut up? You may be older, but I can whup that ass if I need to."

She sighed. "I see you still have that mouth." She turned back to Jeremy. "When things don't go her way, she resorts to violence. You'll see. Is that how DeShaun got kicked to the curb? He didn't do as your highness pleased?"

I clicked my tongue. "Awww, is somebody upset that she never got a husband?"

"If the option is trapping a husband or being single, I'll go with single."

"I'm warning you, Cara."

"Your threats don't bother me. I fear no one but The Lord."

I turned to Jeremy. "The reason I barely mentioned her was because she was never around, so basically, there wasn't anything to talk about."

She smirked. "That's not true, little sis. At the very least, I was around long enough for you to steal my boyfriend and marry him."

DeShaun and Jenn

DeShaun woke up early the next morning. It felt like someone had put a gun to his dome and pulled the trigger. His throbbing head was exacerbated by a healthy dose of guilt. He looked down and saw Jenn sleeping on her stomach beside him, her bare-naked body exposed from the waist up. The turquoise satin sheet only partially covered her smooth skin from the waist down.

DeShaun struggled to remember what happened. If they polished off those three empty bottles of wine overturned on the nightstand like he thought they did, there was no way he was ever going to recall the events of last night.

"What happened?" DeShaun asked as Jenn stretched herself awake.

"We tried to have sex, but we were so drunk and high that you couldn't get it up. Don't you remember? Our naked bodies were hanging halfway off the bed and we fell, landing in that spot right there." She pointed to the foot of the bed. "You banged your head and that was it."

That's why his head hurt so much.

"We were smoking too?"

"Boy, did we," Jenn said, shaking her head. "I thought I was the master with the ganja, but you smoked circles around me. Must be your Caribbean roots."

"Stereotype much?"

They both laughed.

DeShaun reached up and grabbed his aching head. "Remind me not to laugh again."

"I overheard you talking to your wife on the phone," Jenn said. "Is everything okay?"

He struggled to remember the conversation. The only thing he recalled saying was something about divorce papers and calling her out her name a few times.

She pulled up the covers under her chin and propped up on her pillow. "Is it really over between the both of you or can you see yourself getting back together with her?"

DeShaun thought about it. Some of the hurt was disappearing—and it wasn't due to the fact that he had smoked a blunt and drank away several bottles of wine. He was actually getting over Naomi, something he didn't think would ever be possible. Maybe hearing that dude answer her phone was the last piece he needed to realize his marriage was done. "It's over between us," he said. "I'm ready to move on."

He kissed her, softly at first, but as the kiss lingered, the connection became hungrier. He laid her down onto the bed and eagerly kissed her neck and chest. He whipped off the sheets and climbed on top of her. He was ready to make his move when he heard a voice calling from downstairs.

"Hello???? Is anyone home?"

Later that evening, the setting sun created a beautiful deep auburn sky. There wasn't a cloud to be found. DeShaun put Jenn's Range Rover in reverse and backed down the driveway. He liked the feeling of power he had behind such a large vehicle. His rental car, although a luxury vehicle, was in no comparison to a four-wheel drive. He could get used to this.

"Where do you want to go for dinner?" he asked, backing out into the street. He placed the car in drive and stepped on the gas.

"I know this fabulous place on the water," Jenn said. "You're going to love it, I promise."

"Tell me where it is and I'll get us there." He pulled out of the cul-de-sac. They drove past the neighboring houses, each one looked larger than the last, with huge backyards and two—sometimes even three—luxury cars parked in the front.

He pulled onto the main road. She turned to him. "I'm sorry about what happened. I completely forgot my housekeeper was coming today."

Earlier, when he had heard the housekeeper's footsteps heading toward the master bedroom, by instinct, he quickly hopped off Jenn, grabbed his pants at the foot of the bed and scrambled to get them on before the housekeeper busted in. Luckily, Jenn had locked the door the night before, so the housekeeper stood outside, banging on the door, asking in broken English if Jenn was okay. Eventually, they surfaced from the room, walked past the housekeeper and headed down to breakfast, as if nothing had happened, which in actuality, it didn't.

"Do you think she'll say anything?" he asked.

"Rosaria? No way. She's seen much worse."

"What do you mean by that?" He was slightly put off by her comment.

"Not like that. I simply mean when Berti and I have parties, there are usually one or two overnight guests parading around."

He had spent the entire day with Jenn. First, they went shopping downtown for some bargains. Apparently, Jenn had a bargain-hunting obsession, if that's what she called it. She picked up a lamp priced at $437 and an oriental rug for over $2,000. She even purchased a $500 shadowed image of Isaac Hayes, which according to the salesperson, was a collector's item. "This is for you," she had told him. He didn't have a place to put the picture yet, but when he got his own spot, that would be the first thing he hung up.

They ended the afternoon at a winery, which she visited frequently, and bought a bottle of Burgundy wine for $300. When they returned to the house, they spent more time together watching movies and eating popcorn, something he and Naomi used to do. He introduced her to the movie, *Juice*, and she made him watch *Sabrina* with Harrison Ford, which he rather enjoyed.

"You're not at all like I expected," DeShaun had told her while sipping on wine and munching on popcorn while watching his movie pick.

"You're exactly what I expected…thank goodness."

DeShaun reached forward and switched on the radio. He hit the first preset button, then the second and third. "You sure love country music, don't you? What happened to Biggie?"

"I love country music, too" Jenn said. "Berti always listens to it and I sort of ended up enjoying it. Don't tell me you don't listen to country music?"

"Not if I don't have to," DeShaun said. "It's too twangy for my taste. I used to be down with the Dixie Chicks, though."

That was only a half-truth. Naomi was the one who bought all of their CD's. Every Sunday on the way to the bird sanctuary, she'd pop in the CD and they'd listen to "Landslide" at least four times. Just thinking about it made him sad, so he popped it out of his mind as quickly as he could. That was the past. He was concentrating on the future.

"How do you feel about animals?" DeShaun asked.

Jenn rolled her eyes. "I hate all critters. They're gross and do nothing but mess up expensive furniture, kind of like kids. You're lucky, you don't have kids, DeShaun." She thought a moment. "You don't have any kids, do you?"

"Not that I know of."

"Don't get me wrong," Jenn said. "I had one, Kyle, when I was younger and Berti had two from a previous marriage. Kids take up all your time and rob you of your youth. I found that out the hard way."

"I kinda like kids."

"Those that don't have kids always claim to like them. If you actually had them, you'd be telling a different story." She pointed a finger to the left. "Turn here. It's right down the road."

DeShaun turned onto a dirt drive. He could hear the pebbles kicking up underneath the Range Rover's tires. "Are you sure this is the way?"

"Uh-huh."

He kept driving until he reached a tiny wooden shack-like hut, overlooking the water. There were no spots designated for parking so he pulled the vehicle off to the left, in the grass, and put it in park.

"Is this it?" he asked.

"This place has the best hotdogs around. Bet you didn't know you could find a place like this around here, huh?"

"More like hoped."

"Oh, wow," Jenn said. "You are snobbier than the Whitmans, and you know how picky they are with their parties."

"I know you didn't just say I was worse than the Whitmans." He reached out to grab her arm, but she swerved and took off running toward the waterfront. "You think you can beat me?" he said, taking off after her. He caught her at the front of the restaurant.

"You look astounding in that suit I bought you today," she said.

"I appreciate it." He wished he could dress like this all the time. When people said designer clothes were like regular clothes with a higher price tag, they probably had never dressed in the more expensive gear. His pants hung perfectly, accentuating his manly goods. The shirt, a breathable cotton, draped over his pecs and shoulders like it was specially designed for him, which in a way, it was. Jenn had insisted the outfit be tailored to fit his physique and now he understood why. Even the Calvin Klein underwear was softer against one of the most important parts of his anatomy. As ridiculous as it sounded, walking in the clothes gave him an excitement that, before today, only women could do.

He kissed her. After the great day they'd spent together and under the golden sunset, it seemed like the perfect thing to do. He was thankful that a woman could make him feel good again. He hadn't expected that to happen anytime in the near future and here it was, under a sunset with the winds coming up from the water, gently whispering between them.

"What was that kiss for?" she asked.

"You didn't like it?"

"I loved it. But it came out of nowhere."

"It came from a genuine place. I enjoy being with you and I hope you feel the same."

"I do, Deshaun, but remember I'm moving to Japan. You realized it was coming. I told you before at the party, Berti got a job there and was flying back and forth. I wasn't sure anything was going to come from it, but it has and now I'm leaving."

"I assumed the entire move thing was off now."

"Why would you assume that?"

"I don't know," he began. "I just figured—"

"Figured what?"

"When are you leaving?"

"In two days."

"Two days!" he exclaimed. "Why didn't you tell me about this?"

"I did."

"Not that you were leaving in two days! You said the date kept getting pushed back."

She sighed. "Let's just go in and enjoy a good meal. I don't want to think about it right now. I want to have some fun tonight." She took DeShaun's hand and led him into the tiny restaurant that smelled like scented vanilla candles and raw seafood.

Reluctantly, he allowed Jenn to lead him to a tiny table in the corner. "We're going to make the best of the situation while we can." She gently rubbed his arm.

DeShaun nodded, but he wasn't in the mood to eat. He felt like a kid on the verge of a tantrum who just found out his best friend was moving away. Not only was he going to miss Jenn, he now had to bear being alone once again.

Naomi and Jeremy

*I*t took every ounce of my being not to slap her. I was so sick of her blaming me for everything gone off track in her life, when in essence, Cara had gotten everything she ever wanted. Mom and Dad saw to that.

"I can't help it you could never keep a man," I said. "Maybe if you had paid a little more attention to your boyfriends, they wouldn't be so eager to start sniffing in my direction."

"Real mature, little sis," Cara said. "You are such a—"

"Such a what?" I goaded. "Finish the sentence, Cara."

"Thank goodness I'm a Christian. If I wasn't, I'd remind you about certain things I'm sure you don't want me to mention ever again."

"You bitch!" I lunged forward. My fingers were an inch from her neck when Mom stepped in between us.

"Stop it, now!" Mom yelled as my cousin, Sarita, grabbed my arms and pulled me back. "This is the worst possible day you two could have decided to pull this mess. You are disrespecting your father's memory and I won't have it!" Mom took a deep breath to regain her composure. "Knock off this mess before I kick you both out."

"I'm sorry, Mom." I shot Cara one last dirty look before heading toward the kitchen and out the back door. I needed time to cool down.

Jeremy followed. "Hey, you all right?"

"That girl pisses me off every time I see her. I shouldn't let her do it but somehow I do and every single time this is the end result. The last time I saw her was nine years ago, before I was married and even then she had something smart to say. We never got along."

"She didn't even attend your wedding?"

I shook my head. "Nope and I didn't expect her to either, which was why I didn't bother to send her an invitation."

"What did she mean about you stealing and marrying her boy-friend."

"It's a long story."

"What? You got somewhere to be?"

I took a deep breath, preparing to give the condensed version. "Years ago, when I was twelve and Cara was fifteen, we used to come out here every day after dinner and swing until the sun went down. Then when the stars appeared, one-by-one, we would wish on each one, telling each other what our wishes were. One of my wishes was that my sister and I would be best friends forever. I mean, it was unheard of for a fifteen-year-old to allow her preteen sister to hang around with her and her friends. I had the best sister in the world."

"What happened?" Jeremy asked.

"As all good things do, it came to an end. At sixteen, Cara started dating a guy, Derrick Santangelo. Derrick was my first crush and she knew that, but she didn't care. They dated for about a month and then he stopped coming around. One night, my sister invited her friends over and I overheard their conversation. Cara told her friends that she was tired of Derrick and was ready to dump him. She had met another kid, Marcus, and they had already had sex."

"What did that have to do with you?" Jeremy asked, confused.

"Nothing at the time, but three years later when Cara went off to college, Derrick asked me out and we started dating. At first, it was only a fling, but then I really started liking him and he liked me, too. He was my first."

"So, that made you fifteen, then?"

"I was about to turn sixteen when we first had sex. I was in love. I wrote everything down in my diary, professing that one day we were going to get married and have four or five kids."

"Cara found out?"

I nodded. "One Thanksgiving, she came home from college and she was different. She had morphed into this angry, self-absorbed, self-righteous person. When I would ask her if she wanted to hang out at the movies, like we used to, she'd laugh, telling me that she didn't hang with 'pain-in-the-ass little bitches anymore.' And that was a direct quote."

"She said that?" Jeremy asked. "I've only just met her but she doesn't strike me as the type to say something like that."

"She wasn't always the holy roller she claims to be now," I told him. "According to her, she was a woman and couldn't be bothered anymore. One night after dinner, I caught her in my room, sitting on my bed, reading my diary like it was her right. When she looked up and saw me in the doorway, she looked at me with such hate it made the devil look like a saint. She had read my entry about Derrick."

"Ouch," he said. "But didn't you like him first?"

"That didn't matter to her. When she started dating him, even though she knew I liked him, I wasn't angry because she was my sister. I loved her, regardless. I thought it would be the same for her, but it wasn't. I'll never forget that night. She whipped past me, practically knocking me over, and headed straight for my parents. She told them everything. She must've memorized the entire thing, too. She rattled off how many dates I had snuck out to, how many times we Frenched and told them how many times we had sex. She even detailed the times we had it—when my parents went out to dinner for their anniversary, the time we came back from the beach, you name it, she told it. She even read that Derrick and I had crossed the state line and gotten married. The legal age in Georgia is sixteen and I was only fifteen."

"You were married before? What did your parents do?"

"It was ugly. I had never been beaten before, but my father whipped off his belt and beat me for ten minutes straight. They had the marriage annulled and I was grounded for a month. I didn't care about any of that. It was when they said I could never see Derrick again that tore me apart. The entire time, my sister sat there and watched with an evil grin on her face."

"Wow. That was bad."

"That wasn't even the end of it," I told him. "The last night Cara was home, I picked up the phone to call my girlfriend, but instead of a dial tone, I heard my sister's voice. I listened to her beg Derrick for another chance, promising him that she would 'give him some' like he's never had it before."

"What did he say?"

"Derrick told Cara he loved me." I smiled at the sweet memory. "He said someday he was going to marry me…again, and no one would be able to do anything about it. She was so angry that she promised him that he would never see me again. I couldn't believe the words coming out of her mouth. This was my sister, my blood, and yet, the way she spoke about me, it was like I was her worst enemy. All this for a guy she didn't even care about."

"Didn't matter," Jeremy said. "You had something she wanted."

"I never told her I had heard her on the phone, begging Derrick for a second chance. As soon as she went back to school, I continued sneaking around with him."

"I thought your parents had you on a tight leash."

"Never underestimate a girl in love. They were busy working all the time, so I pretty much had free reign to do as I pleased."

"So what happened?" Jeremy asked. "Why aren't you two together anymore?"

"About a month later, I found out I was pregnant. When I told Derrick, we decided to keep the baby and get married. We told my parents in the hopes of getting their blessing. Plus, I was still underage and needed their consent."

"Did you really expect them to give you their blessing?"

"I hoped, but, of course, that wasn't to happen. They called the cops and because he was eighteen, Derrick was arrested for statutory rape. He spent two weeks in jail and eight months on probation."

"What about the baby?"

"My parents dragged me to the clinic for an abortion, three days after his sentencing. That was the beginning of the end. I haven't seen Derrick since."

"Did your sister ever find out you were pregnant?"

"Hell no. You see how she's acting after all these years and that's just about Derrick. Put a baby into the equation, and it's World War III."

"Does your husband know about all of this?"

I shook my head. "He knows Cara and I aren't cool, but he figured that was just sisters being sisters."

"Why did you tell me?"

I shrugged. "I don't know. I guess because with you there's no judgment. You accept something for the way it is and move on."

"I'm glad you feel that way," he said. "I want you to trust me. It's imperative that you do."

"Imperative?"

Jeremy leaned forward and kissed me. When he realized I didn't resist, his lips parted and he stuck his tongue inside of my mouth, but then he pulled back. "Imperative as in I think I'm in love with you."

"Well, well, well, it looks as though my little sister has spun her web and trapped another unsuspecting fly. Poor thing," Cara said, standing in the back patio doorway. She had a plate full of pasta in her hands and was daintily pecking away at it with a plastic fork.

"Why are you even listening to my conversations?" I asked. "You really are some piece of work, aren't you?"

Cara turned to Jeremy. "Which girl did she steal you from? A best friend, a co-worker maybe?"

"Why don't you let up?" Jeremy said. "That was so long ago. She's your sister."

Cara raised her brow and switched her attention back to me. "She's pulling the confiding card so early in the game? You must've screwed her already. Good for you, although, that small feat doesn't take much effort."

"You do not wear bitter very well, Cara," I said.

"Bitter? What a joke. If anyone is bitter, it's you."

"And why is that?" I took the bait, hook, line and sinker.

She narrowed her eyes and gave a crooked grin. "Cousin Salina mentioned you aren't with DeRay anymore. Looks like you're single too now, huh?"

"It's DeShaun," I corrected. "And so what? That's none of your business."

She turned back to Jeremy. "Don't let her pathetic eyes and innocent face fool you. While she was confiding in you, did she give you the sad puppy dog look?" She turned back to me with so much hatred in her eyes, I felt like she would plunge a knife into my chest if she felt like she could get away with it.

"Get out of my face," I warned. I was beginning to feel sick and felt like I wanted to throw up.

"Gladly." She turned and went back inside the house, slamming the screen door behind her. As soon as she did, I bent over and let it fly. Vomit splattered all over the place. I threw up three times and when I thought it was over, I threw up again. This time, I remained bent over until the dizziness subsided. When I caught my breath, I slowly stood up.

Jeremy put his hand on my shoulder. "Are you all right?"

I nodded. "That's what happens when you're pregnant. I suppose I should get used to that."

"What do you mean you're pregnant?"

Oh God! I wasn't even thinking. The words just slipped out and now it was out there. Before I could explain, I was doubled over again, releasing a mixture of deviled eggs and bile—not a good combination.

DeShaun and Jenn

DeShaun hugged the curve doing forty-five. He was eager to get back to Jenn's house; the uncomfortable silence in the Range Rover was deafening. The trip to the restaurant had only been thirty-five minutes, but the ride back seemed twice that.

During the meal, Jenn made small talk, like it was the first time they met. She asked how the business was going and what his plans were for the future. He took offense to that and only gave curt answers, like a pouting child would.

Yup, nope, maybe, I don't know.

He turned onto the Herjavecs' winding driveway and pulled up to the garage. As soon as he put the vehicle in park and pulled out the key from the ignition, Jenn reached for the knob on the passenger side.

"You act like you don't care," DeShaun said, before she opened the door.

She pulled the door close and sat back, listening.

He finally had her full attention. "You barely said anything to me at dinner, Jenn. Then you give me the silent treatment all the way home. What's up with you?"

"Me? I was trying to talk to you all through dinner and you kept brushing me off, so I gave up."

"Gave up, huh?" DeShaun said. "Yeah, you're good at that, aren't you?"

She threw her hands up in the air. "What do you want me to do, DeShaun? Tell me. What would make you happy?"

The truth was, he wasn't sure what he expected from this relationship, but one thing he knew for damn sure, he didn't want it to end so soon. "I don't know."

"How about I leave Berti, and you and I run off together," she said. "Is that what you want? Where would we live? I highly doubt Berti would give me the house so we could live happily ever after. What would we do for money?"

"Sounds like you already thought this through."

"It doesn't take a lot of pondering to figure out there is no way we could have that happy ending you're looking for, DeShaun. I don't want it to end so quickly either, but my husband is moving out of the country. I need to go with him."

"You don't *need* to go with him," he said. "You *want* to go. You don't want to lose all your fancy clothes and cars and all that other bullshit."

She laughed, which only angered him more.

"You think this is funny?" he asked, his lip curled up in irritation.

She gently ran her fingertips up and down his arm. "No, actually it's sad. It's incredibly sad that I have to leave a man that I've grown to enjoy. It's sad that we'll never know what could've happened with this relationship. I'm also sad that you're hurting, but so am I, DeShaun."

His gaze dropped to the gray speckled car mat underneath his feet. "Are you ever coming back?"

"That's the good news," she said. "With the sale of the house pending, I'll be back next week to tie up loose ends. We'll be able to see each other then." She cradled his head in her cupped hands. "I promise." She leaned over and gently kissed him on the lips. "I will call you the minute I'm back in town."

He looked into her green eyes in search of the truth, but he couldn't find it. With Naomi, every time he looked into her brown eyes, he felt her truth, and realized that she was sincere. With Jenn, he couldn't read her expression.

She opened the door and hopped out the car. "We have one last night to spend together. Let's make it good."

"Where's your husband?"

"He's in Japan waiting for me."

"Why is this our last night then?" DeShaun asked. "I thought you weren't leaving for another two days."

"As much as I would love to spend the next few days with you, I have packing I must get done."

"I can help."

She grabbed his fingertips and kissed the back of his hand. "No distractions. You've already set me back a few days. Besides," she added, "I thought you were servicing a party tomorrow night?"

He completely forgot about Kitty and Craig Nielson's party in Olde City he had scheduled a week ago.

"I know what you'd like," she said, quickly changing the subject. "I recently bought this incredible bottle of wine I want you to try. You'll love it." She went around to the driver's side, grabbed his hand and pulled him out of the car. They headed toward the house, but suddenly, her hand released his and fell to her side like limp spaghetti. She stopped walking, and stood there, stiff as a board. Her tanned skin had turned ashen. DeShaun followed her gaze and immediately understood.

Under the dimly lit chandelier porch light, Berti stood there with his arms crossed and an irate expression on his face. "Where in the hell were you all day?"

Naomi and Jeremy

"I was going to tell you," I told Jeremy. "But there was so much going on. Plus, I wasn't sure how you would react about the entire situation."

"I have to ask this," he said. "But—"

"I'm not sure who the father is," I interrupted. "I was with only you and DeShaun."

"So there is a chance it could be mine?"

I nodded, carefully watching the expression on his face. His brows were raised, but there were deep frown lines buried in the corners of his mouth.

"There's always that chance, but I don't know," I admitted. "I thought those times I was feeling sick had something to do with it."

"I remember that day at lunch when you passed out," he said. "Were you pregnant then?" Like I had earlier, Jeremy was calculating his chances.

"Not according to the doctor. When I found out, I was only about six weeks pregnant."

"That's after that night in my car."

I nodded. "Yeah."

"So, you broke up with your husband soon after," he cautiously remarked. "Did you—"

"One time."

"Where does this leave us?"

"Honestly Jeremy, I don't know."

He let out a long, exasperated sigh. "I don't know what to say."

"I don't expect anything from you," I reassured.

"What do you want me to say to that?"

Before I could respond, my mother called from the kitchen.

"Yes, Mom, I'm coming." I turned back to Jeremy. "What are you going to do?"

He shrugged. "I'm going to go back to the hotel, I guess. I need time to think. I'll take a cab and leave the car for you."

"You take the car. I'll find a ride."

He stared at me blankly. "Okay. Tell your mother 'bye' for me."

I went back into the house while Jeremy headed back to the car. I wouldn't have been surprised if I got back to the hotel and found his bags gone.

Mom and I sat at the kitchen table. Everyone had left and the house was completely quiet. Cara was dropping off a few of our cousins that lived nearby, so she would be back soon. I wasn't looking forward to that.

"So how is life in PA?" Mom asked.

"It's going okay."

She dipped her tea bag into a cup of hot water. "That's good. I hate the circumstances, but I'm glad you're here, you and your sister."

I nodded, not wanting to get into a conversation regarding Cara.

"She missed you, you know," Mom said, taking a sip of her tea.

"When she calls, she always asks when was the last time I heard from you."

"Are you sure she meant me? Why?"

"I just told you. She misses you."

She was probably only monitoring how many calls I made to Mom and Dad and trying to top that. Then she would be the good daughter while I was the ungrateful brat she always claimed I would turn out to be.

"Your father used to brag about you all the time," Mom said, taking another sip. "He kept telling people how proud he was of you."

"For what?"

"He bragged about Cara too, but there was a glow on his face whenever he talked about you. The day you came to us and said you were moving to Pennsylvania really hurt your father."

I had no idea. "Really? What did he say?" My father was a quiet man. I was sure he had many secrets. Not bad, life-changing ones, more like secrets that made me see him in a better light and realize why he did some of the things he did. There was so much I never knew about him but wished I had when he was alive. Him being proud of me was one.

"He never said anything to me," Mom said. "It was more like the way he walked around the house, sad and depressed. He even took a few days away from his practice."

"Daddy never took days off, even when he was sick."

"I know. That's how I knew he was hurting. He never did admit it to me, but I knew."

A single tear fell from my eye, but I quickly wiped it away with the back of my hand. "I miss him."

"So do I." Mom gave me a hug. "No more depressing stuff."

She reached across the table and slid a plate of a half-eaten sweet potato pie in front of me. "Tell me about this new guy, Jeremy, right?"

I took the large slice she had cut for me. "Yes. He's nice, too." I shoved a forkful of sweet potato goodness in my mouth. That's really all I wanted to say about him, considering an hour ago, he may have walked out of my life for good.

"Are you ever going to tell me what happened with DeShaun?" Mom asked, taking a bite. "I thought you two would be married forever."

"You hated him. You should be happy he's gone."

"I didn't hate him." She took an extra long sip of her tea. "I simply thought you could've done better."

"Same thing."

"So what happened with him?"

"We made bad choices—that's all."

"Well, Jeremy seems like a good guy who really cares about you." She paused to shovel in another large bite of pie. "I like him almost as much as I like this pie."

"But?"

"DeShaun loved you so much. That man would've died for you. He looked at you the way your father looked at me. There was so much love. I can't imagine what happened to break up the two of you."

"He's not the only man that can love me like that. DeShaun has changed. He used to be so strong and confident and now..." I picked up the remaining pie crust and shoved it into my mouth. "It doesn't matter. That chapter is over. DeShaun doesn't feel that way about me anymore."

"What about you?"

"Of course I don't feel that way anymore. It's over. Way too many things were said and done that can't be taken back. He's moved on and I most definitely have moved on." I avoided my mom's stare. She was in psychologist mode.

"I'll pray for you," Mom said. "I'll pray for you both."

"Thanks, Mom."

I really appreciated her saying that. Something told me I was going to need something short of a miracle to get through this.

DeShaun and Jenn

DeShaun continued up the walk, fearing that if he left now, Berti would be suspicious. Although he didn't want Berti to know about his relationship with Jenn, he would find out eventually. DeShaun planned to continue corresponding with her while she was in Japan. He meant no disrespect, but it is what it is.

"Act natural," Jenn whispered. "He's totally oblivious to all of my indiscretions, as I am to his."

DeShaun turned to Jenn. "What do you mean *all of my indiscretions?* I thought you said you never cheated on your husband."

"Not now. We'll talk later." She forced a smile as she waved her hand high in the air. "Berti, dear, what are you doing home so early? I thought I was to meet you in Japan."

Berti sized up Deshaun, starting from his expensive shoes right up to the designer shirt. "Don't you look dapper. I almost didn't recognize you."

"Thank you."

"And you," Berti said, turning back to his wife. "I'm here because I thought you'd need my help, tying up all the loose ends." He turned back to DeShaun. "But I see you were in good hands while I was away. Speaking of which, where were you all day?"

Jenn casually tossed her hair back. "We were out scouting locations for DeShaun's business."

Berti shot a look at DeShaun. "Is that so? Good for you."

"Well," DeShaun began. "I guess I'd better head out."

Berti grabbed his arm with what DeShaun thought was excessive force. "Oh, no, you don't. You can't leave without having a quick drink. Don't know when I'll see you again."

"I really shouldn't."

"I don't take kindly to rejection," Berti said, still holding onto DeShaun's arm. "One drink and you may go on your merry way."

DeShaun glanced over at Jenn.

"I'm sure she'd love you to stay as well," Berti said. "Wouldn't you, dear?"

"Of course," Jenn said as she squeezed past Berti still standing in the doorway. "I'll make us some drinks."

"Just one," DeShaun told him. He followed Berti into the house, quickly shuffling around thoughts of what belongings he may have left in their bedroom. "One drink and then I have to go."

Berti led him through the foyer. "One and then you may go." He led DeShaun to the study and nodded toward a plush chair in the corner. "Have a seat."

DeShaun took a seat on the lounge chair. Jenn came from behind the bar and handed him a crystal glass containing Hennessy.

"Neat, correct?"

From the other end of the room, Berti chuckled. "Jenn, dear, how would you know what he likes to drink?" He turned to DeShaun. "Women always thinking they know everything."

"This is fine," DeShaun said.

Jenn tipped a bottle of Russo-Baltique and filled another crystal glass, halfway. "I'm a professional, at this." She handed the glass to Berti. "It's my job to know what men like."

DeShaun choked on his drink.

"Take it easy," Berti said. "This stuff is expensive. Don't want you wasting any of it, even if you are choking to death." He laughed as he reached behind the bar and pulled out a rectangular, sandal-wood-colored box. "Cohiba?"

"No. Thank you."

Berti took another gulp. "Jenn, honey, maybe you should finish packing."

"Finish? I haven't even started."

"Really?" Berti asked. "I went up to the room and it looked like a cyclone hit it, clothes and empty wine bottles all over the place. You must've really missed me to drink all that wine by yourself."

Just then Berti's phone rang. He picked it up, said a few "uh-huhs" to the person on the other end, and then excused himself and walked out of the room.

When he was gone, DeShaun quickly turned back to Jenn. "He knows."

She casually shook her head. "Berti may be a smart guy when it comes to business, but in real life, he's an idiot. He could've found your boxers stuffed between my legs and still wouldn't be suspicious, poor guy." She kissed DeShaun on the nose. He pulled away.

"Sorry about that," Berti said, returning to the den. "It's like there's never a day off when you own your own business. But then again, you would know about that, wouldn't you, DeShaun?"

"I just started, but I'm glad to report it's going well."

"That's good," Berti said. "So what places have you seen?"

"Places?"

"Yes," Berti said, taking another gulp. "You said you went scouting locations today."

"We were looking in the Conshohocken area," Jenn jumped in. "But we didn't really find anything worthwhile. Then we found a nice property in Center City but decided not to go ahead with that one either. Too much traffic and noise."

"What about the Main Line?" Berti asked. "It's close to the city, but without the congestion."

"Something to consider," Jenn said.

"I'd better go." DeShaun stood up. "Good luck with your move to Japan."

"Yes, yes, thank you," Berti said. "Take care of yourself."

"You too, Mr. Herjavec."

Berti gave a stern look.

"I mean, Berti," DeShaun corrected.

Jenn stood up and gently took DeShaun's elbow. "I'll show you out." When they reached the front door, she gave DeShaun a quick peck on the lips. "See? I told you. Completely oblivious."

Naomi and Jeremy

I entered into the hotel room and immediately checked the corner by the sofa, where we had dropped off our bags before heading to the funeral. Jeremy's bags were gone.

Just then the bathroom door opened and he walked out. "I didn't hear you come in. Is everything okay?"

I let out a breath of relief. "I should be asking you that. I'm glad you're still here."

"You expected otherwise?"

"Honestly, I didn't know what to expect." I scanned the room once again. "And then when I didn't see your bags, I assumed you left."

"I stuck them in closet to make more room. I would've put yours there too but I didn't want to touch your things without permission."

I smiled. "My mother is right. You really are a great guy."

"Tell you mother I said I know." He walked up and kissed me on the nose.

"Jeremy, I am so sorry I put you in this position."

He shook his head. "Hold on a sec. Let me say this quickly and then you can have the floor. I love you, Naomi. I want to be with you. I don't care whose baby you are carrying. I want to take care of both of you. I know you've had some issues with men in the past, but I'm not like that, Naomi. Let me prove it to you. I can make you happy. I can make us happy, including the baby. I'm going back to school, but I'll get a part-time job. You can live with me and maybe sell your house for extra income. If you don't want to do that, that's fine, too. Everything will be okay, Naomi, you'll see."

He paused and I thought he was finished. He wasn't.

"I love you so much and I hate to see you hurting like this," he continued. "We can make this work. We can be a family, if you'll give me the chance." He paused again. "What do you think?"

On the way over here in the cab, I thought about what I would say to him, if he was still here. It may have been easier for me if he had left. I wasn't sure how I felt about this entire situation. After what he just told me, it put me in an even more awkward position.

His eyes pleaded for an answer, the right answer, the one he desperately wanted to hear. I didn't know if I could give him that.

"I want to be with you, too," I finally said.

He smiled and released a long deep breath. "You have given me the answer I prayed for. You have no idea how happy you have made me." He wrapped his arms around me and gently kissed me. A tear ran down my cheek as he whispered into my ear, "We are going to have a baby together."

"About that," I said, wiping away my tears. "I'm not having a baby."

He looked confused and scared at the same time. "But, I thought—"

"I'm having *two* babies, twins."

His eyes bulged open, but there was a smile on his face. He was overjoyed. He knelt down and placed his ear to my belly. "We're having twins?" He looked up at me. "Can you believe it? We're having two babies. Does anyone else know?"

"Just you."

He kissed my belly and then rose to his feet. Our bodies pressed together as he rubbed my shoulders and kissed my lips. He bent down and scooped me up, carrying me over to the king-sized bed where he gently laid me down. We made love until the sun dipped completely below the horizon. Unlike the first and only time in the car, it wasn't awkward, but rather sweet and gentle. This time, our being together wasn't based on anger or seeking revenge. We were two people who genuinely cared for each other.

His body moved slow and methodically, making sure I was enjoying it as much as he was. But an important piece was missing. Even with all the tenderness and love I felt coming from him, I couldn't help thinking about DeShaun.

My cell woke me up. I glanced over at Jeremy, who was still tucked under the sheets, fast asleep.

"Hello?" I whispered, looking out the sliding glass patio doors. The full moon created dark shadows throughout the room.

"Naomi? It's DeShaun. How are you?"

My eyes bugged open. To say I was surprised to hear from him was an understatement. A part of me was cautiously glad to hear his voice. The last time we spoke, he was threatening me with divorce papers. Tonight, DeShaun's tone sounded less incensed.

"I'm okay. Is something wrong?"

"Everything's cool. I just wanted to see how you were doing. I tried calling the house first."

"I'm not home."

He laughed. "I figured that when I didn't get an answer. Where are you? No wait. It's none of my business. You don't need to answer to me anymore. I was just—"

"I'm in Atlanta."

"Everything okay?" There was concern in his voice.

I looked over at Jeremy, who was still sleeping. I lowered my voice and said, "Dad died." I tried to steady my tone, but my voice cracked.

"Oh, man. I am so sorry, Mimi. Was he sick? Do you feel okay to talk about it now?"

"He had a heart attack." Tears formed in the corners of my eyes. "It hurts so much, DeShaun. We're hanging in there though."

"How's Mom?"

"She's managing, but it's a struggle for all of us."

"Man, I am so sorry to hear that, Mimi. You should've called. I would've gone with you."

I checked on Jeremy, who flinched a couple of times but commenced his loud snoring. I leaned over the side of the bed and lowered my voice even more. "I was going to call, but then when you called that time, you were so angry and told me you had divorce papers in the mail."

"Shit! I'm sorry, Mimi. I was being an asshole. I was just—I don't know what I was," he said. "I'm sorry. Were all your relatives at the funeral?"

"Everyone, including good ol' sis."

"Cara was there?" he asked. "Did someone have to call nine-one-one to pull you off of her?"

I laughed through my tears. "Almost. That girl got on my last nerve."

"Remember when she came to the family reunion and busted her ass playing badminton?" DeShaun said. "You couldn't tell her it wasn't the Olympics. She was going for the gold, too."

"I remember that. She tried to get a foul on me for that point, saying I was illegally spiking the birdie."

We both started laughing. Jeremy stirred and then opened his eyes. Rubbing his tired eyes, he looked up at me and asked, "Who's that?"

I quickly covered the speaker with the palm of my hand. "I'll be off in a second." I removed my hand, turned away and whispered, "I have to go."

"Okay," DeShaun said on the other end. "Look, Naomi, I want to meet up with you when you get back. Is that okay?"

"We should be home tomorrow evening."

"We?"

"I have to go," I said, quickly. "I'll call you when I get back."

"Okay, but tell your mother and Cara I said hello, even though your mother probably doesn't want to hear it."

"You'd be surprised."

"I bet I would."

I felt him smiling through the phone.

I hung up and shoved the phone back into my purse, careful to avoid Jeremy's inquisitive stare. "You hungry, Jeremy? I'm starving. Want something to eat?"

Jeremy sat up and swung his legs over the side of the bed. With his elbows resting on his knees and his head hung low, he asked, "Was that him? Was that DeShaun?"

I stepped out of bed. "I don't want to get into it now."

"Was it or wasn't it him? I'm asking a question."

"Does it matter?"

"What do you mean does it matter? Of course, it does. Why would it not matter that I just told you I loved you and within hours after having sex, you're talking to your husband, ex-husband, whatever? Of course, it matters."

"Yes, it was him. There. Are you happy now?"

"Do I look happy?"

"We are finally on speaking terms. He called, asking where I was, and when I told him, he wanted to make sure everything was okay."

"I don't get why he's calling you in the first place. I thought you said he sent divorce papers to your house. That should be it."

"It's not that simple."

"That's because he's not making it that simple. He doesn't need to call you and next time he does, I want to tell him that."

"What is wrong with you? Why are you acting like this?"

"I love you, remember? I want to be with you and the babies. He doesn't. I don't want him disrespecting me like that again, like I'm some fool. I'm not the one and next time I see him, he's gonna know it."

"Jeremy, it's not like that. He wasn't disrespecting you. He doesn't even know about you."

"Oh really? Tell me this. Are we or are we not going to be together?"

"Jeremy—"

"It's not a difficult question."

"Yes, we are going to be together. Would you please relax? I'm with you, okay?"

The tense creases around his eyes relaxed a little, so I figured everything was cool. "I want to go back to the house to say good-bye to my mother. Are you coming?"

"I'll drop you off," he said. "I have an errand to run before we head back to PA."

A nagging suspicion told me that this topic wasn't even close to being finished.

DeShaun

DeShaun grabbed the platter of shrimp and practically sprinted out the glass patio double doors. As he hurried past the party-goers relaxing on the veranda, he noticed several other guests holding empty champagne and wine glasses.

Dammit, where the hell was M.J.?

He spotted M.J. across the patio, surrounded by several women, serving hors d'oeuvres and chatting it up like he was one of the guests, instead of the help that DeShaun had brought along to make sure this party was a success. DeShaun hadn't secured a solid party in two weeks and he was getting worried. Aside from Countess Vargas' Thanksgiving party coming up, he only had one or two smaller gigs lined up. He was pulling in over $2,500 for a larger private function, but that money had to also pay for the guys he brought along to help him serve. It didn't matter that he was still bunking on M.J.'s lumpy pull-out couch. If M.J. didn't pick it up, he was getting a smaller cut. If anyone, including his boy, was messing with his money, that was going to be a big problem.

"DeShaun," the Countess said, holding his arm in a death grip. "Would you like to come back to my place tonight to service my *private* party?" The old woman was slurring and her eyes practically rolling back in her head as she spoke.

DeShaun smiled politely. "I can't. I have a million things to do after this party."

"Really?" she asked. "What about tomorrow night?"

DeShaun kept his focus ahead, still in search of M.J. "We'll talk about that another time. Let me get you another drink." As expected, that trick earned him his freedom. She released his arm and he headed toward the bar to get the Countess another drink.

"DeShaun," she called after him. "I'm really sorry, but I'm going to have to cancel my Thanksgiving feast. I won't need you after all."

"Excuse me?" This got his full attention. "What do you mean cancel? We have a signed contract."

"The recession is killing me," she said. "With everyone losing money, no one feels like celebrating anyway. I will keep you in mind for future engagements."

"You can't do that. What about the contract we signed?"

She shrugged. "Take me to court. I'm not throwing the party."

"Does this have anything to do with the fact that I won't sleep with you?"

"It has everything to do with that," the Countess said matter-of-factly. "You can fuck that fat cow, Jenn Herjavec, but you won't have me?"

"What are you talking about?"

She waved her bony, manicured hand in the air, like she was shooing a fly. "Oh, please. Spare me the denial. Everyone knows."

"But, but—" He was desperate. "I saved your life."

"I'm an old, drunk woman. I fall into the pool at least once at every party. If it wasn't you, it would've been someone else." She turned and started walking away. "Take care of yourself, DeShaun, darling."

He watched her stumble away. Now what? He'd really have to hustle to get another gig to replace that one.

"Yo, DeShaun." M.J. came running up. "We're out of Patron and Zinfandel. People are beginning to complain."

"I have reserve bottles in my car," DeShaun said. "It's not a lot, so fill the glasses halfway instead of two-thirds. And tell those ignorant assholes who are supposed to be working for me to stop drinking it, and that includes you!" DeShaun knew the guys dipped into the bottles and snuck glasses here and there during the service.

"Man, we don't want that mess," M.J. said, darting off toward the car. "We like the good stuff."

"Hello, DeShaun."

DeShaun turned around. Berti stood there in a casual pair of khakis and a cotton button down shirt. "How are you?"

"Mr. Herjavec, I mean Berti. I wasn't aware you would be here tonight."

"Last-minute thing." He took a sip from the wineglass he was holding. "The Nielsons and I are good friends and they insisted I come, so here I am."

"That's good." He looked beyond Mr. Herjavec and toward his car to make sure M.J. grabbed the correct cases.

"Looking for my wife?" Berti asked.

"Oh, no, I was just—"

"She won't be here tonight. It's better that way."

DeShaun chose his words carefully. "Why is that?"

Berti threw his head back and chugged down the remaining contents in his glass. "What is the saying? Something like, never biting the hand that feeds you?" He thought a moment. "I don't know, something like that. But, if you're more of a biblical man, how about, thou shalt not covet thy neighbor's wife? Does that sound more familiar?" He shook his head. "On second thought, you seem like you'd favor the 'don't shit where you sleep' saying. Am I right?"

DeShaun kept his face straight. "I don't know what you're talking about." If he had to, he was prepared to battle with this man, right here, right now.

"I think you do," Berti said. "I fed you and you bit me…hard."

"I don't—"

"Please stop. I know."

DeShaun raised his head and squared off his shoulders. He realized this day was coming. It was inevitable. "I've only worked one of your parties, so, in essence, you have never really *fed* me, so to speak."

Berti's face turned red. DeShaun expected him to ball up his fists and throw a punch any second. He was surprised when Berti simply stood there, shaking his head. "Let me help you understand. You see these people? These people are *my* friends, not yours. I've allowed you to work for them and squirrel away some nuts for the winter, but not anymore. The Countess didn't cancel her party, you ninny. In fact, my wife and I will be there for Thanksgiving. You won't. I made sure of that. You really should check your messages more often. As we speak, those two other parties *my friends* booked are being cancelled."

DeShaun stared him down. "You bastard."

"And you're an asshole who has no respect for another man's property."

"Like you care. Aren't you busy with your own side projects? I know about you and those young black guys."

"By the time I'm finished with you, you'll beg me to be one of those young guys."

"You're sick."

Berti reached up and scratched the tiny stubble forming on his chin. "Aren't you tired of losing? When will you realize that some of us win in life and some are like you. Your wife left you and now my wife is gone, too. You have no work. If I have anything to do with it, you will never work around here again. You neglected to realize that no woman is ever worth your livelihood. You can lose a woman and find another one, but if you lose your livelihood, you're done. No woman wants a broke loser. Now, if you will be so polite as to pack up your shit and go. This party is over for you."

Berti turned and started walking away. He stopped, turned back to DeShaun and said, "Great party, but don't expect to get paid for it. If you got a problem with that, take it up with my lawyers."

"My men working here have nothing to do with me," DeShaun said. "At least they should get paid."

"That's what happens when you associate with trash—you all get thrown away. Like I said, if you have a problem, take it up with my lawyer. You dug your own grave; lie in it."

Naomi and Jeremy

"Where's Jeremy?" Mom asked. She was in the kitchen, fixing turkey and cheese sandwiches for Jeremy and me to pack into our bags for the car ride back to Philly.

"Mom, you don't have to do that. We can get something on the road."

"Too expensive." She slathered low-fat mayonnaise onto a slice of whole wheat bread. She grabbed two slices of turkey, a slice of tomato and some shredded lettuce and placed it onto one slice of bread. "You want cheese?"

"Two slices, please."

She grinned as she reached for a slice.

"Hey, if you're going to make it, I'm gonna eat it," I told her. "Got any bacon?"

"You know I do." She opened up the refrigerator and pulled out a piece of tin foil. "Courtesy of your sister."

"Cara cooked? Grab your sweater, folks. Hell is about to freeze over."

Mom shot me a quick, disapproving look. "Behave yourself, please. She brought the bacon over from her hotel's breakfast bar. You know I raised me some non-cooking, non-cleaning girls."

"Is she here, now?" The question barely left my lips before the front door opened and I heard stilettos clicking on the wooden floor.

Cara came sauntering into the kitchen. "I didn't expect to see you here this early, little sis."

"Don't you mean you were hoping?"

"Tomayto, tomahto." She looked around the kitchen. "Where's Loverboy?"

"None of your business."

"Don't worry." She grabbed a glass container full of orange juice from the refrigerator and poured herself a glass. "I won't try to steal him from behind your back. I'm not you."

I rolled my eyes. "Gee, thanks. I was worried."

"Girls," Mom said. "I wish you two would stop bickering all the time. It's only us now. You're father is gone and I would appreciate a little more family unity."

"It's her fault," Cara whined. "It's always been her fault. She needs to say I'm sorry."

"Sorry for what?"

"For stealing my boyfriend!"

"He was never your boyfriend," I shouted back. "He was a decent guy and you cheated on him. And if you remember, I had a crush on him first, so technically you stole him from me."

"Oh, that's right," she said. "I'm the bad guy."

"Okay, you want me to say I'm sorry? I'm sorry he fell in love with me, someone who actually loved him back."

"You bitch!"

"Girls!"

"In fact," I continued. "You should apologize to me for giving me hell all these years when all I did was fall in love. You're the one who deserted me when I needed you the most. I've always hated you for that."

"So you get back at me by marrying my boyfriend?"

"HE WASN'T YOUR BOYFRIEND!" I shook my head. This

girl was clueless. "This has nothing to do with some guy fifteen years ago. It's about you and me and you broke that. Even before Derrick, you treated me like dirt, like I didn't matter, and now, years later, you still treat me like dirt under the guise of being angry over some boy from years ago. Trust me. If it wasn't Derrick, you'd have some other excuse to hate me."

Cara always had something to say, but not now. For once, I silenced her.

She rolled her eyes and huffed. "Oh, please."

I looked over at Mom, who was standing in the corner of the kitchen. Her expression was a combination of shock, horror and sadness. "I should've done better," she said. "I should've gotten you both together when you were younger and I didn't. It's my fault you both are so angry with each other."

I came over and wrapped my arms around her. "You did an excellent job. Cara and I will work this out, you'll see. It's going to take some time, but we will work this out. I promise." I looked back at my sister, sitting at the kitchen table with her arms folded like a pouty schoolgirl. "Right, Cara?"

She mumbled an unconvincing, "Sure."

"See?" I told Mom. "Everything will be fine."

I was still embracing Mom, trying to calm her down when the doorbell rang. It rang a second and third time. I turned to Cara, who was still sitting at the table. "You gonna get that?"

She sucked her teeth and hopped up from the table, clicking her stilettos all the way to the front door. A few seconds later, she barged back into the kitchen. "Your fresh meat is here."

When Jeremy entered into the kitchen and saw all of us, his face beamed. "Good. I'm glad you're all here." He was breathing hard, beads of sweat dewing on his forehead. He grabbed my hand and led me toward the center of the kitchen. He took a deep breath and finally said, "I love you, Naomi. I haven't made a secret out of that. You mean the world to me and I trust that you want to make me as happy as I want to make you. You're the one for me, and when a man finally realizes that, he wants to scoop up the woman of his dream and make her his."

"What are you doing, Jeremy?" I asked, concerned.

"I'm doing what I need to do." He took in another deep breath. "I love you, Naomi. That's why I'm asking for your hand in marriage." He reached into his back pocket and produced a small black box. He held it up under my nose and asked, "Naomi, will you make me the happiest man in the world and be my wife?"

I looked at my mother, then I glanced at my sister, who sat at the kitchen table with a smirk on her face.

"Congratulations, sister dear. You are the first woman I know who collects husbands like she's collecting stamps." She got up and walked out.

Naomi and Jeremy

The entire car ride home, I was so angry I could barely even look at Jeremy. When we had pulled into the rest stop in Garner, North Carolina, Jeremy kept asking what he'd done wrong. I simply glared at him and cut my eyes. When we stopped for gas in Baltimore, he practically begged me to tell him what was wrong. At that point, I was able to mumble an irate, "Are you kidding me?" That was the extent of our conversation, up until now. I had let my rage fester inside for the entire trip home, but as we stepped into the house, I was ready to let him have it.

"If you ever pull some shit like that again, I will kill you." I heard the trembling in my tone.

"I don't get why you're so mad."

"You have embarrassed me with your phony proposal. Everyone knew it was bullshit—including me."

"I love you and I want to marry you. What's the problem?"

"The problem is," I took time to steady my voice, "you're only proposing to keep me on a leash. You don't want to marry me and, if you haven't noticed, I'm already married." In case he still didn't get it, I threw up my hand and flashed my ring finger. "See? Still married!"

"I do want to marry you and yes, I know you're still married, but you're getting a divorce."

"Stop pushing me. Let me conclude my first relationship before I enter into another one."

"Enter? I thought we were already well into our relationship. You said you were only waiting for the divorce papers to come through. Speaking of which—" He walked over toward the small antique table I kept the mail on and began rifling through the stack of envelopes. "Where are the divorce papers?" He went through one stack and tossed the envelopes onto the hardwood floor. He picked up another stack and began rifling through those. "You said he told you he was sending them, so where are they?"

"Stop it!" I told him. "This is not your house. You have no right to go through my things."

He set down the mail stack in his hand. "Oh, I forgot. This is you and your husband's house. Outsiders aren't welcomed."

"It's not even like that."

"How is it then?"

"Why are you making this so difficult for me?"

"For you?" he asked. "What about me? I fell in love with you the day you started working at the bank, but I stayed away. You were married and, aside from that, you hated my guts."

"I didn't hate you. I thought you were an egotistical jerk."

"And that's better?"

I was relieved when he cracked a smile. I never wanted to hurt him, but I was in a weird place right now. Unfortunately, he was caught smack dab in the middle of my marital chaos. I blamed myself for that.

"I get it," he said. "I pushed too hard. You're not ready."

I wrapped my arms around his neck and kissed his cheek. "Thank you."

"I don't know about you," he said. "But all this relationship crap has made me hungry. I'd go buy us something to eat, but I spent all my money on the ring."

I waited for him to laugh before I cracked a smile. I was so thankful that he was no longer angry. I needed more time to sort it all out. Everything came at me so quickly in such a short span of time, my marriage ending, pregnancy and now Jeremy. It was too much. I needed to breathe.

Jeremy pulled out his wallet from his back pocket and opened it up. "I need to get some money from the ATM. You relax. I'll be back in a few with something to eat. Chinese good? Oh wait, is that too spicy for a woman in your condition?"

"Chinese is fine."

He walked to the front door and I followed. Before he walked out, he turned and said to me, "I'm holding on to this ring. I'll wait for you and the babies until the day I die."

Naomi, DeShaun and Jeremy

While Jeremy was gone, I took a long, hot bath. I stepped out of the tub and looked into the mirror, trying to imagine a burgeoning belly. I twisted to the left and turned to the right, inspecting my profile. According to the doctor, I was almost two months' pregnant. I was beginning to show. I ran my fingers up and down, over the tiny bulge in my lower belly. This wasn't the first time I entertained the idea of "fixing" this with one quick trip to the doctor, but then I'd remember being seventeen and the pain of an abortion, physically, but more so mentally and emotionally. I decided to keep these babies, even if I had to raise them by myself. I had no job, no husband and was quickly running out of money. I no longer wanted to count on DeShaun to pay my bills. I needed to do it myself, then I would cut ties from him completely. I had finally made my choice; I was divorcing DeShaun, and Jeremy and I would start a family together. It scared me thinking about it.

When I heard the key in the front lock, I quickly threw on a pair cotton pajama pants and my favorite tank. "Thank goodness you're back," I said, heading for the front door. "Please tell me you brought back sweet and sour chicken."

When I got to the door, I was surprised to see DeShaun, not Jeremy. He was holding a bouquet of red roses.

"I didn't know you were back yet," he said. "I was going to surprise you."

"You have to leave," I told him. "You shouldn't have come."

He handed me the roses, but when I didn't take them, he let them drop to his side. "I need to talk to you, Mimi. I am so sorry for what we're going through. It should've never gotten to this point."

"You have to leave," I said again, this time with a little more authority. "We can talk about this tomorrow."

He gave me the once over. "You look good."

Was he not hearing me? "DeShaun, I—"

"Let me say this and I'll leave. I promise."

"Fine. Hurry."

"We both made mistakes, but we can work on getting us back, Mimi. We had so much there. I'll even go to counseling if that's what it takes." He took a step toward me. "We owe it to ourselves to at least try, don't you think?"

I looked into his hopeful eyes and was thankful that he didn't hate me anymore, but getting back together didn't really seem like an option. If we could go back, before we made that immoral fateful decision that we both knew was wrong, I wasn't even sure the outcome wouldn't be the same. Going back to what we were was impossible. We had said and done too much.

"We tried, DeShaun. We loved each other. We would've died for each other, but that wasn't enough."

"Don't let us go, Mimi. We can work this out."

It hurt my heart to see him defeated like this. It hurt me even more to see our marriage defeated. "I wish we hadn't done some of the things we did or said some of the things we said," I told him. "But it happened. We can forgive, but we'll never forget."

"It doesn't have to be like that, Mimi. We can create a new chapter, a happy one that exposes our mistakes and helps us come back."

"Things are different, DeShaun. We're not the same people. I've started seeing someone and we're trying to make it work."

"That doesn't matter. " He took a step closer. "It'll never work with anyone else. You know that. Baby, please?"

"You won't be saying that when you hear what I have to say," I told him. "Trust me, things *have* changed."

"What are you talking about?"

I shook my head. "I can't do this now. You've got to go. We'll talk tomorrow."

He reached over and grabbed my hand. "When tomorrow?"

"I don't know." I forced my hand from his, took him by the shoulders, and began rushing him toward the door. "I will call you. I promise, but you have to leave now."

"Wait." He turned around. "Who is this guy you're seeing anyway?"

"Just go, please."

Right on cue, Jeremy walked through the front door with two large bags of Chinese takeout in his hands. He was fumbling with the lock, so he didn't see us standing in the foyer right away. "That rain is really coming down," he said. "Luckily, I brought the umbrella, or I would've been soaked." He set the umbrella down and shut the door. He looked up and saw DeShaun first. Then he looked at me. "What the fuck is going on?"

"DeShaun just came over and I told him he had to go," I said. "Everything is cool."

"It's cool, huh?" Jeremy took two steps toward us. "So why the hell is he here?"

"Wait a minute," DeShaun said. "This is *my* house you're walking into. I need to be asking you who the fuck you are, walking up in to *my* spot like you own the damn place. Look at you. You got my key and everything."

Jeremy slammed the bags onto the hall table, keeping his eyes on DeShaun. "That ain't all I got that was yours."

"What?" DeShaun took a step toward him and squared up. "What did you say?"

"Jeremy," I said, "everything is cool. Just relax. I'm handling this."

DeShaun laughed. "Oh, yeah. I thought I recognized your corny face. Man, you couldn't wait 'til I was out of the picture before you snuck in the back door like the snake you are."

"I didn't have to wait long, did I?"

"You also don't have to wait long for this beat down you're about to get, if you don't get outta my face."

"DeShaun!, Jeremy! Stop it!" I yelled. "This isn't a who-has-the-biggest-balls contest. Knock it off!" I turned to DeShaun. "Please, just go."

"Yeah, go," Jeremy chimed in. "You ain't wanted around here. You fucked up and you're out."

"Stop it, Jeremy!" *Why wasn't anyone listening to me?*

DeShaun balled up his fists. "Says who? You?"

They stared each other down. DeShaun, at least four inches taller than Jeremy, looked down on him like a ferocious lion about to tear apart his prey. Jeremy wasn't backing down either. He stood toe-to-toe with DeShaun, staring up at him like he was about to enter a championship cage battle. DeShaun would probably tear Jeremy apart with his bare hands, but, to Jeremy's credit, he would come back at DeShaun with every bit of strength he had.

I grabbed DeShaun's arm and pulled him toward the door. "Go before it gets worse. We'll talk some other time."

DeShaun pointed to Jeremy as he headed toward the door. "You are a lucky man, today. That don't mean I'm not gonna find you."

"Yeah, you're right," Jeremy said calmly. "I am lucky. I am lucky enough to be having twins with your soon-to-be ex-wife. That's how lucky I am."

DeShaun stopped in his tracks. He turned, looked at me and then back at Jeremy. "What did you say?"

Both men glared at each other, waiting for the other to make the first move. It was only a minute, but it seemed like forever.

DeShaun lunged at Jeremy and both men fell to the floor, beating and punching each other like their lives depended on it—and for one of them, it did.

Epilogue

I didn't believe it possible, but the other side of the prison gate was even more dismal than the gray, water stained concrete of the outside. I headed toward a guard who opened the gate and led me through to the caged world of anguish and despair. I smelled the faint scent of Pine Sol and fresh paint with wafts of urine permeating through.

Each step down that long, black and white tiled hallway brought on more tears. This was the third time I had come to see him. The first time, I had missed visiting hours by ten minutes and the guard wouldn't let me through even though I had traveled from Pennsylvania to New York. The second time, he was detained in a surveillance cell. He had gotten into a fight with another inmate and was under twenty-four-hour close supervision. This time I made sure to call ahead first.

"First time here?" the supervising guard asked me. She was young, looking no older than her late twenties.

I shook my head, scanning the immaculately cleaned walls and floor corners. "I've been here before."

"A regular, huh?" We walked halfway down the corridor before she turned and asked, "What's your dude in here for?"

"Second-degree murder."

"Oh, sorry."

We stopped at a heavy metal door with several keyless locks

attached. In the top center of the door, there was a square tiny glass window with thick metal bars running down it. She stood on her tippy toes, peeked through the glass window, then banged on the door twice, yelling, "Open up!" She turned back to me. "This is where you get off. The guards will take you the rest of the way."

There was a loud buzz and then the heavy door swung open. Three guards—two male and one female—motioned for me to come over. The male guard took my purse and placed it onto a scanner. The female guard told me to raise my hands. When I did, she ran a plastic gadget up and down my entire body, front and back.

After her very thorough search, another male guard came up and asked me to follow. He took a key fastened to his belt and unlocked another solid metal door. The guard led me down yet another hall and to another secured door. Before he opened the door, he rattled off a list of rules and then asked if I understood. I nodded. He unlocked the door and I walked through, into a large room with several people sitting in sectioned off cube-like structures. On the opposite side of the bulletproof cube, inmates wearing navy blue jumpsuits sat and talked with their visitor via telephone.

Halfway down the line, I spotted him.

DeShaun's hair was cut lower and he was smaller than when the trial began. Like the other inmates, he was wearing a blue jump-suit with neon orange lines running up and down it. His eyes lit up when he saw me.

I sat down across from him and he nodded toward the black, worn-looking phone, fastened to the wall of my cube.

"Hey, Mimi," he said, when I picked up the phone. "You're look-ing good. You're letting your hair grow, huh? It suits you."

"You look good, too."

"Thanks."

Our eyes connected. We were trying to read each other, trying to find that connection that we held for so long. On my way here, I had a million things to say and to ask. Now I couldn't think of one.

"How's baby Mia?" he finally asked.

"She's getting so big," I told him. "I'm having her second birthday party next week." I thought of the picture so I reached for my purse, but then remembered I had to leave it at the guard station. "I'll send you a picture of her."

He looked disappointed. "Good. I'll look for it."

"How are you doing?"

He smiled weakly. "The best I can. How about you?"

"Good. It's been rough. I think of Mia's sister often."

DeShaun shook his head. "I'm so sorry that you lost the twin. So much bad happened that night. I wish I could—"

"Don't worry about it," I interrupted. I never wanted to think about that night ever again, but I did often. It wasn't as frequent, but I still had reoccurring nightmares about Jeremy lying on the floor in a pool of his blood.

"I came today to let you know that Mia and I are moving back to Atlanta next week to be with my mother," I told him.

"Is she still sick?"

"You know my mother. She says it's not too bad, but doctors tell me different."

"Sorry to hear that," DeShaun said. "That means you and Mia are going to be farther from me."

I nodded. "That may be best for awhile."

"Are you ever going to bring her for a visit?"

"I don't think that's a good idea. Not right now."

He nodded. "I understand. Will you ever tell her the truth?"

I sighed. "I suppose, when she gets older."

I looked into his eyes, still searching. It pained me to see him hurt like this. When I relocated, he would have no one to visit him. But, I had no choice. I had to take care of my mother and my baby. I had to move on.

"Remember when we first met in the Bahamas?" he asked, laughing.

"How could I not? We were at that bar, having a good time and you punched out that dude."

"You took off after that," he said. "But I didn't blame you. I was a nut."

The thought made me smile. "You weren't that bad."

"And then when I called you after you left." His eyes sparked with the recollection. "I'm surprised you picked up."

"I almost didn't."

"Are you sorry you did?" he asked.

"Never."

I didn't know what to say next. "I guess I'll write you and send pictures of Mia."

"I'd appreciate that."

DeShaun was in jail for another six years for involuntary manslaughter, and I wasn't sure where our relationship would stand after that. Our divorce became final two months ago and I was under no obligation to continue to trek up to New York and see him.

But my heart didn't want to let go.

Months ago, I was ready to release all of those unanswered questions. As time went on, I felt like I had to know, for closure. "DeShaun?"

"Yes?"

"Did you ever sleep with her?"

He shook his head. "I never ever slept with Jenn. I promise you. I may have wanted to, but for some reason or another, it never got to that point. She left for Japan and I haven't seen her since. I swear, Mimi."

I didn't know what to believe anymore.

"That night and the fight with Jeremy," I said. "I blacked out and don't remember anything after that. What happened?"

"I knew you'd eventually ask."

"Of course I would, DeShaun. I need to know."

"I told both you and the cops what happened."

"I know what you said, but it doesn't add up. I blacked out." I searched his eyes for the answer, anything, but he wouldn't look at me. "Before I passed out, the last thing I remembered was Jeremy's body on the floor, lying in a pool of blood. Did you take the bloody shard out of my hands? Tell me. Did I do it? Was I the one that stabbed Jeremy? Please, DeShaun, tell me the truth."

He looked up at me. I searched deep within his eyes..

"No," he said. "It's the same as I told the police. He attacked me, I pulled the broken vase from his hands and then I stabbed him with it. That's all. Now go and take care of Mia."

I nodded. "I love you, DeShaun, more than you'll ever know."

"What's done is done," he said. "Just know that I love you, too, and would do anything for you."

A single tear ran down my cheek. "Even go to prison?"

"Naomi, if you love me like you say you do, you'll take Mia and move far away from here. Take care of her and your mother. Most importantly, take care of yourself."

"DeShaun—"

"Go." He stood up. "Don't worry, we'll see each other again when I get out of here. I promise." The guard came up and escorted him out of the room, leaving me sitting in my tiny cube, watching after him. The guard led him through the doors and he was gone.

I walked outside the rusted prison gates just as tiny droplets of rain splattered onto the sidewalk. I reached into my purse and pulled out my compact umbrella to shield me from the rain. I hopped into my car and set off down the long, winding road leading away from the prison and to the freedom of the outside world, where a new life awaited me.

About the Author

Nicole Bradshaw was born and raised outside of Philadelphia, Pennsylvania in a quaint little town called Malvern. She currently resides in Freeport, Bahamas, with her husband and three children. During her college years, she needed funds for books, so she came up with the bright idea of starting an on campus advice column. She charged students $7 for her witty advice on dating and relationships. That year she made $14. Nicole is the author of *Unsinkable* and author of the ebooks, *A Bond Broken* and *Caviar Dreams*.

Visit the author at www.writernicole.com and on Facebook at Nicole Bradshaw Books.

If you enjoyed "Champagne Life,"
be sure to check out the e-book prequel

Caviar Dreams

by Nicole Bradshaw
Available from Strebor Books

Naomi

I took a step off the plane. As soon as I hit the airstairs, the sun's rays burst through my dark shades, exposing its radiance. I shielded my face with my hand. The warmth felt good against my skin, in contrast to the forty-five-degree weather I left behind in Philly.

"Why does it have to be so sunny?" Laeticia, my best friend since fourth grade, reached inside her way-too-much money, oversized designer bag and pulled out her sunglasses.

"That's because we're in the Bahamas," I told her.

She lifted her head to the sun, and in movie star mode, carefully placed the sunglasses on her face. She reached up, tucked a small section of her weave behind her left ear and said, "You ready, Naomi, girl, 'cause I sure enough am."

I laughed. "Look out, Bahamas. Here comes Laeticia The Superstar. Shall I call the paparazzi and let them know we've landed?"

"That's right," she said with a smirk. She reached into her bag and pulled out a floppy sun hat. She jammed the hat so far down on her head, she covered up the entire top half of her face. The hat combined with the glasses *really* made her look like a star now. "I do not play when it comes to getting sunburned," she said, slathering on greasy sunblock all over her exposed arms. "That's how Bob Marley died, you know?" She worked the white creamy glop into her hands, in between each finger. "My auntie Gertrude got skin cancer, too. Black may not crack, but it does burn, especially us light-skinded folks." She looked me up and down and thrust the sunscreen tube in my face. "That's why you may need this. Sure you don't want none?"

"I put mine on already. And would you stop talking like that?"

"Like what?"

"Light skin-*ded*," I said. "All the way over here, you kept talking about what you *seent* and *what you be like*. Why are you talking like that? You're a grown woman speaking Ebonics. I hate that!"

Laeticia was twenty-eight, a year older than me, but from the way she acted, you wouldn't know it. She graduated from Texas A & M with a degree in Marketing and was one of the smartest women I knew. She worked for one of the largest medical insurance companies on the east coast and was going to law school in the fall. This was precisely why I couldn't figure out why she insisted on speaking like she was a day out of the hood.

"Girl, please. I done heard you talk like this all the way down here, so shut up."

"Oh, no you didn't." I grinned. "You done never heard that mess comin' from me."

She laughed and smacked my shoulder.

I was finishing my degree in Finance (one semester left) at Temple University. I planned to apply to Wells Fargo for a Business Analyst position in the fall. I couldn't wait to finally kiss my crappy customer service job goodbye.

"You got any more of those cookies you baked?" Ticia asked. "I'm hungry as hell but I wasn't about to pay extra for that nasty plane food. Did you smell that fried chicken that chick brought on the plane?"

"I think the whole plane smelled it." I reached into my purse and pulled out a brown paper bag. I went to open up the bag, but before I could, she snatched it from my hand.

"I love these things," she said, taking a huge bite of a chocolate chip cookie. "You can bake your butt off. You should be selling these things. You could make a billion dollars off the chocolate chip alone."

She shoved the rest of the cookie into her mouth, dug her hand inside the bag and grabbed another one.

"If you were that hungry," I told her. "You should have gotten something on the plane."

"So I could have the entire plane smelling like chicken, too? No thanks." She popped the last bit of cookie into her mouth.

"Oh, please, Ticia, you know you wanted that."

"Don't misunderstand, Mimi. I didn't say I didn't want it, but there's no way you're gonna ever catch me slobbin' down some chicken on no plane. Oh, hells no."

I laughed. "You are so stupid."

"Last chance," she said, waving the sunscreen tube back and forth. "Sure you don't want some?"

I shook my head. "I'm good, thanks."

"Okay then, let's go!"

I glanced down at Ticia's floral, strapless peach and yellow sundress. "If you're so worried about sunburn, why didn't you wear sleeves?"

"Sleeves in the Bahamas? C'mon, now, that look is not cute."

"And neither is shellacking grease all over your arms and legs. Couldn't you have done that on the airplane?"

"I could've, but didn't." She carefully navigated her way down the last step off the plane in her Jimmy Choos. "Now stop your complainin' and let's go!" Ticia grabbed my arm and pulled me toward the airport entrance. "Finally, we're in the Bahamas, baby! Feel that beautiful sun." She lowered her sunglasses an inch and peered over the top, "And check out all those yummy Bohemian men!"

My eyes followed her gaze. Two dark chocolate men in pristine uniforms, medals included, stood at the gate leading into the airport. One guy was well over six feet with broad, stiff shoulders. The other guy, a little shorter, looked just as physically fit. Even through his starched white shirt I could see his chiseled chest.

"It's Bahamian," I said, still checking out the guys. The shorter guy whispered something to the taller one. They both looked over at us.

"Huh?"

"It's Bahamian, not Bohemian. The men here are not some hippy, retro seventies throwbacks."

"You are a straight buzz kill," she said with a toss of her weave. "You're here for the same thing I am…to find a guy."

"I have a guy," I reminded. "Did you forget about Kevin?"

I actually missed Kevin a little bit. He and I had been dating for seven months. In fact, he dropped me off at the airport to catch the flight for our Girl's Weekend in the Bahamas. However, if someone were to ask how our relationship was going, I couldn't tell ya. Even though we had been exclusively dating for several months, our relationship seemed to be *regressing* instead of *pro-gressing*. He lived in Philly and I lived further out in the suburbs so we decided to see each other only on weekends. I would go down to his spot on Saturday mornings and hang out until Sunday evening. Fridays were another story. Fridays were not happening with Kevin. At first, I believed he only wanted to hang out with his buddies on those nights, but when I told Ticia, her immediate reaction was, "Girl, are you stupid? He's seeing other chicks!" After the fifth month, we—mostly he—decided to only hang out on Sundays, like when we first started seeing each other. When I told Ticia that, she said, "Girl, are you stupid?" That was her mantra. She needed to write a book with that title. I was certain she'd make a million bucks off the title alone.

She so eloquently informed me that Kevin wasn't interested in "only my black ass." In Ticia's words, *he's pretty much banging the entire northeast.*

Ahhhh yes, tact was so overrated.

"Girl, are you stupid?" she asked with another toss of her hair. She was trying a new style and decided on curly instead of straight this time. "So what he drove you to the airport? He probably couldn't wait to get you out of town so he could get his dirt in."

I hated talking about Kevin with Ticia. I hated talking about *any* guy with her. I changed the subject as fast as I could. "Did you see those guys staring at us?" I smirked when I realized the irony of my question.

"Yup, and I plan to get me one of those Bohemian guys too."

"Bahamian."

"Whatever!"

We headed into the airport terminal and toward the big red sign titled, *Customs.* "You'd better be careful. These dreadlock-wearing people will lock you up in a minute. They smoke ganja all day long while listening to Bob Marley and Beres Hammond and then want to lock you up for having a coconut in your suitcase." She looked down at my bag. "You ain't got a coconut in your case, do you?"

"First off," I began. "That sentence had at least four derogatory stereotypes in it. Second, how would I have a coconut in my suitcase? We're coming *from* Philly. Ask me that dumb question when we leave! Wait, on second thought, don't."

"Good morning, Ladies."

Ticia leaned her head back and whispered, "Keep an eye out for these guys too. They are desperate to get a hold of some unsuspecting American chick to wife up so they'll get a green card."

"Are you serious?" I asked incredulously. "Would you stop, please? I don't know which is worse, insulting them with that green card mess or insulting me by even thinking I'm that stupid."

"You are the one that is dating Kevin, not me. I'm just sayin'…"

I grabbed her elbow and steered her toward the *American Citizens* sign, the longest line, of course.

After having our bags ransacked—her word, not mine—by Bahamian custom agents, we stepped out once again into the dazzling sunshine. Not a cloud in the sky.

I thought about telling Ticia that Kevin and I decided to take a break right before he dropped me off at the airport, but then rethought that. The night before the trip, he told me he needed "time to himself to get his thoughts together." He never mentioned another woman.

"With everything that's going on," he had said right after coming out of the movies one night. "I need time to concentrate on my job."

The funny thing was, I never even broached the subject in the first place. You can best believe I called him out on his lie, though. Apparently, he forgot he told me two days prior that he'd been laid off from his job. He quickly retracted his statement. "I meant that I was concentrating on my job *search*."

Reluctantly, I agreed with the intention of getting back with him when I returned. Desperate, I knew, but what else did I have? But as I stood in the warm tropical breeze, I felt a sense of relief that Kevin and I were on the outs. Call it intuition, but it felt like I was destined to meet someone here. Ticia must've felt my fate too, because at that exact moment, she leaned over to me and whispered, "I think I'm gonna get me some here. Watch."

Close enough!